AF580600

ALEX, BY PROXY

KAREN MYNA CANTOR

Printed and bound in March 2026 at RRD, Dongguan, China.
www.holidayhouse.com
First Edition
1 3 5 7 9 10 8 6 4 2
ISBN: 978-0-8234-6116-5 (hardcover)

Library of Congress Cataloging-in-Publication Data

Names: Cantor, Karen Myna author
Title: Alex, by proxy / Karen Myna Cantor.
Description: First edition. | New York : Holiday House, 2026. | Audience: Ages 12 and up | Summary: "Sixteen-year-old Alex, a victim of Munchausen syndrome by proxy, starts a true crime podcast to tell his side of the story"— Provided by publisher.
Identifiers: LCCN 2025019232 | ISBN 9780823461165 hardcover
Subjects: CYAC: Podcasts—Fiction | Munchausen syndrome by proxy—Fiction | Mental illness—Fiction | Trials—Fiction | LCGFT: Thrillers (Fiction) | Novels
Classification: LCC PZ7.1.C3743 Al 2026
LC record available at https://lccn.loc.gov/2025019232

EU Authorized Representative: HackettFlynn Ltd, 36 Cloch Choirneal, Balrothery, Co. Dublin, K32 C942, Ireland. EU@walkerpublishinggroup.com

To Taz: You make it all worth it,
even if you steal all my good socks.

PART 1

MONSTER MOMMY MANIA

SEPTEMBER

CHAPTER 1: 88 DAYS TO TRIAL

HARROWING NEW DETAILS IN "MONSTER MOMMY" CASE.

That was how the local paper wrote about it. All caps and bold font. Today's edition was sitting on the table in the stuffy law office of Evans & Everston, pricking Alex's neurons every time he looked at it.

If it were up to him, he could've come up with a million better headlines. Like **SON FROM POISONING CASE IS AN ASTRONOMY EXPERT,** or **KID FROM "MONSTER MOMMY" CASE UNREASONABLY GOOD AT GERMAN CROSSWORDS,** or **WAY MORE INTERESTING NEWS: SMALL-TOWN ESTONIAN MAYOR LOSES BID FOR REELECTION.**

But it wasn't up to him. Instead there was just this newspaper, whispering from afar. *Did you remember this detail? Hey, what about that one? Don't forget to make eye contact when you provide your testimony!*

Testimony. Alex had just attempted to practice his with the lawyer, who was now staring at him, gaze dispassionate and profoundly unimpressed.

"That was...an attempt," said the lawyer.

Of course Alex had screwed up. The only question was how: Had he gone back and forth too much? Messed up the sequence of events? Or maybe it was something else, something in his body language. A shifty look in his eyes, his hands tapping the table. People would squint and think, *He's a little off, that one.*

The worst possibility was that it was something deeper, something he couldn't fix. Something in his vibe that made it obvious what was wrong with him. Something that made people say, *This boy is sick in the head and you'll never be able to trust him.*

There were so many delightful options—all Alex had to do was spin the wheel and find out. "Just tell me how bad it was."

His dad grimaced in the chair across from him. "You're speaking too quickly, as if you're trying to get everything out in one breath. I could barely understand you."

Their lawyer—Mr. Evans—jotted down some notes on a yellow legal pad. "Try to go slower next time, Alex. We only have three months before the trial. We need to know ASAP if you're going to be able to get on the stand."

Alex sighed. Testifying about the worst thing that had ever happened to him—how hard could it be?

Though sometimes he wondered which part of the story was *really* the worst. The answer seemed obvious: His mom had poisoned him for ten years, in order to pass him off as severely ill. His childhood had been a cascade of medical drama after medical drama that ended with him falling into a coma last year, in true soap opera fashion. He'd almost died, but then she got caught.

So if someone asked *What was the worst thing that ever happened to you?*, that was the obvious answer.

Still, he wondered. He combed through memories of his mom, the way her smile was so warm, the way they had a million inside jokes, and he thought, *The worst part was when they took you.*

He should've been bitter. He should've been angry, resentful. And part of him was. But another part of him missed the way they used to spend a Thursday afternoon, hanging out in the park or watching ridiculous horror movies with titles like *Attack of the Giant Tomato* or *Space Reptile Worms Strike Back!*

Yes, he'd been severely ill. But he hadn't felt like his entire life was a lie.

"Okay." Alex looked back at his notes. "I'll try again."

"We've already run through it three times today." Mr. Evans shook his head. "Just get some rest. Think about how you want to be perceived on the stand. When you rush through it, when you don't make eye contact, you sound guilty. I'd hoped you would have a better handle on this by now."

Alex's throat tightened. As if it was an easy thing to get up in front of a jury and who-knew-how-many onlookers in the public benches and recount every gruesome detail, spilling his secrets as if he were relaying the latest episode of some reality TV show. He was supposed to look out at dozens, possibly hundreds of strangers, and say something like *When I was thirteen, after my second brain surgery, my mom made me soup but I think she dosed it with mercury.* And he was supposed to not burst into flames while doing this.

Mr. Evans was being paid to help Alex prepare, but he kept his distance. Rarely addressed Alex directly. Rarely even looked at him.

It was easy to imagine what his lawyer had heard. A boy with a long history of mental illness, of hallucinations and psychotic episodes and talking-to-walls incidents. A boy who had been dragged out of school screaming about creatures sending him telepathic signals over electromagnetic waves. Yep, that was the kid Mr. Evans had to prep for trial testimony in order to ensure Maryland's latest true crime spectacle went to prison.

When I was thirteen, after my second brain surgery, my mom made me soup but I think she dosed it with mercury. You can totally trust my perspective on this, because I've only been hospitalized for "acute psychotic illness" several times.

It didn't matter that the trial was in three months. It could be in three hundred years, and Alex still wouldn't be ready.

Mr. Evans glanced at Alex's dad. He lowered his voice, which was ridiculous, because of course Alex could hear him. "Are you sure he'll be able to..."

"I'm sure." His dad's voice was firm.

People always said he and Alex looked alike. And when Alex was younger, whenever he looked in the mirror, he'd hunted for those signs of his dad. With his dad deployed in one place or another, Alex had been looking for a connection, a physical link. Once his dad came back home, the similarities were obvious—along with the differences. Same brown hair, but cut short and dusted with gray. Same brown eyes, but something sad in them now, distant. White skin, lined with wrinkles, a long scar peeking out from his collar. His dad had come into sharp focus, and it was disorienting.

Mr. Evans nodded. "Alex, I need to speak with your father about some of the trial logistics. Can you step outside?"

They wouldn't be talking about logistics. "Yeah, okay."

Outside the door, Alex pressed himself against the wall and listened. He couldn't help it—if Mr. Evans had doubts, then maybe, just maybe, Alex could unravel what they were and pick them apart.

The alternative was letting Mr. Evans pull him off the witness stand and leaving his dad to explain the whole story to the jury. That couldn't happen. His dad hadn't even been there. The case would become thin, easy to flip. And if his mom walked free...

Alex wasn't worried she would poison him. No, he knew her (definitely, possibly, maybe), and she probably (most likely, maybe) wouldn't try that again.

The real risk was far more complicated. Alex wasn't sure if his dad even recognized it.

There was no way out but to testify. It was Alex who had seen every IV line, every syringe held between two fingers. Alex who had listened to her explain what all the new "medicines" were. Alex who had gone through every procedure, every surgery—and Alex who was left wondering how much of it had ever been necessary.

"Matthew." Mr. Evans's voice was faint behind the door. "We don't have much time."

"We have until the middle of December, technically—"

"The defense will need a witness list long before the trial starts. Look, we need to make a decision soon. It's already September. And I just don't know if he's stable enough to go on the stand."

A moment of hesitation.

Alex's dad's voice came next, uncertain: "He's still recovering, you know."

"He woke up from the coma in May."

"But—"

"I know. Potential brain damage, long-term effects and all that. But that's the problem, isn't it? What does he really remember?"

Alex gritted his teeth. That wasn't the problem. Yes, being poisoned for ten years had left its mark—a collection of mental and physical issues that were simultaneously familiar and annoying—but the problem wasn't his memory. It wasn't that his version of reality was warped. Well, sometimes it was. But the real problem was that everyone *believed* his version of reality was warped.

This was something Alex had known for years: It didn't really matter what was true. It only mattered what everyone thought was true.

What everyone thought was true, what everyone had seen, was a devoted mom with a severely sick child, a mom who did everything in her power to keep her son healthy. A mom who always greeted people with a smile, a mom who somehow still managed to make it to the PTA meetings.

And Alex was supposed to convince the whole world that that woman was a liar. It was a hard story to swallow, and he knew it.

He settled into the couch in the law office's waiting room, the leather rough and cracking. Another copy of the newspaper lay on the side table. Out of the corner of his eye, a pale hand reached out and flipped through the pages.

"Well." A woman's voice, smooth and familiar. "Can you believe what they're saying about us?"

His mom looked just like she had back in January, when he last remembered seeing her. Soft, curly brown hair, skin so pale it was as if she never went outside, that one blotchy freckle on the corner of her cheek.

He knew she was in jail. This was a hallucination, a fake. But he couldn't look away.

"It's not about us," Alex said before he could stop himself. "It's about you."

"Alex?" The door opened and his dad stepped out. "Who are you talking to?"

Crap. "No one."

I just don't know if he's stable enough to go on the stand, Mr. Evans had said.

Alex stood up, and when he looked back at the spot where he'd seen his mom, she was gone.

CHAPTER 2: 88 DAYS TO TRIAL

"We don't have to talk about it," Alex said as soon as he got into the car.

His dad met him with a long look. The shadows under his eyes suggested he already wanted to drop dead, which, relatable. "Look, I know this is intense," he said. "It's a lot. It's personal. I wouldn't blame you if you decided not to take the stand."

That wasn't an option. What other evidence did they have? A few police reports detailing mercury and other substances in the hospital bathroom, but his mom could claim they had been planted; all sorts of people came in and out of hospital rooms, and she could pretend they had come from a nurse. His dad would testify, except he'd been deployed overseas for the better part of ten years. Logan could maybe testify, but the whole thing had started when he was a baby. He probably didn't remember anything. And even if he did, the idea of Logan having to testify made Alex queasy.

The evidence that pointed to his mom was still so ambiguous. It was up to Alex. If his mom came back—

Alex took a slow breath. "It's fine. I'm going to testify."

His dad peered at him. God, he was so hard to read. It didn't help that Alex only sort of knew him. Alex knew how his dad hummed to himself as he made coffee, how he leaned forward with intense focus when watching cooking shows, how he had an eclectic collection of T-shirts advertising video games from the 1980s. But he didn't really *know* his dad. He was, at best, a friendly acquaintance.

It was his mom who had been there. Every quirk, every flick of her wrist, every laugh. Alex had it all memorized.

His dad pulled the car into the elementary school pickup line. Logan was attending an after-school program while they did trial prep—as if that was a perfectly normal way to pass a fall afternoon.

"You could try writing things down," his dad offered. "It might help you sort out what you want to say."

That was unlikely, but the alternative was going on the stand and instantly combusting, so Alex would have to consider it.

The door to the back seat was flung open, and Logan leaped inside. "Go. GO!"

"Kiddo, there's a dozen other cars—"

"I'm being pursued!"

In the front entryway of the school, a handful of kids pumped their fists, their tiny mouths forming words. *VIDEO GAME! VIDEO GAME! VIDEO GAME!*

"Oh no," Alex whispered.

"They want the beta version of the game done so they can play it. But I haven't finished debugging the script!" A Fruit Roll-Up slammed into the car window. Logan locked the door and shuddered. "And I still have to render the monsters!"

Monster Bash Crash Murder—Logan's video game in progress—was hotly anticipated by his peers. Apparently even the first graders wanted to play it, though they were probably too young for all the bashing, crashing, and murders. Logan was ten, and Alex suspected he'd be running a tech start-up by the time he started high school. He'd design robots that cleaned your house, or maybe robots that would survey all the weaknesses known to humankind and then destroy civilization with nanobot-level precision. Alex didn't care which; personally, he thought humanity deserved the latter.

"Give! Me! Murder!" a girl with curly hair shouted.

Logan rolled the window down a crack. "You must let the artist finish his work!"

Alex twisted around to face him. "Have you fixed the bat problem yet?"

"Listen, kiddos," their dad cut in before Logan could answer. "There's a lot going on. Let's do something fun. How about ice cream?"

Alex was sixteen now, but his dad talked to him like he was a little kid—like he was frozen in time, still a normal six-year-old bumbling around talking about asteroids and the impending heat death of the universe. On second thought, maybe he'd never been "normal."

"YES," Logan blurted out, just as Alex said, "Sure."

Their dad drove toward downtown Frederick. It was a city, really, but it had the trappings of a small town: low-slung redbrick buildings, little shops, even a creek running through downtown that was flush with lily pads. The storefronts were decked out with Maryland flags—and most of them sold state-flag bumper stickers, pins, T-shirts, mugs, and hats.

This was the sort of cheesy thing Alex might've been tempted to mock, except he, like every Marylander, was deeply proud of the flag. It stood out, with its four quadrants, each one a jumble of colors and patterns in red, white, yellow, and black. Outsiders insisted it was an eyesore, even "painful to look at." Alex had heard it all, and he didn't care: He wore his Maryland-flag sweatshirt all the time. Or at least on cooler days, when it wouldn't make him boil to death.

Alex's dad parked, and the three of them stepped out into the heavy September heat. At this hour, downtown was busy, crowded with teenagers hunting for something to do and adults heading home from work. In downtown Frederick, "something to do" might mean counting all the Maryland flags, buying an overpriced scarf at a boutique, or throwing stones into the creek. You could even harass a goose, if you were particularly daring.

So far, no one seemed to have noticed Alex. That was progress. Two weeks ago, someone had stopped them in the grocery store and insisted that Alex's case had been fabricated by his dad for some vague, nefarious purpose. It'd been so awkward they'd fled the store and forgotten to get milk.

Inside the ice cream parlor, Logan strode up to the counter.

"Hello," he greeted the cashier, who seemed taken aback by the ten-year-old's professional tone. "I would like three scoops of chocolate chunk, peanut butter, and…hmm. What would complete the trifecta? You need a hint of acid to cut through all that, but would lemon do? No, that would clash with the peanut butter…"

Alex glanced around the ice cream shop, feeling weirdly conspicuous, and not because of Logan's monologue. Several people from school were here. Michael Florentine and Armando Garcia sat at a nearby table—Alex had been on a group project with them freshman year. And there was Amelia Washington—he'd taken Algebra with her. She'd shared her notes, and he'd returned the favor by tutoring her in French. It had gone well enough until the homework load grew so enormous that they'd just started copying each other's answers.

None of them would make eye contact now.

He knew what they'd heard. The rumors had spread like an algal bloom, and eventually found their way back to him through social media posts, whispers in the hallways, and lingering stares.

They didn't believe he'd been poisoned. They thought he'd done it to himself.

The shop door swung open, and immediately Alex ducked behind his dad.

Freaking *hell.* It was Ella McIntire. Even if she got a face transplant, Alex would recognize her by her distinct taste in sweater vests, always emblazoned with a million pins and buttons, usually merch for *Rosé and Decay,* a TV show set in old-timey England with zombies. She had a tight, serious expression on her face, brows lowered, and dark hair framing her pale cheeks. She looked the same, but she'd changed. Alex knew she had.

"Right, so um, I'm gonna grab a table," Alex said.

His dad frowned. "But you haven't even ordered—"

Alex scurried off to a chair in the corner. It was a relief to sit down—standing for that long, plus walking from their parking spot, had started to make him dizzy. The joys of dysautonomia, a neurological condition that wreaked havoc on his heart rate and blood pressure. His pulse would fly through the roof if he so much as broke into a light jog. It was one of the problems that hadn't gone away, and it caused occasional fainting episodes that his dad politely referred to as *incidents.* Alex had only passed out a few times since coming out of the coma, but the last thing he needed was to collapse on the cold tile of the ice cream shop. Especially in front of Ella.

Alex lowered his head. Maybe Ella wouldn't see him and—oh crap, someone was approaching his *dad.* It was a middle-aged white woman he didn't recognize. Her face was cold and angry. Alex leaned closer, straining to catch fragments of the conversation.

"Ridiculous that you should have him out of the house, after everything—"

"He's allowed to go outside, same as you," his dad said, sounding tired.

"You don't think he should be punished for lying?"

Logan, luckily, was oblivious. "—kiwi wouldn't do, because we aren't in New Zealand, and I think that's the only place where you're allowed to eat the—"

Alex put his head in his hands. Of course that woman thought he was lying.

Chronic poisoning—years and years of ultraconcentrated salts and mercury, hidden in food and pill capsules—had made a mess of his brain. Lesions in some places, scarring in others, according to the neurologist. These things didn't heal. But his mom was in jail, so the fact that he was still sick fueled the fire of the rumors.

What Ella had said over the summer made it worse.

Logan kept going. "Now one option would be banana, the classic. It depends on whether your banana flavor is the Gros Michel variety or the Cavendish—"

Let's leave, Alex texted his dad. The woman was saying something about how Alex's behavior was an insult to sick people, an insult to disabled people. An insult to his mother. He took slow, deep breaths, but he couldn't breathe away the feeling that he'd been stabbed.

That was, of course, when Ella spotted him.

She gave him an appraising look, as if cataloging him from top to bottom. His skinny frame, his too-large T-shirt. Maybe she was comparing him to her memory of that day back in January.

Alex wanted to look away, and he almost did, but he stopped himself. That would make him seem guilty.

Ella came toward him, maintaining eye contact. She always walked so fast; Alex was taller, but he'd never been able to keep up with her, even before he got really sick.

"So." She folded her arms over her chest. "Frederick's most infamous compulsive liar came out of his hiding place."

It was hard to believe they'd actually been friends once. "Nice to see you too."

Ella leaned toward him. "Alex," she whispered. "Just admit the truth. I *saw* you do it."

"We've been over this. You saw me taking my meds." Months before Alex's mom had been arrested, Ella had come over to drop off some homework for him. She'd gone into the kitchen for a glass of water, and spotted him refilling his IV line from the doorway—though Alex didn't find this out until later. Admittedly, he could see how it might look kind of weird to a non-disabled person. But so what? "Weird" was not the same as poisoning himself.

"Filling an IV with a mystery serum?" Ella rolled her eyes. "Okay, so if it was just your medicine, then why did you hide it from me? You only started setting it up after I went to the kitchen."

Because non-disabled people freak out about needles. Nah, best not to say that.

"I couldn't believe what I saw," Ella continued as she shook her head. "I had to hold on to that for *months,* Alex. It kept me up at night! Wondering what was going on." She lowered her voice. "It only made sense after you got your mom arrested. Then I knew the truth. You were doing it to yourself. For attention."

And instead of telling me what you thought you knew, you blasted it on TikTok. It was Ella's fault that half the town didn't trust him, that a random woman was lecturing his dad in the ice cream parlor, that online forums buzzed about the "real" truth of his case. They said it wasn't Munchausen syndrome by proxy, but Munchausen syndrome, full stop.

Technically, the illness was *factitious disorder imposed on another.* But it wasn't like anyone was going to listen to him about that now.

He needed to get out of here. "Listen, this has been great, but I have to make sure my brother doesn't get kicked out of this place for taking too long to order."

Ella took a deep breath, and—were her hands shaking? That was weird. Alex had never seen her tremble. "I need you to tell the truth. Put an end to this," she said.

His dad and Logan were walking toward the table now. Logan had a quadruple-scoop monstrosity of a million colors and toppings, and his dad carried a tray with a disturbingly large coffee, a small ice cream, and a sorbet.

"Ella?" Logan beamed when he first saw her, but then his smile faded. "Ella."

Alex rubbed his temples. Sometime after Ella and Alex had become friends, she'd started babysitting Logan whenever their mom had to stay with Alex in the hospital. Logan had been thrilled every time Ella came over, probably because Ella never bothered to enforce a curfew. But then she went and torched Alex on the internet, and now everything was weird.

His dad waved halfheartedly at Ella, as if seeing her was just another reason to make a long day even worse. "Ah, Ella. It's... good to see you. How are you? Still into that TV show?"

"Yeah." Ella's gaze flickered around the ice cream parlor. And something became clear to Alex: Except for his family, no one was saying hi to her, either.

Why, Alex couldn't guess. She was Frederick's "truth teller," after all. Everyone ought to adore her.

"Screw you," she hissed at Alex under her breath, low enough for his dad and Logan not to hear. She hurried to an empty table.

Alex's dad sat down next to him. "Haven't seen Ella in a while."

The last thing Alex needed was to talk about the disintegration of his social life. "You got coffee?"

"No. I got…" His dad spooned a dollop of something into his coffee."Coffee with ice cream. It's Italian! They call it *affogato*."

He seemed so proud of himself, Alex decided not to tell him he'd accidentally scooped in the sorbet.

Logan dove into his ice cream with impressive abandon while their dad glanced at Ella's table—ugh, he was going to keep talking about it after all.

"It's a shame you two aren't close anymore," he said. "Those videos were terrible, but I wonder if there's some way to talk it out. And Bryce, whatever happened to Bryce? You two used to do everything together."

Ah. Bryce.

Alex wasn't talking to Bryce either. Although that was his own fault.

It would be easy to come up with a lie. *Bryce moved to Nunavut. Bryce was sent to a military boarding school.* The truth was simpler. *Bryce kind of hates me.*

His dad must've read something in Alex's expression. "Well. Maybe we'll just focus on the testimony for now."

No pressure. If Alex messed up during the trial, it would fuel Ella's theories. If his mom was let out of jail, Ella would tell everyone she'd been right all along. People would probably believe her too. His mom would sigh, shake her head, and say, *I never thought he was capable of this.*

"Totally," Alex said, as if the concept of the trial didn't make him want to disintegrate.

It was amazing, really, how quickly someone could torch your whole life.

CHAPTER 3: 88 DAYS TO TRIAL

After dinner, Alex took Logan to the park. He wasn't ready to start his testimony notes, but maybe fresh air would help clear his mind. Logan paced back and forth in front of the bench where Alex sat, talking out a new idea for a video game level. Not that Alex was really listening.

It all began when I was six, when I had a seizure and fell off the jungle gym.

He couldn't know if it had really started then, and the last thing he needed was to be caught in a lie.

I don't know when my mom started poisoning me, but I was sick for most of elementary school.

Too dull.

My mom was supercaring and sweet, except for the hundreds of times she—

"Ice cream inspired me, by the way," Logan said. "I realized I need a banana level. One where the Gros Michel and the Cavendish duke it out to find out which one is superior."

"Isn't one of them gone?"

"Well *duh*, but this is a *fantasy* where the Gros Michel *comes back*. Keep up." Logan kicked a rock into a bush.

"Right. Uh, I guess they should have banana powers." As if the testimony wasn't enough of a mess, then there was Ella to deal with. Their encounter in the ice cream shop had been strange. At first she'd been her usual self, demanding her fake truth, her forced confession. But then there was that unsettled look in her eyes, a tension in her shoulders. Almost as if she'd been afraid.

Except she didn't seem afraid of Alex. She seemed afraid of everyone else in the shop.

Ugh. If only he could ask someone at school about it, see if something had happened since Ella's posts over the summer. But school felt like an alien planet these days. Sophomore year, round two—since he'd been in the ICU for all of spring semester, he'd needed to be held back. His former classmates, now juniors, had been decent enough at the start of the school year. One person had given him a card that read *Glad you're well?*, and Alex had never related more to a question mark in his life.

But the sophomores…after he'd had a passing-out "incident" the first week of classes, they kept their distance. They were probably Team Ella.

Putting together a decent testimony could fix that. He could show the world the real truth. No pressure.

"Dropping a peel for people to slip on is *way* too stereotypical for banana powers," Logan said with a sanguine nod, as if this was what Alex was thinking about.

It was a disease in its own right, the obsession with the Monster Mommy case. If they lived in Germany, this thing would have its own word by now: maybe *ObsessingOverCrimesBecauseYouHaveNothingBetterToDoWithYourLife*, or *ThinkingYou'reADetectiveSoYouInterrogate-OneKidUntilHeWantsToExplode*, or even just *MonsterMommyMania*.

"Alex?"

A girl was coming down the park path with her phone in hand, a clipboard tucked under one arm. She had thick black curls in two buns, strands of hair framing her face. Deep brown eyes, dark skin, 12.2 billion freckles. A shirt that read: THE ROMAN EMPIRE IS DEAD.

Oh God. It was Naomi Shawna Green.

Alex forced a smile and met her gaze. He could still avoid a lecture if he was careful. "Hey," he said. "Can you believe this weather lately? That tornado last week was wild."

"I wish it took out the Latin classroom."

Great. He was going to get the speech. Bryce called it the Naomi Monologue, and it'd been around for ages; Alex had heard three versions of it in last year's English class alone, and one in French—actual French.

"It's *ridiculous* that our school still requires Latin." Naomi shook her clipboard in the air. "Are we going to tour Pompeii? Speak to a Roman noble? Of course not. The sooner we start teaching Mandarin, the sooner we'll be prepared for China's new position as a global power. I'd be happy with just Mandarin, but we'd be better prepared if we added Cantonese too."

"Uh-huh," Alex said politely as Logan wandered off to throw rocks into a stormwater pond.

Naomi watched him carefully. "You agree with me, right?"

Naomi was a lot. But it was kind of nice that she wasn't keeping her distance from him. Maybe she didn't think he was lying. She didn't know him, not really, and yet here she was, railing against the injustices of the Foreign Language Department.

His shoulders sagged with relief.

"*Right?*" Naomi repeated.

"I mean, yeah, I guess." She had a point about Latin, even if everyone in Frederick was tired of the lecture. "But I don't think I could learn—"

Naomi was already tearing through her backpack. She yanked out a pencil case, and a few notebooks fell to the ground. One was labeled LATIN, but as it splayed open on the grass, Alex saw nothing but page after page of beautiful Mandarin characters.

He leaned closer; the strokes must've taken hours to perfect. "You take your Latin notes in Mandarin?"

Naomi huffed, digging out a pen. "I've got to practice my script somehow. Since they're forcing me to take this dead language, I figured I can study Mandarin at the same time. You know, reading Latin grammar tips in Mandarin, reviewing Latin verb conjugations in Mandarin, stuff like that. It's called *laddering*. Learning one language from another."

Alex actually recognized that term. "I tried to do that once!"

Great, now he sounded like an overeager child. If he wasn't careful, it would become painfully obvious that he'd lost all his social skills after the coma.

Naomi sat down next to him. "Really?"

"Uh-huh. I tried to learn Russian from German. That ended up being too hard, so then I tried to learn Russian from English. But it turns out Russian cases are incomprehensible in any language."

Naomi broke into a laugh, her freckles bunching up. "I didn't know you liked languages."

"I make an attempt," Alex said. A few feet away, Logan glared at ducks in the pond.

Alex did like foreign languages, despite being absolute garbage at them. He loved the utility of Spanish, though the regional variations were enough to make his head spin. He'd been fascinated by the rich history of Russian, but the silent *b* tripped him up. He'd been obsessed with Albanian for a while—it was so unique it wasn't connected to any language family in Europe—but it was nigh impossible to find free resources on it.

In the end, the only one that stuck was German. Ah, *Scheiße*.

Naomi held out her clipboard. "You should sign my petition to fund a Mandarin Chinese class."

"Um."

"Unless you're afraid. Everyone's scared to learn it. But once you land the tones, you can't go wrong."

"Uh..."

"Though if you *don't* land the tones, you will always go wrong."

"Well..."

He gave in and signed the petition.

Looking pleased, Naomi tucked her books away and popped an earbud in. Alex glanced at her phone screen, which had a GIF of blood dripping down a windowpane, pale white hands pressed against the glass.

"It's a podcast," Naomi said without fanfare.

Alex's cheeks burned. "Sorry, I didn't mean to snoop."

"No, it's fine. It's something I'm working on," she said. "A true crime podcast. It's called *The Gruesome, Ghastly Goal*."

Oh dear. "How very alliterative."

Naomi nodded. It was a factual nod, as if she were saying, *Yes, it is indeed alliterative, thank you for noticing.* Then she watched him for a moment, as if waiting for him to say more.

It occurred to Alex that she might've wanted him to look at

her screen, to notice the podcast. He wasn't sure what to do with that—understanding the way other people dropped hints, or tried to ask questions without asking, was a code he'd never managed to crack. Bryce used to joke that Alex's go-to response in any social situation was the blue screen of death.

Naomi pulled out the earbud. "Do you like true crime?"

"Not particularly."

"Want to give it a listen?" she asked.

The Gruesome, Ghastly Goal, Episode 1: "Bloodstains on the Pitch"

(Ominous piano music plays. A note is out of key.)

NAOMI In a charming town in central Maryland, a wind blows. It passes over a local high school, ruffling dead leaves on a soccer field, scattering them in a chilling dance. Little does the town know that the soccer field will come to remind them of the horrors that struck their community—

FEMALE VOICE Horrors that will shake them to their bones.

NAOMI Welcome to *The Gruesome, Ghastly Goal.*

(Piano music again.
Something smashes the keys, creating an ominous thud.)

NAOMI Now you might be asking yourself, "Wait a minute. I know about every true crime story the minute it hits the news. I have the NeighborhoodMom app specifically for crime reports. I've even installed a police radio in my car to keep up on the latest incidents. Why haven't I heard of this one?"

FEMALE VOICE It's so horrifying, even CNN doesn't want to tell you the details.

NAOMI But we're here to give you the scoop. So listen on . . . if you dare.

FEMALE VOICE We'll be investigating the mysterious disappearance of a high school student—a soccer player, beloved by everyone in town, at the peak of his game. That is, until the very last goal he made.

NAOMI The gruesome, ghastly goal.

(Sound of a soccer ball being kicked, followed by a high-pitched scream.)

CHAPTER 4: 88 DAYS TO TRIAL

Alex pulled the earbud out of his ear. "A kid *disappeared*?"

Logan, fortunately, was too far away to hear—he stood by the edge of the stormwater pond, skipping stones.

"Oh yes," Naomi said in a creepy whisper. "Someone from our school."

"When?" Had he been so caught up in his own drama that he'd missed this? That was kind of shameful. "A soccer player?"

"Yeah. He was on the varsity team. Very tragic." Naomi wiggled her eyebrows. Her tone felt decidedly un-tragic. She dug into her bag and retrieved a business card. "Use the link at the bottom to listen. Episode one releases October first."

Alex turned over the card in his hands. It looked professionally printed. Some people really had their life together.

"That was just a draft," Naomi went on. "I'm still workshopping it, but I'll have a final cut soon. I'm conducting a full investigation. Well, with a team. We're going to get the truth out. At any cost."

"That's great," Alex managed. The only way to get his truth out would be in front of a scrutinizing jury.

Naomi cast him a sideways glance, as if something was computing in her brain, formulas running in the background. "You must know what that's like," she said. "Being on a quest to find the truth."

"I know what happened to me," Alex said, a little too sharply.

Naomi put her hands up. "Right! I get it. I know what it's like to not be trusted. No one believes me when I tell them people will be able to speak over ten languages in the future. They just say they're going to have translating chips in their brains! But translating chips can't—"

"Wait," Alex cut in. "You believe me?"

Naomi blinked. Then she shrugged, her curls bouncing. "Sure, why not? I mean, poisoning yourself sounds so extra. Plus, where would you even get poison? Although if you do have a source, that might be helpful for my investigation, so I'd love to know the details—"

"That's a no." Alex leaned back.

A podcast sounded like something Bryce would do. Of course, maybe Bryce had changed—Alex hadn't spoken to him in months. He hadn't even seen him since last December. But they'd been inseparable for most of a decade. Years of video games, surviving Gym, and designing an increasingly elaborate tabletop RPG together didn't vanish overnight.

It would be easy for Alex to say things had fallen apart as he got sicker. At a certain point, he wasn't healthy enough to go out anymore, wasn't strong enough to get out of bed. And that was part of it.

But the part that mattered was this: Bryce's parents had split—a nasty divorce that ended up in the newspapers, a dad thrown out of the house with the neighbors watching—and Alex, feeling like he was drowning in his own mess, had kind of shut Bryce out.

Okay, mostly shut him out.

Well . . . totally shut him out.

"I know a guy who'd be into your podcast," Alex said without thinking.

"Who?" Naomi asked. Next to the pond, a duck approached Logan and flapped its wings in fury.

Alex rubbed the back of his head. "Oh, just a—" *Friend* didn't feel accurate, since they weren't speaking. "Just a guy. His name is Bryce. Bryce Miles. Actually, he probably knew the kid who disappeared, since he's on the varsity team—"

Naomi grimaced.

"What?" A horrific thought floated into Alex's mind. "Wait. *Bryce* isn't—"

"No! No." There was another pause, which might've convinced Alex that Bryce *was* the victim if not for the fact that he knew Bryce had scored some huge goal at the first Varsity game last week. "No, I know Bryce. He's... already helping me."

Oh. *Oh.*

Of course. Bryce had other friends. A true crime podcast was exactly the kind of spaghetti project he'd throw at the wall to see what would stick—he just wasn't doing it with Alex.

The stinging in Alex's chest was so intense that for a moment he couldn't focus on anything else.

"Right." He swallowed hard. "Yeah, that makes sense."

Naomi tilted her head to the side. "You guys go way back, right?"

"Yeah." He couldn't get into this now. The logical thing to do would be to walk away. Let Bryce work on the podcast, and let whatever was left of their friendship disintegrate like a meteor burning up in Earth's atmosphere. There was no point in trying to get involved. Bryce probably didn't want to talk to him anyway.

Naomi tucked her clipboard into her bag. "I should get back. I'm sure Ella is going to need help with the—"

"Wait." Alex's voice came out harder than he intended. "*Who* needs help?"

"Ella McIn—oh." Naomi frowned. "I forgot she was posting that stuff about you."

"It's not true," Alex blurted out so desperately it for sure sounded like it was true. He rewound his conversation with Naomi—the other voice on the podcast must've been Ella. "Ella McIntire is working on this podcast with you and Bryce?"

Naomi gave him a weak smile. "She's really good at asking probing questions?"

No way. He couldn't let this happen. He wasn't sure what was happening, exactly, but it was a problem. His former best friend, plus one of the few people in Frederick County who didn't think he was lying, were in cahoots with *Ella freaking McIntire* on a podcast.

Sure, it wasn't like Ella, Bryce, and Naomi would start out by talking about Alex, but the show was about local true crime. Of course it would circle back to Alex at some point! Of course Ella would unload her theories on them! How many times would Ella have to lay out the "evidence" before Bryce and Naomi believed her?

It was one thing for Bryce to be an ex-friend. It was an entirely different thing for him to be an enemy.

And Alex was so, so sick of being alone.

Ella and Bryce had always run in different friend groups—though Alex had been friends with each of them on their own, they'd rarely crossed paths. It was hard to guess what Bryce thought of her, or if he knew about the stuff Ella had posted. He had to know, right? Except maybe not. Bryce wasn't that active on social media, and he was notoriously bad at texting; back when they'd been friends, if he wanted to hang out, he would just show up at Alex's door.

Alex couldn't lose him to this podcast. To Ella. But he couldn't barge into Bryce's house after months and launch into a tirade about Ella and her lies. He'd come off as a conspiracy theorist.

No, he needed an in. Something—

"Hey," Naomi said. "Do you want to...draft an episode with us?"

Whoa, that was easy.

Yes was the obvious answer, but he couldn't help being suspicious. "Sure. But...why me?"

Maybe it was because he'd signed her petition. Or maybe she thought he had some kind of true crime "expertise." Or maybe she just felt bad for him.

"First, I need you to promise not to tell anyone about this podcast."

Alex nodded. "Sure. Are you worried someone's gonna poach the story, or—"

"And you can't talk to *anyone* about the missing soccer player."

This was getting weird. "But isn't it on the news—"

"That's the deal." Naomi folded her arms over her chest. This conversation had taken a turn. Still, it was an opening. If he got involved with the podcast, maybe he could keep Bryce from falling in with the likes of Ella. Maybe he could have at least one friend back.

"Fine," Alex said. "I promise."

"Meet me by the Foreign Language trailers tomorrow after school," Naomi said, and before Alex could think twice, she was gone.

He stood up—carefully, always carefully, to avoid an incident—and made his way over to Logan. "Time to head home."

"That duck wants to kill me."

Alex was going to deny it, but one look at the duck made it clear Logan was telling the truth.

As they walked home, he mulled over his plan.

Step 1: Get on the podcast.

Step 2: Convince Bryce that Ella was a liar.

Step 3: Figure out how to become friends again?

Step 4: Launch himself into the sun before the trial.

It was all okay. He could do this.

There were only two billion ways this could go wrong.

CHAPTER 5: 87 DAYS TO TRIAL

Alex played by Naomi's rules the next day at school. He didn't ask anyone about the missing soccer player, or say a word about the podcast—honestly, it was bold of her to assume he had someone to tell—though he did google it during his free period.

Missing soccer player, missing student, disappearance frederick county.

Half an hour of different search strings left him with nothing. There wasn't a single article about a missing student from their high school, or any high school near Frederick, for that matter.

It was baffling. He'd assumed that he'd missed the story because of his ongoing medical and legal nightmare. But everyone else? It didn't add up. He trudged down to the Foreign Language trailers, thoughts swirling into nothing.

His daily medication sat in his pocket like iron weights. Antipsychotics. The only pills he was supposed to be taking, after everything.

He'd take them later today. At some point. Definitely.

A few students were lingering by the trailers behind the school, chatting before they headed off to sports practice, club and group meetings, or whatever it was normal kids did when they weren't the center of a true crime fiasco. It was hard to make out what they were saying. *Mommy* or *Tommy*? *Police* or *puh-lease*? But then ice cut through his veins. Someone had *definitely* mentioned mercury—

"What's up?"

Alex startled and fell against the trailer. "Naomi?"

She tilted her head to the side, tight curls bouncing over her shoulders. "Well, you look profoundly un-good."

Alex rubbed the back of his head. "Sorry. I thought I heard mercu—something."

"Oh yeah. Dr. Chen had us doing mercury experiments today. It's wild how it turns into a sphere! Such a shame they squeezed her class into one of the trailers. Though I guess I can understand it, after the ethyl alcohol explosion."

He'd missed all the cool stuff while he was in the coma. "That... makes sense."

"Yeah. Anyway." Naomi hiked her backpack up high on her shoulders, as if she was about to venture on an Arctic expedition. "Want to see this podcast come to life?"

Absolutely not.

"Let's do it," Alex said with a fake smile, which Naomi seemed to buy. Amazing—he was figuring out how to talk to people again. Or at least how to lie to them.

Naomi led Alex into the woods behind the trailers. Apparently other students also spent time here, because the area reeked of weed.

"Sorry, I just have to..." Naomi smoothed her hands over her jeans and then took off her backpack. She pawed through it—looked inside every pocket and undid every zipper—before mumbling to herself and pulling it back on. "Whatever. Let's go."

"Forgot something?" Alex asked as they stepped over a fallen log.

Naomi let out a sigh. "I thought I did."

But then, just a few more minutes into the forest, she stopped to open up her bag and check everything again. It seemed like every compartment had to be opened, every item had to be touched. This time, she even went through her pencil case.

Alex stood awkwardly next to a tree. He was grateful for a break; his vision was already starting to wobble. Walking through the rough, hilly terrain of the woods was more physical activity than he was used to.

"Soooo," Alex said, "do you want me to help look, or—"

"No." Naomi pulled her bag back on. "It's just—forget about it."

"Did you forget something you need for the podcast?" Alex asked.

Naomi watched him for a long moment, her brow furrowed. "You haven't heard about me."

"You might overestimate the social contact I have these days."

"I guess I should tell you. You're gonna find out anyway." Naomi tightened her grip on her backpack straps as they started to walk. "I have OCD. People always think it means I'm superneat and organized, or that if I touch a bug I'll explode or whatever, but that's not the kind of OCD I have. It's more..." She trailed off. "I check things. A lot. My bag, door locks, homework, schedules. Everything."

"That sounds kind of inconvenient," Alex said, which was a useless response, but it was already out there.

She shrugged. "Yeah."

"And people talk about it?"

Naomi made a face. "Of course they do. Some kids try to mess with me. Steal a pencil or something to see if I'll notice. Copy my homework because they think it'll be perfect. They act like I'm hearing voices telling me to sharpen a pencil exactly twelve times. But that would be totally—"

She cut herself off.

"Sorry," Naomi blurted out. "I forgot that you... you used to..."

"Hear voices?" Alex offered, and Naomi squirmed. "It's fine."

The last thing Alex needed was for Naomi to feel bad. Her podcast could be his only path to reconnecting with Bryce—or, at least, preventing Bryce from taking Ella's side.

"I'm sure it's better now," Naomi said hastily.

"I don't know. I mean, I..." Part of him wanted to lie, to say that he was 100 percent better now, but what was the point? She'd find out eventually, just like he'd have found out about her OCD. At least she'd been brave enough to tell him the truth.

"Sometimes I still hear things. Or see them. Like... at times it's hard to know exactly what's real." He couldn't look at her; it was too weird to talk about it and meet her gaze. But it felt important to tell Naomi, in case it blew up in his face.

Naomi clambered over another log. "I thought you weren't sick anymore."

"It doesn't work like that." There had to be a good way to explain it. "It's like, if you took shots of arsenic every day, and then one day you stopped, you wouldn't be fine overnight, right? It would mess you up. Maybe permanently."

Naomi raised an eyebrow. "You were taking shots of arsenic?"

"Not arsenic." His fingers were turning blue from the exertion of navigating the woods, but he shoved them into his jacket pockets; the last thing he needed was to explain two diagnoses in one day. "Anyway, the long-term effects mess you up. That's where I'm at. And it's not like psychosis turns you into some chain-saw-wielding horror-movie villain. It just makes you... kinda sick."

This was more than he'd ever said about it to anyone, and it was exhausting.

"Well," Naomi said, "if it helps, *I* never thought you were a chain-saw-wielding horror-movie villain."

"The highest compliment I could ask for," Alex half joked, though he appreciated it more than he could say.

They walked on in silence. This part of the woods was so far from school that you couldn't hear cars. The leafy, open forest floor gave way to dense stands of trees, oak and beech all aching for the sky. Leaves arranged themselves in crowded groups, and branches stretched toward the light. Any sunlight that made it through was muted.

The world felt different here. Heavy.

Naomi stopped and turned to face him. "All right! We're going to have to be careful on this next part."

Alex staggered to a stop, clinging to a tree trunk.

Naomi frowned. "Are you . . . ?"

"Never been better." His heart was pounding so fast it hurt.

"Okaayyyy." Naomi spun back around and pushed aside a thicket of branches. "Look."

Alex took a stumbling step forward, and—holy crap.

There was a steep drop-off a few feet ahead, the ground plummeting into a deep ravine. Rocks jutted out across the sloping ground, with dark, rich earth exposed between them. Spindly trees clung to the hillside as if hanging on for dear life, and leaves fluttered down into a creek at least thirty feet below, where water rushed over jagged, shimmery stones.

That, and there was a half-wrecked wooden riverboat lying in the middle of the creek.

Alex did a double take. A boat? In the middle of the woods? That had to be a hallucination.

It took a minute to catalog the various dangers. Trees with

alarmingly jagged, bladelike branches? Check. Sharp-edged rocks at every turn? Check. A thirty-foot drop? At least if this killed him, he wouldn't have to testify.

"You ready?" Naomi tightened her backpack straps. "We'll slide down into the creek."

"We're going *down* this?"

"Ya-huh." Naomi began scooching down on her butt. "You can walk down, but if you fall, it'll hurt way more than if you slid."

If he backed out now, he might never work up the nerve to speak to Bryce. The podcast would give them something to talk about, a starting place. Rather than, *Hey Bryce, I'm sorry for ignoring you for a year, but also, there were days when I was so out of my mind I didn't believe you existed.* Yeah, that would go over well.

Alex took small, halting steps down the rocky slope. He'd barely made it a few feet when, of course, he stepped on something slippery and skidded.

For a second, it was like he was in a washing machine, gray sky and dark dirt spinning around each other—Sky! Dirt! Sky! Dirt!—until the world blended into itself like a painting. It was almost beautiful, the sum of those colors swirled into a single work of art. It would've been great, except it freaking hurt.

When he thudded to a stop just before the creek, every part of his body sang with pain. Aches radiated up his arm and along his back, and something warm and damp lingered on his elbow, his knee, his ankle. Alex groaned and wiped blood off his face.

"Holy crap!" Naomi hurried down the rest of the hill and jerked to a stop beside him. "Are you okay?"

He winced. "How did you even find this place?"

"I like exploring! It's beautiful out here, except for the mosquitoes."

Naomi pulled him to his feet. Standing up quickly made his vision go out, but he took several steps forward anyway.

The black spots cleared. And the boat came back into view.

It was a small riverboat, maybe forty feet from bow to stern, the hull painted a perfect-day blue. Toward the back, the rudder lay exposed, with flecks of paint and rust peeling off the dented blade. Ropes and life preservers hung limply from the bow, like the boat had been rushing headlong into a future that then stripped it bare.

"Welcome!" Naomi did jazz hands. "To... the Shitwreck!"

Holy hell. It was real.

Alex blinked a few times, but the image didn't resolve into something that made sense. "I'm sorry, the *what*?"

"Isn't the pun self-explanatory?"

Alex groaned. "Where did this come from?"

Naomi shrugged. "I think it washed up here from Lake Linganore, after the flood a few years ago. The boat must've even gone a little upstream, the flooding was so bad. Of course, the lake's dammed up on the other side." She stepped up to the bank.

Alex frowned. "Does anyone else know about this place?"

"No," Naomi said. "And I didn't want to tell anyone else, because—"

"You're using it as a hideout."

"Not exactly. It's just a good base of operations for our investigation." Naomi picked her way across the creek toward the boat, which rested mostly on the opposite bank. She stepped across stones toward a large hole in the hull, big enough to climb through. The water was a few feet deep at the creek's center. Alex stepped from rock to rock, following Naomi's path like a lost duckling.

"Is the boat stable? Seems kind of dangerous," Alex said.

"Only if you're the type of person to trip all the way down a hill."

Naomi reached the hole. The wood was twisted and mangled at its edges, like the boat was actively fighting against intruders. "Try not to get impaled."

Inside, there was nothing but darkness and a damp smell pervading the air, the reek of mildew and rot. The planks underfoot heaved with every step. Something skittered in the dark.

Naomi clicked on a camping lantern, and a warm glow suffused the space, casting the wooden beams in hazy orange light. It was almost like a sunrise coming to life inside the boat.

A figure resolved in the shadows, and Alex took in a breath.

There, on the other side of the boat, was Bryce Miles.

CHAPTER 6: 87 DAYS TO TRIAL

Seeing Bryce for the first time in almost a year was at once familiar and disorienting. His hair had grown out a bit, but his tan was as aggressive as ever, and he was—of course—wearing a soccer T-shirt and shorts. It somehow made perfect sense that he was standing inside a beached boat fifty miles inland.

"Whoa." Bryce's expression was part bafflement, part *I-just-ate-something-sour.* It was not encouraging.

"So, uh," Alex began. He should've planned better for this part. "You look...sporty."

Bryce raised an eyebrow. *Classic blue screen of death,* Alex imagined him saying. "You look kinda messed up."

Alex touched the scratch on his face. He wanted to ask Bryce so many questions. *Are the screaming matches over? What happened to your dad's doomsday bunker? Did your mom sell his junk like she threatened to? Are you okay?* The vitriol in Bryce's house had gotten so bad last year that Bryce had spent most of his time at Alex's place; it felt safer. That was weird to think about, in hindsight.

And now they were in a boat. The most logical thing for Alex to do would be to apologize, but he felt frozen in place. It was a very

Schnapsidee sort of situation: launching into an idea thinking it was genius, then realizing you'd messed up.

"So," Alex began, "you're into podcasts now?"

That was when Ella entered through the hole in the hull.

She turned to Alex, opened her mouth, and then closed it, meeting him with a cold glare. Alex wished he could disappear.

"Hey Ella!" Bryce said cheerfully, as if Alex wasn't there at all.

"What's *he* doing here?" Ella jabbed a thumb in Alex's direction. She turned to Naomi. "I told you, this has to be kept under wraps."

"Why?" Alex blurted out before Naomi could answer. "I mean, doesn't everyone already know about the kid who disappeared? It has to be on the news." Admittedly, Alex hadn't found anything, but maybe the internet had reorganized itself while he was in the coma.

"A kid who disappeared?" Bryce asked, looking confused. "I thought the podcast was about that serial killer up in Minnesota. You know, the one that used maple syrup."

Alex turned to Naomi. "But the podcast you showed me—"

"*The Maple Syrup Murders*!" Bryce cut in. "Your draft was amazing. It's sort of weird I couldn't find anything about it online, but I guess podcasts are great for cold cases."

Naomi wrung her hands, and Alex started to get a bad feeling about all of this.

"Naomi." Ella met her with a hard look. "This was not the plan."

"Okay, don't kill me." Naomi set her backpack on the floor. "But both of those podcasts were fake. They were early drafts Ella and I recorded while we were still brainstorming, when we thought we'd make something up. But then Mrs. Richards said we had to work on something real. A nonfiction narrative."

This was not moving in a good direction. Alex sat down on an overturned crate. Bryce narrowed his eyes and leaned against the wall of the boat, which let out a creak.

"I agree *The Maple Syrup Murders* podcast would've been fantastic," Naomi said, "but it never actually happened, which is a shame, because it would've been—"

"Naomi," Bryce cut in.

"Right." Naomi cleared her throat. "Well, Ella and I *are* making a podcast. About, well, um..."

And then she looked at Alex. So did Ella and Bryce, and in a flash it felt like they were just faces in a crowd, eyes watching him: *Alex, do you solemnly swear that you will tell the truth, the whole truth, and nothing but the truth—*

Blood rushed in his ears. He sputtered out, "You're joking."

Ella groaned and threw her head back. "Naomi! Why would you tell—"

"Because we can't do this by ourselves, can we?" Naomi asked. "That's what *you* said."

"Oh my God, I said loop in *Bryce*." Ella dug her fingers into her hair, which was up in a topknot. "Bryce and Alex were friends, so of course Bryce would have intel. Not Alex!"

Intel? They were going to use Bryce against him. Alex's heart thundered in his chest and he leaped to his feet. But he didn't know what to say—there were too many words in his head, all fighting for space, and the gist of it was *what the hell.*

"Who would have better intel than Alex?" Naomi asked as if Alex wasn't even there. Story of his life.

"We talked about this," Ella shot back. "There's no way we can trust him to tell the truth."

Naomi put a hand on her hip. "I told you, I'm not doing a podcast about a real person without having that person involved. It would be gross to do this without him."

It was unbelievable that Naomi and Ella had planned to launch a podcast about *his* life, about *his* family. He could only imagine what they'd say. *When Alex was ten, he had a seizure in school, but as soon as everyone came running he was fine!* None of it would be true. But Ella would sound so believable: *I used to babysit his little brother. I can tell you exactly what went on in that house.*

Bryce's shoulders sagged. "Aw, Naomi, that *Maple Syrup Murders* podcast would've done numbers."

"I didn't think you'd come if I told you what we were really doing," Naomi admitted. At least she had the decency to seem ashamed.

"Yeah, no kidding," Alex snapped before he could stop himself. "Why are you doing this? I know why Ella would want to. But you?"

"It's complicated—" Naomi began.

"There's a scholarship," Ella cut in. "For Media Studies. We found out about it in our Journalism class. Students can get a chunk of their college tuition covered. There's even a study abroad component, and you can go to some school in like, Beijing."

"Harbin," Naomi corrected.

Alex wrapped his arms around himself. Well. His life blasted on every audio streaming service, all so Naomi could go to Harbin.

"Is it cool there?" he asked at last, not knowing what to say.

Naomi rubbed the back of her head sheepishly. "Literally. They have ice sculptures."

"I'm glad to know that's what it takes for you to ruin someone's life." Alex turned his back on them and climbed out of the boat, stepping across the rocks and onto the bank at the foot of the ravine.

But then he paused. Sure, he could ditch this podcast. Except

Naomi and Ella—and maybe even Bryce!—would probably still make it. A series tailored to ruin his life.

He stood next to the creek, caught between decisions, when he heard Ella say, "Okay Bryce, if you're in, we're gonna get started today."

Bryce's voice was harsh. "Why did you think I would be cool with this?"

It was a bit of a relief to know that Bryce wasn't eager to blow up Alex's life on-air.

"Come on," Ella said. "Don't you think there's a story here? Don't you think we're missing some of the facts?"

"I don't know, and I don't care, okay?" Footsteps sounded from inside the boat. Alex knew he should walk away, but he couldn't do it.

The podcast was going to happen with or without his involvement. Maybe this meant there was an opportunity.

He could *join* the podcast. If he found a way to get Ella to let him stay on, then he'd be able to craft the story, provide his own take. Maybe he could even use it to pull his testimony together.

It could be like free trial prep—running his testimony by Naomi, Bryce, and Ella. Ella probably wouldn't be willing to hear his side, but Naomi and Bryce might take it seriously. Eventually he could even try it on the podcast listeners. He could see, in real time, what landed and what didn't. What made sense, and what got lost. What might be understandable to a jury, and what would get thrown out immediately.

There was the question of whether sharing stuff before the trial would be a problem for his case—but he was sure Mr. Evans would be okay with it. It could mean Alex might come up with a testimony that wouldn't make the man regret his career path.

Not to mention this would give Alex the space to break down every rumor. Tear apart every lie.

He's not in class again—I wish I could get school to take pity on me that easily.

No way his mom did it. She was so nice. She gave me a free cookie at the bake sale!

If she was really poisoning him, she would've been supercreepy, like in those movies.

He'd seen the posts, read the accusations in letters to the editor of their local newspaper, heard them in whispers in the hallway. He felt them swirling around in his chest.

I'm conducting a full investigation, Naomi had said. *Well, with a team. We're going to get the truth out. At any cost.*

So, okay. He'd join their podcast about his life. He'd give them enough detail to make it authentic, though they'd have to keep his involvement a secret or else everyone would assume the podcast was biased. And then—then he'd finally have something he could take on the stand. Something to push back against the swirling mess of hate and lies Ella had created.

And maybe he'd be able to stop holding his breath all the time.

This was his chance to bring the world back into balance before the trial. A chance to make sure that when the jury heard him, they actually listened.

The only problem was Ella. He'd have to come up with a plan to fix that.

Alex stepped back into the boat. Naomi and Bryce turned to him, Bryce with his bag slung over one shoulder as if he was about to leave. Naomi's eyes lit up when she saw Alex. As if she knew.

"I changed my mind." Alex tried to throw some confidence into his voice. "I'm in."

CHAPTER 7: 87 DAYS TO TRIAL

Ella immediately burst into laughter. She'd always had a nice laugh, sort of like tinkling bells. No wonder everyone believed her.

"Look," she said. "This was a misunderstanding. I obviously wasn't clear with Naomi about our plan. Sorry that you trekked out here, but you aren't a reliable source for this podcast. I want to tell the truth."

"Haven't you already posted your side of the story?" Bryce asked. "That stuff about Alex being a liar or whatever."

Ella's expression hardened. "People have a right to know."

"Okaaayyy." Bryce shook his head. "This has been awkward. I'm out."

"No, wait." Alex stepped forward. He couldn't jump on a podcast with just Ella and Naomi. And having Bryce around would give Alex a chance to apologize. To find some way to say, *I didn't mean to blow everything up.*

"We should do this podcast," Alex said. "Well, not the version where Ella makes up stories about me—"

"I never—"

"But the real version. My side of things." All the social media posts, all the glances in the hallways, all the tabloid articles: They would disappear. Mr. Evans would look at him, let out a relieved sigh, and say, *I'm so glad you figured out your testimony. Now we can put her behind bars.*

"Naomi, you'll still be able to apply for that scholarship," Alex went on. "You might even have a better shot, because your podcast will be more accurate. You'll have access to the original source material. Me."

"That's what I was trying to tell you," Naomi said to Ella in a matter-of-fact tone. Her eyes were gleaming; she seemed pleased that her idea was working out. Alex had to look away.

"And, Bryce, uh..." Alex swallowed hard. "I want to clear the air. Between us. Maybe this is one way I can do that."

Bryce met him with a skeptical look. "You could do that without a podcast."

Alex's palms went sweaty. "Yeah, except, uh..." How could he explain things? Bryce had known Alex was mentally ill, but he hadn't seen the worst of it. The days Alex had spent convinced televisions and computers were talking to him, the times he'd been certain even *he* wasn't real. His mom had warned him how bad it might get. *You're hallucinating more and more, and we both know the meds aren't working as well as they used to. Are you sure you want to go to school today? Are you sure you want to see Bryce? I don't know if you want anyone to find out—*

She'd been the one thing that always seemed real. The one person Alex knew would be there—not a trick of his mind—even while his psychosis gnawed at his reality and made him feel like a pale illusion of himself.

If Bryce knew this stuff, he'd freak out. The best way was to explain it slowly, episodically, which he could do via the podcast. Maybe by the end, Bryce would understand.

"And what do I get?" Ella's interruption seared Alex's nerves.

Alex shrugged. "I was sort of hoping you'd drop out."

"Oh no. I need this thing," Ella said. "I've got people ignoring me at school, talking behind my back. Last night I got a DM saying I should kill myself for spreading rumors about a dying kid. Even my mom thinks I made it up."

Whoa.

It hadn't occurred to Alex that people would go after Ella—that for every person who thought he'd poisoned himself, there was another who thought Ella was trying to drag Maryland's tragic tabloid story through the dirt. A bubble of vindictive glee rose in his chest, and he almost blurted out, *Boo freaking hoo.*

Except he didn't want people blowing up Ella's DMs telling her to kill herself.

"I get it," Bryce said. "People avoid me now, because they think I must've known about what was going on with Alex. Honestly, it was kinda nice when Naomi brought up working on a podcast. Like, maybe I'd just get to hang out with someone and have things be normal. For once. For the first time, maybe."

Oof.

Naomi sighed. "This is what I get for taking journalism instead of sewing. My cosplays would've been next-level if I took sewing. But I don't know if they have scholarships for—"

"We're doing the podcast," Ella cut in. "It's done—we already told our teacher we'd be working together, and *as you know*, the projects have to be done in pairs so we can share the recording equipment." She turned to Alex and Bryce. "If you guys try to kick me off, Naomi won't have a partner."

Naomi grimaced, hugging her arms. Alex let out a sigh.

"Okay." He jammed his hands in his pockets and tried to come up with a solution. If Ella was going to be on the podcast, he had to find a way to work with her. "Then maybe—"

"Tell you what." Ella stepped forward. "Prove it to me. Prove to me that your side of the story is right. If you're so convinced I'm lying, then convince me of your side. If you do that, you can stay on the podcast."

Alex let out a slow exhale. This was something. This was a start.

"I don't know if anything I say will convince you," he said. "You've already decided what you want to believe."

"I like evidence. Details. Build your case." Ella folded her arms over her chest. "Unless you don't have one."

Evidence. Details. Maybe this was just a way for Ella to dig deeper into his life so she could build her own case—but so what? If she was giving him this opportunity, he had to take it.

"I do. And I'll prove it." It was the first glimmer of progress Alex had made with Ella in months, and he couldn't help pushing it. "I'll prove it to you. And then you need to come clean and say you've been lying about me the whole time."

Ella wrinkled her nose. "I'll take down the posts. But I'm not publishing some notes app apology."

Alex rolled his eyes. "If I prove it, then you should—"

"Taking down the posts will be good enough." Naomi stepped between them. The anxious look in her eyes made it clear that she wanted to make this work. "Right, Alex? She'll take down the posts and you'll both move past this."

It wasn't enough, but it was better than nothing. "Okay."

"So how are we going to do this? We can't have four narrators on the podcast," Ella said. "It'll get confusing."

"We won't have four," Alex cut in. "I'll help you out with details and stuff, but I won't go on-air. You can say you got them from an anonymous source. A cop, or someone at the hospital. Then boom. Podcast."

Bryce grimaced. "Dude, you really want us talking about what happened to you? You want the whole *world* talking about what happened to you?"

Alex let out a breath. "They are already."

But the truth went deeper than that.

The odds were high that the defense would use his mental illness against him. *The boy has a psychotic disorder, he's out of touch with reality.* He knew what his mom was capable of—the stories she could tell, the lies she could weave. She could play the jury with that gentle look in her eyes and her casual sense of scatterbrained disarray. *How could I poison my son when I can't even find my keys, ha ha!*

To counter that, he needed a bulletproof strategy. One that, unfortunately, meant telling his side of the story to whoever would listen.

And if he could convince Ella? It would mean he could convince a jury.

If Alex failed, if he botched his testimony at the trial, well. His mom would come back.

He wasn't worried about her poisoning him again—what would she do, slow dose the medicine he wasn't even taking?—but her presence in the family was its own kind of poison. A festering rot.

For years, while his mom had obsessed over Alex, she'd ignored Logan. She barely acknowledged she had a second son at all. It had pushed Logan to the breaking point more than once. How many times had he threatened to run away? Alex had lost count. He couldn't let her come home—for Logan's sake.

Ella leaned against the wall, and Alex had the sudden and disorienting fear that the ship would capsize, even though they were in a shallow creek. Nausea roared inside him. *Please, please, please.* This had to work.

"Well?" Alex fought to keep the pleading out of his voice. "Are you in?"

Bryce squinted at him. "You seriously want this?"

No. "Yes."

Bryce's expression didn't change. "Okay."

A grin tugged at Naomi's lips. "Yes!"

The three of them turned to Ella.

"Fine," Ella said. "Prove it to me, and I'll help you."

"All right." Alex had to fight not to lose his nerve. "Let's do this."

That night, Alex walked home along the creek, since it flowed in the direction of his house. At some point, it had to meet the woods behind his backyard, and he needed the extra time to think, to breathe. At least the ground was more level here, so he didn't feel like he was going to collapse.

A podcast. A podcast. *A podcast?*

This was an opportunity, he reminded himself. A chance to make things better, if he played it right.

Once he was sure he was alone, he sat down on the bank and fished the two daily antipsychotic pills out of his pocket. Ran his fingers over the waxy gelatin capsules, tested their weight. As if he'd be able to tell if they were one milligram off.

You only have to take these now, his dad had told him. *They'll help with the hallucinations. With those... thoughts you have.*

You have to take these, his mom had said, year after year. *Don't you want to be able to trust your own mind?*

Yes. He did.

Of course he wanted to trust his own thoughts again, after feeling like there was a film between himself and reality, like his world and the worlds of other people never quite converged. Hallucinations of monsters and fantastical creatures when he was younger, followed by recurring visions that his dad had been killed overseas, not to mention those months when he'd been sure everyone could read his mind. Through it all, his mom's voice had been steady. *I know you're seeing it, but it's not real.*

Followed by another pill.

I know you're seeing it, but it's not real.

Each pill a promise that maybe, one day, it would get better.

And yet here he was.

His dad—and his psychiatrist—wanted him to believe that the pills would iron out his thoughts and put his head straight, but Alex knew better. And he couldn't ignore the tiny, insidious thought that kept worming its way into his mind, taking root in his neurons. *You don't know what's really in those.*

Alex twisted one of the pills open.

White powder spilled over his fingers, some drifting into the wind like a cloud. It was too fine to be salt. It definitely wasn't mercury: no silvery blobs. Who knew what it was, though. The pill bottle said ziprasidone, but the possibilities were endless. Sugar. Flour. Cocaine—that would be something—ground-up bones, baking soda, pulverized chalk, anthrax.

I know you're seeing it, but it's not real.

It looked perfectly normal. But that didn't mean anything.

He dumped the pills into the creek.

CHAPTER 8: 87 DAYS TO TRIAL

Over dinner, Alex's dad went on a merry-go-round of attempts at conversation: *How was school? Any interesting classes? Any extra-curriculars you'd like to try?* Alex tried his best to answer, but Logan didn't bother. It was awkward, as always.

"Logan, how are you managing to avoid your rabid fans during the school day?" His dad swirled his spoon in a bowl of soup.

"Ya-huh."

Alex took a few mouthfuls of soup. This was going to end the same way it always did.

His dad's eyes narrowed. "Are you stuck on your video game?"

"Yep."

A sigh. "Do you know what your next level is going to be?"

"Totally."

His dad set down his spoon. "Logan. You're not listening."

"Huh?" Logan looked up. "Oh, sorry. I gotta do homework. Linear Algebra and stuff."

"Kids your age don't take Linear Algebra."

"For sure." And Logan was gone, pushing his chair away from the table and jogging up the stairs to his room.

His dad put his head in his hands. "I don't know how to get through to him."

It wasn't clear if he wanted sympathy, an explanation, or advice. The most awkward part was that Alex had heard the same conversation a million times before, but in reverse.

Logan asking their mom, *Hey, do you have any cool ideas for monsters?* —Not now, honey.

Can we go to GameStop and see if they have the new racing game? —I'm busy, Logan.

Do you want to check out my newest level? —Uh-huh, uh-huh. Sorry, what?

Until Logan had simply given up. He'd retreated into his own world long before their mom got caught. He still let Alex in, against all odds, but he showed no sign of trusting their dad now that he was back.

If Alex screwed up his testimony and their mom came home, then Logan would be right back where he was before: the boy who never mattered.

"I'm not hungry either. I'm gonna do, uh, homework." Alex grabbed his phone and trudged upstairs. He cracked open the door to Logan's room. "Hey, you all right?"

"Yeah, just superbusy." Logan was sitting in bed, surrounded by sketches and concept drawings for his game. His room was plastered with video game posters—*SHARK RACE 2.0*, *ZOMBIE VAMPIRE WOLF FOREST*—and a robot he'd made for tech club last year sat in the corner. Its red eyes watched them intently.

"Uh-huh." Alex stepped in and leaned against the door frame. "Dad's not trying to be annoying, you know."

"I guess." Logan didn't look up, balancing a sketchbook on his knees. "I just don't wanna deal with it."

"Deal with what?" Alex asked. "Him asking you questions?"

"No, like..." Logan waved a hand in the air. "The fakeness."

This caught Alex off guard; he'd never thought of their dad as fake.

He sat down next to a pile of sketches. One of them featured two bananas locked in mortal combat, surrounded by dozens of ducks.

"The ducks eat the bananas at the end," Logan said. "It's like, tragic and stuff."

"Dude."

"Anyway." Logan shrugged. "Dad's asking questions because he thinks he's supposed to, but it's not real. He's no better than Mom. Sometimes she'd pretend to care, and I thought things could be different, but she was never actually listening to me. I changed my answers every time and she didn't notice." Logan stood and went over to his computer as if that was the end of it.

Alex's heart sank. He should've done something about this years ago. Maybe he could've talked to his mom about it, showed her how neglected Logan felt, gotten her to treat him like a son too. Now it was too late.

At least she's in jail and you can finally recover, a teacher had said to him. As if he didn't stand a very real chance of bombing his testimony, ruining the case, and putting Logan back where he started.

"This thing is just so weird," Logan said, settling into his chair.

"Tell me about it," Alex muttered.

"Although I'm glad you're not dying. That's cool."

"Appreciate it."

"But it also kind of messes with your head. She was too busy for me because she had to take care of you, right? Except it turns out you weren't sick. So what does that mean?" Logan sounded like he'd been thinking about this a lot. "She made you sick because she hated me that much?"

It hurt to think of Logan believing this, though Alex had no evidence to refute it. Still, he said, "I don't think that's why she did it."

"So she hated you? That doesn't make sense either, because she could've just smothered you when you were a baby. And if she hated me, she could've smothered me when *I* was a baby. Instead, we both survived being babies, and then this happened." Logan frowned, putting his head in his hand and leaning on the armrest. "It's so confusing."

Alex let out a sigh. "I'm with you there. But I'm pretty sure Dad is doing his best. Try to give him a chance, okay? I don't think there's a manual for what to do when it turns out your wife was poisoning your kid."

Logan gave a half smile, and Alex left him to debug code. When he stepped into his own room, his phone buzzed.

He knew it wouldn't be a social media notification, since he'd deleted his accounts months ago. It wouldn't be a message about podcast logistics, either—they'd already decided to meet in the Shitwreck every Friday afternoon to draft episodes, though the others would meet more often for recording. Ella was dead set on releasing the first episode in the beginning of October, which was just two weeks away.

Alex tapped his phone screen, and his heart dropped into his stomach.

It was an email. From his mom.

Email 1 ★ ↺ ⋮

My sweet son,

I know you probably weren't expecting to hear from me. Maybe you'll want to sit down to read this.

By the time you see this message, I imagine you'll be back in school, back to your classes and your strange (sorry!) obsession with watching poorly made disaster films. Maybe you'll be up to revisiting some old hobbies. I was always fascinated by your collection of children's books in foreign languages. Especially since you couldn't read them. Did you like the pictures? The way the letters were shaped? Did you feel like you were traveling around the world with each new book? I never asked. I wish I had now.

More than that, I hope you're safe. I hope your father knows how to take care of you and your brother, that he knows what to do if you have an episode, if you get caught up in a delusion again. I hope you're doing well in school, and that it's not too challenging adjusting to classes after half a year away. And—though you might not believe this—I hope you're healthy. I do.

I'm writing this in May. You're still unconscious, but everything has changed. The police believe things about me that aren't true, and I think they plan to take me away from you—even though I'm the only one who can take care of you.

I'm writing this because I want you to understand who I am. I don't know what you'll be like after you wake up, who you'll be. Maybe you won't recognize anything of yourself in my words; maybe you'll have thrown away all your books and gotten into EDM. I'm excited for the you that you might become. I really am. But I also want you to know me.

★ ⮌ ⋮

So I'm writing to you. I'm scheduling these emails to be sent to you in the fall—I don't know where I'll be, but I guess that's the point. In case I'm not there.

Take a deep breath. Exhale, and I'll tell you everything. Piece by piece.

I have only one request: Don't show these to your father. And definitely don't show them to the police.

The email didn't end there. It went on for several more paragraphs, but the words blurred together on the screen as blood rushed in Alex's ears.

It was her.

It felt as if he was having the most vivid hallucination of his life. She'd written and scheduled an email—no, a chain of emails—before she was taken away. The reality of that was jarring. How had she had the time to do that? He'd always assumed the arrest had unfolded quickly: a police officer riffling through a cabinet, pulling out a syringe loaded with mercury, and boom, handcuffs. Not his mom sitting in the ICU, a muscle tightening in her neck the way it always did when she was anxious, her dark eyes glancing from side to side as she typed away.

I want you to understand who I am.

They were so similar. They always had been.

Alex closed his eyes. She was a book, and he'd memorized every page, every line. She had always been so easy to read. Until it turned out that he'd been reading the pages all wrong.

He scrolled down.

Email 1 continued ★ ⮌ ⋮

When you were first born, you were so small. I could carry you with one hand.

Can you imagine that? Imagine carrying a creature in the palm of your hand. But not a hamster or a gerbil—a tiny human, with preemie-pink skin and dark eyes like your father's. You were unlike anything I'd ever seen.

You probably don't understand this, but being a parent, becoming a mother, it changes something inside you. Hardwires something so that the only thing that matters is your child. You were a star, my whole universe. You still are.

But you don't need to hear my platitudes. What I want to tell you is that everything I've done, I've done for you.

I've always done it for you.

CHAPTER 9: 80 DAYS TO TRIAL

What I want to tell you is that everything I've done, I've done for you.

For days after the first email, every time Alex's phone buzzed, it felt like a bomb. Even if it was just an app update, or *Pokémon GO* crashing his phone for the fifteenth time—when *would* he delete that—there was always the chance it could be her. Another email. Another message sent from the void of his past life.

I've always done it for you.

A week had passed since the email, and her words were imprinted on his brain. He heard her voice as he walked through the hallway between classes. He imagined her writing the emails on her laptop while he lay unconscious. She said she was going to explain herself—and he needed that more than anything. He needed an answer, a rationale. Something to reconcile the woman who took him to the park for stargazing with the woman who looked at the doctors and said, *Yes, I think we'll move forward with the surgery.*

What could she even say? *I love you very much, but I just couldn't help almost killing you.*

Alex had spent most of the past week trying to avoid Bryce, Naomi, and Ella at school, even while he coordinated with them via text over the direction of the first podcast episode. He couldn't be seen with them at school—if he was, then once the podcast came out, people might realize he was involved. It was bizarre, spotting Bryce in the hall and turning away, seeing Naomi in the library and ducking into an aisle.

After school on Friday, Alex trudged through the woods to the Shitwreck. This time he took the long way, where the ground sloped into a gentle hill toward the creek, instead of that heart-attack-inducing ravine. If he was being honest, he was excited to get started on the podcast, even if it meant seeing Ella. At least it would provide a distraction while he waited for his mom's next email.

Then something moved in the corner of his eye. A shadow walked among the oaks and hickories, flitting behind branches just out of sight.

He knew who it was. Brown hair the same color as his, hanging over her shoulders. Long, elegant strides. That distinct manner of stopping and starting, going and pausing, like she was never sure which path she wanted to take.

She'd been arrested four months ago. And he had no memory of seeing her since January, before the coma. The figure in the woods had to be a hallucination. His rational side, the side that knew he should be taking antipsychotics every morning and that had been taught to question his delusions, knew it wasn't real. She was in jail.

And yet.

He pushed through brambles, past the trees that sent long shadows cutting across the dirt. There she was, a dozen yards out, strolling around as if she was admiring the foliage. Alex took another step, his ears starting to ring, and for crying out loud, was he seriously going to have an episode here?

"Alex!" Her gaze was bright, dark eyes sparkling. "I didn't think I'd see you here, sprout."

"Why do you still call me that?" He threw himself down onto a log just in time; his legs were going numb.

"You like to garden."

Alex made a face. "I haven't gardened since I was five."

"But you were obsessed with that pumpkin." She stared off into the trees for a moment, as if remembering. "It was almost as big as you were!"

Alex's cheeks heated up. He'd been so proud he'd dressed up as a pumpkin for Halloween that year, and the pictures would haunt him forever.

He glanced over his shoulder. He knew he needed to be somewhere, but his thoughts were getting foggy. Where was he supposed to go, exactly? He couldn't leave yet. It'd been so long since he'd seen her.

"What are you doing here?" he asked.

She smiled. "I missed you. My pumpkin." She scooched a few inches closer to him. "I wanted to check on you. I know you've been having a hard time."

How are you here? he wanted to ask. If she was in jail, she couldn't be here. It was impossible to fit together the reality he knew with the one in front of him. She was sitting on the log beside him, and the rest of the world—the arrest, the rumors, the *Glad you're well?* card and the podcast—took on a grainy haze, like it was out of focus.

"Oh!" His mom pressed her hands together. "Maybe tonight we could watch a movie. Something to decompress. I found one you might like!" She broke into a smile. "It sounds absolutely horrendous."

Alex grinned. "How bad?"

"The world is attacked by a giant tomato, and only an eccentric chef can save them."

"Now *that's* storytelling."

His mom laughed. It was refreshing to see her like this. A relief, almost. She'd been so anxious the past few years.

Warmth flooded Alex's chest. She was here, and he was here, and they were going to watch a movie like old times. He let out a breath.

"By the way," he added, "I know that pumpkin I 'grew' was a Home Depot decoration. You guys put it out the night before we were supposed to harvest, so I wouldn't be disappointed. Yeah, Dad finally told me."

His mom made a face. "Matthew swore to secrecy!"

"I know, I know. My fragile heart is broken." Alex put a hand on his chest and threw his head back for dramatic effect. This made him dizzy, because of course it did.

"Wait a second." His mom looked puzzled. "When did your father tell you about that?"

Alex shrugged. "After you..."

After you went to jail.

He staggered to his feet. Leaves crackled underfoot like cracks forming in glass.

No, no no no no no, not again. He closed his eyes, tightened his grip on the backpack straps, tried to remember the tips the psychiatrist had given him that summer. He pressed his fingertips into the scratchy fabric. Crunched leaves under his shoes. Breathed in deep. *Crap, crap, crap.*

Unbelievable. At this rate, he was never going to survive the semester. He would be in class, and something would speak to him from the shadows, and—no, don't think about that.

The obvious solution was to take the pills, but for all he knew they would make things worse. Of course she was in jail, of course she couldn't alter them with something, but she'd also just been right *there*...

Breathe. Breathe.

He stumbled in the direction of the Shitwreck. He'd work on the podcast, it would distract him, and everything would be fine.

Alex turned back toward the log one last time. There was a shadow, but it was impossible to tell if it was her.

CHAPTER 10: 80 DAYS TO TRIAL

Alex stepped into the ship, trying to exude a vibe of confidence. Bryce and Naomi were sitting around the camping lantern writing in notebooks.

"That's a perfect title!" Naomi was saying. "Alliterative *and* spooky."

"Hey!" Alex sat beside them. He hadn't yet decided if he should act normal around Bryce, like nothing had changed between them, or if he needed to keep his distance. So he looked at Naomi and avoided Bryce's gaze, which was a perfectly normal and not weird thing to do. "Sorry I'm late. I, uh..."

Bryce shrugged. "It's fine. Ella's still at SAT prep. Naomi just wanted to get a head start."

"I've already hashed out some ideas." Naomi snapped her fingers. "We need to start with a bang, you know?"

"We threw together a draft." Bryce rubbed the back of his head. "But, like, we don't know what happened. So it's just random junk. Though it's pretty compelling random junk, if I do say so myself."

Alex cracked a smile. *It's garbage, but it's pretty compelling garbage*, Bryce used to say when they'd worked on their RPG together.

"We should flesh it out with the real stuff." Bryce looked right at him. "You know, the stuff that you said you'd tell us."

"Okay." The story of Clarissa Anne Clark's crimes. And there was something else behind Bryce's words: He wanted an explanation for why Alex had vanished from his life.

Hey Bryce, I was deep within a psychotic break last year and I didn't trust myself not to nuke our friendship, so I nuked it preemptively. Hope that's cool!

One step at a time. Focus on the podcast. "We shouldn't reveal everything at once, though."

"What does it matter?" Naomi asked. "Everyone already knows the outcome."

Alex ran his fingers over the knotted wooden slats of the boat. "But isn't that a problem for a serialized podcast? You need suspense."

Bryce shrugged. "Actually, lots of true crime podcasts are about cases where people already know what happened."

"Uh-huh." Alex nodded. Crap, now he had to give them something to work with. He racked his brain for a good starting place, but somehow he was back at his testimony. *My mom was pretty cool, if you forget about all the—*

"Alex?" Naomi waved a hand in front of his face. "You went spacey for a second there."

"Sorry." Alex cleared his throat. "Uh, I guess we could start with my pediatrician?"

"That seems boring." Bryce drummed his pencil against the notebook, scrunching up his face the way he always did when he was concentrating. "We've got to open with your mom. I mean, she was a borderline helicopter parent when we were little, right? Like, she was always there. At the playground. At the school pickup line. At the bake sale."

Alex frowned. "But we were kids. Isn't a parent supposed to be around for that stuff?"

Oops. Bryce's parents hadn't been there for much—his dad had been busy building a doomsday bunker for the end of the world, and his mom had resented her husband's descent into survivalist media. "Ah, sorry."

Bryce's brow furrowed. "Yeah, I guess a parent is supposed to do that."

Naomi winced. "Alex, we need something more than *she was around a lot.*"

"Right." It was hard to breathe, but Alex needed to say something. "She, uh, she liked to lecture my doctors. Insisted that she knew more than they did. She brought up her chemistry degree a lot."

"She had a degree in chemistry?" Naomi's eyes lit up. "That's great stuff. She definitely knew a lot about poisons."

"Honestly, I don't think it's related—"

"I'm here, let's get started!" Ella stepped through the hole in the boat like a wraith, autumn light catching loose strands of hair, as if she was about to ignite. The buttons on her vest caught the afternoon sun, glowing like searchlights. "Sorry, test prep ran over. Where are we?"

"Mapping out episode one." Bryce kicked his legs out, gangly limbs splayed across the rotting wooden floor. "Man, this is so weird."

"What is?" Naomi crossed something out in her book.

Bryce shrugged. "Doing a podcast about someone who was my friend."

A terrible, squirmy feeling took hold of Alex's gut. He wanted to say, *We could still be friends.* He wanted to say, *This is supposed to make it better.*

"I thought you liked doing things like podcasts" was what came out.

Bryce tilted his head. "I dunno, maybe? The *Maple Syrup Murders* one would've been fun."

"If only the *Maple Syrup Murders* had actually happened," Naomi said with an almost dreamy sigh.

"This feels *too* real," Bryce added.

"It's supposed to be real." Ella sat down beside them with a thunk, slinging her book bag onto the ground.

"How many episodes are we planning? Six?" Naomi chewed on her pen, a charm bracelet dangling from her wrist. One charm was a violin, one a zombie face, one a broken heart—apparently she was also into *Rosé and Decay.*

Bryce frowned. "I don't know if we'll be able to stretch the story out that far."

"I thought we decided a lot of it was going to be dramatizations," Naomi said. "I've been practicing."

Oh no. "Dramatizations?" Alex asked.

Naomi beamed and grabbed her notebook. "Let me show you what I've got."

Lethal Lullaby, Episode 1:
"Monster Mommy at Midnight" (TEASER)

(Children laughing, the sound distant and faint. Wind chimes can be heard over their voices.)

NAOMI	*(In a little-kid voice.)* Mommy? I feel . . . sick.
ELLA	Oh, sweetheart. But we just got to the playground!
NAOMI	But . . . my insides . . . they feel . . . like they're melting! What's happening to me?
BRYCE	Welcome to the saga of Clarissa Anne Clark. Though you might know her as the Mercury Mama, the Maniac Matriarch, or most commonly . . .
BRYCE, ELLA, AND NAOMI	*Monster Mommy.*

(Children's laughter fades out into a single scream.)

"I'm thinking we can pinch Ella's little brother to get the scream," Naomi suggested after her dramatic reading.

Alex felt like self-destructing.

"That's what you've planned for the opening?" he asked. It was so ludicrous that it had moved past embarrassment, beyond offense, and into the realm of the unreal. He felt like he was listening to someone else's story. Which maybe was the point.

Naomi beamed. "What do you think?"

She looked so earnest that Alex didn't know what to say.

"I actually kind of like it," Ella admitted.

"Of course you do," Alex muttered.

"The playground? It's the perfect *juxtaposition*." Ella's tone informed the others that they should be impressed with her for knowing what *juxtaposition* meant. "Something sweet, innocent, but beneath the surface there's terror! We'll hook them."

Alex had a million questions about the teaser, so he settled on the most basic one. "Why is the title 'Monster Mommy at Midnight' if the playground scene takes place during the day?"

"I warned you he'd complain about that," Bryce said to Naomi.

"Whatever. We can change the title." Ella leaned forward, a gleam in her eye.

You just have to convince her, Alex told himself. *Convince her, and things might suck less.*

"What matters is the content," Ella went on. "Naomi, I like what you're doing with the teaser. People love an innocent setup when they know something's about to go wrong. *Dramatic irony.*"

Bryce leaned back on his hands. "Oh man, that was on our Lit test last week, wasn't it?"

"Bryce, focus." Naomi lay on her stomach on the floor and drew a line across a blank page, adding little perpendicular slashes as if making a timeline. Her brow was knit with concentration. "What comes after the teaser?"

Ella flipped open her notebook. "After the opening—"

Alex cut in. "Just so we're all on the same page, I never approved—"

"—we'll talk about your mom." Ella met him with a smile that made Alex feel dissected. "The first episode should focus on her. We'll barely need to talk about you at all."

That was so much worse.

It was obvious what would make good content: things like *She seemed so happy every time I collapsed*, or *She had to restrain me when she jabbed the needle in*, or even *She pulled out all my teeth and made a necklace with them, for kicks!*

None of it would be true. But half of the things in the news weren't true, either.

There were other things he could say. Honest things. *In the hospital, she found new podcasts for me, so even when I couldn't open my eyes there was something for me to do. When I was feeling better, she'd take me to the park at night so I could use my astrolabe to find my favorite constellations. In the winter, she was obsessed with holiday lights. Logan and I almost got electrocuted when she went overboard—but the show at the end was always worth it.*

His phone felt heavy in his pocket.

"Alex?" Bryce pursed his lips. "Are you..."

"Sorry." Alex forced himself to look up. "Just distracted."

"I get it." Naomi's voice was sincere. "Awful memories, right?"

Except that was the strange thing, the impossible thing, the how-was-he-supposed-to-hold-that-in-his-brain thing. She hadn't been awful. At least not in the way they thought.

"I can get us started." Naomi set her notebook down. "I did some digging. Your mom has a Facebook profile, even though it's locked. She grew up in Pennsylvania and she posted that she'll always be a 'farm girl.'"

"She never lived on a farm," Alex said. "But she always wished she had. She said she was going to convince my dad to buy a horse farm in the mountains."

"She rode horses?" Ella clicked her pen.

A memory of his mom rose to the surface: her at a horse farm upstate, white-knuckled and falling out of the saddle. "Not in the slightest."

"She also posted a lot of..." Bryce worked his jaw back and forth. "I'm not sure how to put this."

Oh God. Alex had never looked at his mom's profile. Would it be photos of fresh-baked bread, his mom bragging about a "secret recipe" that everyone now suspected was poison? Or maybe a picture of the fancy walker she'd found, back when Alex needed support to walk.

Maybe there would even be pictures of him, fragile and pale, surrounded by a universe of monitors and IV lines.

"Mom memes." Bryce winced.

Alex blinked. "Mom memes?"

Naomi turned her phone around to face Alex. There was a picture of a laughing woman, her arms crossed over her chest. Caption: *Thinking about all the junk food I'll eat after the kids are in bed!*

Naomi swiped.

The next one was a child with his eyes half-closed, cuddled up in bed. *Never make eye contact with a kid about to fall asleep... They'll sense your excitement and abort mission.*

Alex had to hold back a snort at this one.

"Oh no." Bryce hung his head. "You think they're funny. You think they're funny! Something *is* wrong with you, and it's not what everyone says it is."

Alex huffed. "Okay, if you had a younger sibling, you'd get that last one."

"Mom memes? The most interesting thing about this woman is that she posts mom memes?" Ella asked. "That won't make much of a podcast."

"We could look for a suspicious mom meme," Naomi said. "Though they probably don't make memes about what happened to you."

"The mom memes *are* kind of weird," Alex admitted. "I mean, I was typically the one who put Logan to bed, if I was healthy enough."

His mom had usually dropped into bed at the end of the day, tired from his appointments and consultations. But when Logan had needed help to fall asleep, it was kind of fun to make up stories with him until he started snoring.

Ella gave Alex a sideways look. "You'd have to tranquilize that kid to get him to sleep."

It was uncomfortable to think that Ella might know Logan almost as well as he did. But maybe this was an opening—if he brought up another piece of the truth, maybe she'd latch on to it.

"My mom doesn't know a thing about Logan." Alex was careful not to look at Ella. "She'd ask him if he wanted a new coloring book, but he's never been into coloring. Or she'd take him to the zoo, except he hates the zoo. Then she'd go around telling people how close we all were."

Naomi jotted something down. "So she was always a liar."

Instinctively, Alex wanted to jump to his mom's defense, though of course Naomi was right. And it was better than Ella calling *him* a liar. Still…

"It never felt that way to me," he said. "It felt more aspirational. She wanted to be the kind of person who rode horses. She wanted to be the kind of mom who put both her kids to bed at night. Who had time for everything."

"So she was living a fantasy life on the internet?" Bryce didn't look up from his notebook, scribbling away.

Ella picked at her jeans. "I mean, that's what the internet is for."

Her tone was matter-of-fact, less judgmental than before. "Yeah, I guess," Alex said.

"But she took it to another level." Bryce stroked his chin. "The question is why."

Alex's mind wandered. Thinking about what his mom might have wanted out of the situation was like pressing needles into his skin, a million stabs in a million places. And no matter what this podcast did for him, it wouldn't give him the answer.

Bryce lifted his gaze from his notebook and said, "I have an idea for the next part."

Lethal Lullaby, Episode 1:
"The Fantasy of Family" (DRAFT)

(Sounds of wind blowing, leaves rustling.)

BRYCE Everyone has a fantasy for themselves. When I was little, I wanted to be a pro soccer player. I joined every team, tried every position, even got a concussion when someone threw a two-liter bottle of Coke on the field. Those soccer moms are a menace.

(Sound of a ball being kicked;
a middle-aged woman screams in rage.)

BRYCE

I bet you have a fantasy too. Maybe you want to date a supermodel—good luck, unless you're also a supermodel, in which case, congratulations! Maybe you want to live in a mansion—land is cheap in rural Alabama, so that might be something to look into. Maybe you want to ace the SATs, which, godspeed, because that test is designed to break your spirit.

(Clicking sounds.)

BRYCE

A lot of us live out these fantasies on social media: Instagram, TikTok—or, if you're over the age of forty, Facebook. We use filters. We create new versions of ourselves. We have better hair, smoother skin, cooler jobs. We travel to amazing places, and we don't even tell our followers that we only got to see the Eiffel Tower for two seconds before some Parisian blocked the view. You live here, man! Come back another time!

(Frenchman saying, "Hon hon HON!")

BRYCE

Clarissa Anne Clark was like that too. No, she wasn't an ornery Frenchman. But she had fantasies: She wanted to live on a farm. She wanted to ride horses in the mountains. And she wanted to tuck both her sons into bed at night, even though she usually only had time for one.

(A child's music box plays.)

BRYCE Clarissa Anne Clark had another fantasy. She wanted a tragically ill kid to nurse and care for: to shuttle back and forth to doctors' appointments, to bring in and out of hospitals and get the doctors' sympathy, to parade around the neighborhood so she could show everyone that she was the Best. Mom. Ever.

(Dramatic beat.)

BRYCE But she made this fantasy come true.

Alex stared at Bryce.

He knew that this angle on the story was personal to Bryce. Bryce's dad was always trying to reinvent himself—first it was achieving the perfect suburban lifestyle, and then he wanted to be a survivalist, a man who could take on the worst the world had to offer. Plus there was the cheating that Bryce had told Alex about. His dad had tried to remake himself, and he'd remade their family instead.

The Fantasy of Family. It wasn't just about Alex.

"I'm going to have to do the French accent." Ella frowned. "Your *hon hon hon* was *hon hon* horrific."

"Remind me to never go to your soccer games," Naomi said.

Alex said nothing, still trying to draw together the two images he had of Bryce—the carefree boy with windswept hair and a lopsided grin, and the boy who was caving in on himself. Bryce read his script so casually, he managed to hide everything that Alex suspected was lurking beneath.

"Alex?" Bryce asked, jolting him out of his thoughts. "What do you think?"

"It's great," Alex managed.

Bryce broke into a grin. "Let's get it done."

CHAPTER 11: 75 DAYS TO TRIAL

Alex spent the next week attempting to focus on school. Ella, Naomi, and Bryce were recording the first episode at Ella's house—they didn't need him there, since he wasn't going to be on-air—and he had to trust that they would follow the plan.

There were ample distractions: On Monday, Geometry was interrupted by an explosion in the nearby Chemistry lab (apparently some students had found leftover ethyl alcohol from the original experiment), and on Tuesday, his History class got derailed by a fistfight between two students attempting to re-create the famed Hamilton–Burr duel. Meanwhile, intrusive thoughts wormed their way into his brain.

People will think the podcast is pathetic.

Everyone's going to say it's full of lies.

People will know you're in on it—

It was enough to make Alex want to peel his own skin off.

One day during lunch, he went to the library instead of the cafeteria. Ella sat at one of the front tables, a pile of books next to her, so Alex ducked into an aisle without making eye contact. He meandered among the bookshelves until he hit the foreign languages section. This, of course, was where he ran into Naomi.

She was sitting on the floor picking at a sandwich and flipping through a workbook. Food wasn't allowed in the library, but most kids ignored this rule.

"Alex!" Naomi waved as if they'd known each other for years. For crying out loud, didn't she realize they were supposed to ignore each other in public? If people saw them together, no one would trust the podcast.

On the other hand, this corner of the library was empty. Maybe, if they were quiet enough, no one would notice them. It would be nice to not eat lunch alone, for once.

"Hey." Alex sat down beside her, dropping his bag to the ground. "Do you always eat lunch in here? I only thought to come because... uh..." *Because no one in this school wants to talk to me.* "Because it's less noisy."

His phone buzzed, but it was just a text about a group project, not an email from his mom. He'd gotten two more emails since the first, mostly talking about his mom's fears for his mental health, plus rehashing a memory or two—baking cookies together when he was little, hanging up Christmas lights until the house seemed to glow. It made his chest ache.

Naomi glanced around the shelves. "You said you tried to learn Russian from German, right? What made you pick German?"

Alex leaned against the bookshelf. "I loved the fairy tales as a kid. They're so perfectly creepy. It's like, 'Don't suck on your thumbs, because if you do, the tailor with freakishly large scissors will come and slice them off. Snip snip, sleep tight!'" Alex shook his head. "My little brother based a level in his video game off that one."

Naomi snorted. "If you ever get back into Russian, you should try *those* fairy tales. I think my favorite is the story of the kikimora. If she sees you, she'll kill someone in your family, and then a sorcerer can take your family member's spirit and put it into a doll."

"Great souvenir."

In an aisle to their left, there was a faint whispering, murmuring. Other students? Could they see him and Naomi? He tensed up, but Naomi seemed unbothered. Like she hadn't heard anything.

Then there were footsteps and Naomi looked up as well. Two girls walked past and shot her a scathing look. "Ugh, you can't even get to these books without running into the school troll."

Naomi's cheeks flushed. "What's the point when you're not even going to read them?"

"At least I won't be mouthing every syllable to myself like I'm still learning how to read," the girl shot back.

Naomi waved a hand dismissively, though her shoulders were tense. "I think the early reader books are in the other aisle. Those might be more your speed."

The girl glowered at her. "Do you have any idea how hard it is to focus in class when you're digging through your backpack, or whispering to yourself, or—"

Alex got to his feet. He ought to do something, say something, but now that he was standing up, he didn't know what his plan was. "Hey, why don't you just..."

The two girls stared at him as if he'd appeared from an alternate dimension. It took a second for them to connect the dots, but Alex saw the recognition in their eyes, the story flashing to the surface as if they'd just punched *Monster Mommy* into Google.

"Well," said the first girl, her voice almost impressed. "Look at that. She's landed a friend."

"Careful, he looks like he might faint." Her friend smirked.

Before Alex could respond, both of them were gone. His heart was pounding, so he gripped the bookshelf and sat down again before he could get dizzy. Naomi didn't make eye contact.

"Um," Alex ventured. "Does that happen a lot?"

Naomi tore the edge of her sandwich into pieces. "Don't people mess with you too?" she said, as an answer.

Alex wanted to say yes, but the truth was, it didn't happen to him in the same way. It seemed like people saw Naomi's OCD as a nuisance, not a threat. It was just something that made the weird girl even weirder.

Psychosis was different. Psychosis scared people—they saw it as the disease of serial killers, people raving to themselves on street corners, and horror movie villains. Kids simply avoided him. Instead of being mocked, he got whispers in hallways, people turning away as soon as he walked past.

"Sort of," Alex offered.

"Mmm." Naomi twirled a strand of hair around her finger. "There's a Chinese quote about this. 'Sacrificing oneself for the pursuit of truth.' Sometimes I feel like I did that. I can't hide my OCD, so I sacrificed my social life for it."

Alex's shoulders fell. "It's that bad, huh? The way people treat you?"

Naomi didn't answer. Instead, she leaned back against the shelf, her curls framed by a dusty French dictionary and a yellowing *Ana Perry's Guide to Mexico!* "I'm ready to get out of Maryland. Leave the States, even."

"You think they'll be more understanding of OCD in another country?" Alex asked.

"Well, no. I'd just like to see something new. For once." There was a dreamy look in Naomi's eyes. She pulled her knees up. "I'll go to Mexico and eat rainbow maize in one of those remote towns where everybody knows everybody. I'll go to a village at the base of Mount Everest and meet all the climbers and Sherpas. I'll go to a Lunar New Year celebration in China and help make dumplings."

It struck Alex that what she wanted was to meet strangers, to peek into other people's worlds, to learn who they were in their own languages. A language built the stage for how a person viewed the world, defined the very words they used to think about things. After all, if you didn't have a word for something like *the mother of all loneliness*—which German, of course, did—would you even know it existed? Would you recognize it when you saw it?

Alex recognized it in Naomi. No wonder she spent so much time in the library.

"That's cool," he said. "The traveling. It sounds amazing."

"Yeah, well. We'll see if that scholarship works out. If not, I guess I'll just rot here in Frederick." Naomi closed her Tupperware without finishing the sandwich.

Behind her, words began unpeeling from the spines of books. They fluttered down to the ground, as if the engraved titles were nothing but leaves blowing off as the seasons changed, settling onto the library carpet.

He wasn't hallucinating. No way. Books probably just did that sometimes.

"Alex?" Naomi's voice seemed farther away now. "What are you looking at?"

"Nothing," Alex answered.

"Hmm." Naomi gave him a skeptical look. "I should go. My next class is out in the trailers."

After Naomi left, he heard a voice from the shadows of the aisles. *So you convinced some kids to tell your sob story on Spotify?*

It wasn't real, it wasn't real, it wasn't real.

Why would you lie to those three? another voice crooned.

Alex clenched his hands. *Crap.* It was a real voice. Except it wasn't. An auditory hallucination.

The pills were so heavy in his pocket.

Before he could think, he had the capsules in his palm, his hands twisting them open. This time, instead of white dust floating out, the substance was red. Red, red, red, more of a ruby color than blood, gem-like and sparkling. The liquid floated into the air, drawn up like thread.

Beautiful, almost.

He dumped them into a trash can anyway, because beautiful could make you sick.

Outside the library, the hallway floor split open in a web of cracks, rich red color leaching out from each fracture. Like liquid gems, reflecting the overhead lights so they glowed in a riot of red and orange. If someone wasn't careful, they were going to break the school open and fall into another dimension.

Alex pulled on his backpack and thought, *Someone better check on that.*

Trial Notes 1: When did you first start to feel sick?

Five, six? Seven? Who knows? It wasn't like flipping an on-off switch, like one day I was a healthy kid who climbed to the top of the jungle gym, and the next I was hooked up to a million monitors in an ICU.

It was more like this: Some days when I came home from school, I felt so worn out that I crawled into bed and slept for twelve hours. But that happens to everyone sometimes, right?

Some days, I threw up so much I had to go home early. But plenty of kids get food poisoning.

Some nights, I came to without any memory of passing out, only to hear Mom's voice saying, "There, there. You had a seizure." Even I knew that wasn't normal.

Some days. Some nights. Once a month. Once a week.

Time began to blur.

CHAPTER 12: 73 DAYS TO TRIAL

By Friday, Alex was ready to get it over with.

Episode one. No big deal. Just a podcast about the worst thing that had ever happened to him. A six-part series that would encourage the world to dissect his testimony before he even went on the stand.

How could he have thought this was a good idea?

They weren't meeting in the Shitwreck today—they'd upload the episode and make their social media posts from home, and then get started on episode two in a few days.

Bryce had emailed the group the final cut. On the walk home from school, Alex put in one earbud and held his breath.

In some towns, everything seems perfect. The trees grow to the exact same height, the gardens are carefully manicured, and people are always smiling—even when you know their lives are falling apart.

Alex wouldn't have described his childhood as seemingly perfect, but maybe there was some truth to Bryce's words. His mom had been supercheerful around other people. At the grocery store, she'd gushed over the seasonal produce, even when he knew she hadn't slept the night before. She'd chatted with the shopkeepers and *ooh*ed and *aah*ed at the new collections hanging in colorful boutiques, even as she'd warned Alex that they had no money for Christmas presents that year—hospital bills added up.

Strange how Bryce had captured that duality.

Most of us want to help others. We want to make this world a kinder, gentler place. Maybe you want to end climate change, ban nuclear weapons, or prevent the imminent AI takeover of humanity—on that last one, big tech can already see inside your house, so it's too late. But some of us want to help so much that we create a crisis where there isn't one.

Was that it? It couldn't be that simple. But it did bring the two sides of his mom into perspective: the sweet, gentle side that always had time to chat, and the side that had uncapped his pills and filled them with mercury.

Have you ever fantasized about coming across a car crash so you could be the one to save lives? Have you ever dreamed about being the one passenger on a plane who could say, "I can fly this thing!" when the pilot gets sick? Have you ever imagined being the hero of the story?

Clarissa Anne Clark did. She made herself the hero—and the villain.

Alex relaxed a bit. Maybe Bryce could pull this off. Maybe he could string together Alex's story so that it wasn't excruciating to listen to. This didn't feel voyeuristic or cruel. Just honest.

Then the sound of a little boy shrieking broke through his thoughts.

Great. They'd gotten Ella's brother to scream.

By the time Alex made it home, he'd listened to the full episode: every philosophical tangent (Bryce went off about existentialism around the thirty-minute mark), shoehorned-in ad (Naomi, plugging online Mandarin-tutoring services), and painful dramatization (somehow Ella managed the voices for two doctors, an EMT, Alex, his mom, and even a clown that made a bizarre and unexplainable appearance).

Over the course of thirty-eight minutes, they covered the details Alex had given them, and some they'd gleaned from the news: where his mom might've gotten the mercury (old thermometers, science kits), how she got it into the pills (with a syringe), and even some facts about Logan (he'd always been the healthy one, though his penchant for violent video games was borderline).

It was strange, it was unnerving, it was rattling.

It was perfect.

No one would think he was involved. No one would even *dream* that Alex would be part of a project in which his childhood self was terrorized into tears by Spunky the Clown.

Alex stepped into the house. His dad was home, thumbing through documents on the couch. Alex didn't have to see the papers to know they were for the trial. It was in just two and a half months, which Alex felt like a ticking bomb in his chest.

"I swear," his dad muttered. "One day, I am going to get my life organized. I'm going to clean out my email inbox, sort my mail, and have one of those accordion folders with the labels for my documents. I'm gonna do it! Hold me to it, Alex."

"I guess I inherited your organizational skills." Alex's schoolwork was jumbled up in a crumpled mess of doodles, homework he'd forgotten to do, and readings he'd never looked at. Only his German notes were in order, and that wasn't even for school.

His dad sighed. "I could do better. Be someone who has it all together. I could be that person."

I could be that person. Like if his dad put everything in an accordion folder, his life would make sense.

I could be that person. Maybe Alex's mom had said that too, preparing the injections, thinking about the sympathy she'd get the next time Alex ended up in the ICU.

I could be that person. Who knew what kind of person Alex could be, now that he was no longer the Tragic Sick Boy? At least, not as tragic, not as sick. A lowercase-*s* sick. The kind of sick that wouldn't kill him.

Alex's phone buzzed as he went into the kitchen for a snack.

Bryce: Are we ready to launch???

Naomi: Don't forget to crosspost!!!

I could be that person. The podcast would clear away the rubble of his history, let people look at him in a new way, as a new Alex.

Alex texted back: *Let's do this.* Naomi, Bryce, and Ella were going to blast the podcast to everyone they knew and post it on their socials. The link to the launch announcement came barely a minute later.

LETHAL LULLABY: A NEW PODCAST ON APPLE, SPOTIFY, AND WHEREVER YOU GET YOUR PODCASTS.

PART 2

LETHAL LULLABY

OCTOBER

CHAPTER 13: 70 DAYS TO TRIAL

The weekend had been excruciating.

Alex had deleted his social media accounts, so it was hard to track the podcast's progress. He kept refreshing Naomi, Bryce, and Ella's pages. Ella was posting the most and she had a sizable following, but she had disabled comments after getting those nasty DMs.

Had anyone listened? Was it trending anywhere? How would he know? Were people talking about it on… Discord? Was that what people did on Discord? He had no idea.

Monday morning, Alex was so jittery he could barely sit still. His dad peered at him when he slid into the car to go to school. "Are you okay?"

"Yeah! Just…" *Drank too much coffee?* That would be a bad lie; he wasn't supposed to drink coffee due to side effects with the antipsychotics—not like he was taking them, anyway. But his dad couldn't know that.

His dad's eyes narrowed. "Just what?"

Crap, he'd forgotten to finish his sentence. "Just stayed up late doing homework!"

His dad nodded slowly. "Uh-huh."

Once Alex reached school, he was on high alert. Walking through the hallway was torture. People glanced at each other, talking, laughing at this-or-that inside joke. Hardly anyone looked his way. Did that mean they'd heard it? Maybe the details were so graphic the other students were uncomfortable? Or maybe—

Maybe no one had listened.

First period: Their homeroom teacher droned on about dress code violations, and everyone stared at Cassidy Harris, who was being reamed out for wearing a tank top with too-thin straps.

Maybe no one had listened.

Second period: Someone had etched a note onto his desk. A circle, with words inside reading *SEIZURE BUTTON*. Ha ha. Very funny.

Maybe no one had listened.

Third period: A girl gave a stirring rendition of a monologue from some Shakespeare play (Alex hadn't done the reading in weeks), and another kid cried.

Maybe no one—

After school, even though it was a Monday, Alex ventured through the woods. He crashed through brambles and branches, staggered over logs, even took the shortcut down the ravine. He got a busted knee for his efforts. But he had to know. He had to.

"Yikes," Ella said when he stepped into the boat. Only Ella. Of course. Bryce probably had soccer, and Naomi might've been tutoring. "What happened to you?"

Alex took a breath and realized his vision was going dark.

"I'm—" he said, but then the blackness crowded closer, and it was like he didn't have legs.

He crashed to the floor.

When he came to, the inside of the boat was a blur, harsh edges smoothed into nothing. It was impossible to know how long he'd been unconscious. The camping lantern buzzed, and its vibration trickled down his spine and into his bones. It felt like the earth was trembling.

Oh, he wanted to throw up.

"Hey, hey, whoa." The voice could've been coming from light-years away. It was soft, almost soothing . . . *Ella?* "You fainted."

Fainted sounded like a thing Victorian women with too-tight corsets did on velvet couches. Characters in soap operas *fainted*; normal people blacked out.

But for once Ella didn't sound condescending. She seemed worried.

Passing out, blacking out, fainting. Maybe it didn't matter.

"Sorry." Alex's voice was garbled. "Went too fast."

"No kidding." Some kind of fabric had been placed under his head, plush and fuzzy. "Do I need to call someone?"

"I'll be fine. Just give me a minute." The last thing he needed was his dad trekking into the woods. Alex cast a wary glance in Ella's direction. "You're not gonna yell at me for faking it? Not gonna ask where I keep the passing-out drugs?"

Ella pursed her lips. "You must think I'm a complete asshole."

"Yeah, kinda," Alex said without hesitation.

"Even if you did this to yourself, I can't let you drop dead in the Shitwreck. I'm not that kind of person." Ella paused. "What were you running down here for, anyway? You know we meet on Fridays."

Alex slowly sat up, leaning against the hull. "I—"

The sound of footsteps and crunching leaves could be heard from outside. Bryce and Naomi stepped into the boat.

"Hey! We got your text. I just think—" Bryce's gaze fell to Alex. "What are you doing here?"

Wait a second. Ella had texted Bryce and Naomi, but not Alex. "She messaged you?" Alex asked.

"Yeah. We need to strategize. This thing has like, no traction." Bryce sighed and leaned against the wall. He must've come right after practice; he was wearing his uniform, and muddy cleats dangled from his bag.

"We have six listeners?" Naomi offered.

"Six is not acceptable." Ella didn't even look at Alex, didn't acknowledge that she'd tried to freeze him out of this meeting. "We need this thing to be front page on Spotify."

Okay, that sounded extreme. They needed listeners, sure—listeners who would comment and give Alex a read on whether his planned testimony was decent—but they didn't need millions, and the idea of having that many people plugged in was terrifying.

Bryce rubbed the back of his head. "Okay, I guess we can try to amp things up a bit."

"All right." Alex tried to brace himself. "How do we get this to more listeners?"

Ella sat down on the floor with a thunk and pulled out an enormous binder. "I think we need to dig deeper into your mom's version of the story. We need to figure out what she would say."

Alex fought the urge to push back. Ella had given him an opportunity to convince her. He just had to use it. "She would say . . ."

Can you believe what they're saying about us?

I never thought he was capable of this.

Alex exhaled. "She would lie. Like she lied to the doctors." *Like she lied to me.*

"It's hard to make sense of," Ella said slowly. "Her lying, even though she was so thoughtful and nice."

"Was she?" Naomi asked. It occurred to Alex that she was the only one there who'd never met his mom. "Nice?"

"Yeah," Bryce admitted.

"Maybe we could run with that. Not in the way Ella was going," Naomi said before Alex could protest. "But, like, we could dig into that duality a bit more. Compare her lies with how caring she was, or how caring she seemed."

"I like that," Bryce said. "I mean, she always made me cookies when I came over. It was great! Scary to think about that, in hindsight. Like, those cookies could've killed me." He directed this at the others, not Alex. Maybe it was too weird for him to speak directly to Alex. To act as if nothing had changed.

"I doubt she would've poisoned you." Naomi balanced a notebook on her knees.

"You're right. I'd be the most obnoxious sick kid ever. Always whining for balloons and video games and shit."

"Bryce." Ella cleared her throat. "Where are you going with this?"

"It's just strange to think about, looking back." Bryce pulled a knee up, staring off into space. "She seemed like she loved being a parent."

"Yeah, she did," Alex said quietly. Her email was lodged in his memory; he could rattle off his mom's words without thinking. "She used to say, *Being a parent, becoming a mother, it changes something inside you. Hardwires something so that the only thing that matters is your child.*"

"Damn." Bryce let out a low whistle. "She said that to you?"

"She wrote it in a note in my lunch box," Alex said, which was kind of true.

Bryce frowned. "Intense."

Ella jotted some words down, her eyes narrowed in concentration. "That's helpful. Her devotion to you."

Alex twisted his hands into each other. "But then I'd have some medical emergency, and she'd get so..." It was difficult to describe what happened. "*Excited* isn't the right word, because she did seem worried. But she sprang into action so naturally. Like she was only alive when something went wrong."

Ella's expression softened for a moment. Maybe she recognized this as truth—after all, she'd been around to babysit Logan whenever Alex had an emergency. She must've recalled the way his mom channeled her energy when he was sick, the way her frazzled demeanor transformed into resolve.

"Maybe your mom was like that because she was persistent," Ella said. "Because she knew that if she didn't fight for you, no one would."

"Maybe." There had to be another way to show Ella the mom he'd seen, the mom he'd known. But the problem was, he'd assumed his mom was just persistent too—he never in a million years would've guessed the real truth. "I just can't bring the two sides of her together in my head. Like, she was so caring, and yet Logan..."

Ella bit her lip. Alex could tell he'd hit on something there; Ella knew just how neglected Logan felt.

Logan, who had been born right around the time it all started. Logan, who had never been interesting to their mother. Logan, who had never been poisoned.

Ella shook her head. "It doesn't make sense. I mean, I guess she was busy with you. But still."

"It seems like we've got a lot to work with," Naomi said, closing her notebook. "We'll put together a draft, and then we should be in a good position to record and release on Friday. What do you think?"

That wasn't nerve-racking at all.

Ella snapped her fingers and said, "Episode two will be brilliant."

CHAPTER 14: 66 DAYS TO TRIAL

Lethal Lullaby, Episode 2: "A Cold Day for Justice" (FINAL CUT)

(A music box plays.)

ELLA	A chill begins to fill the air. A brutal wind rips leaves off the trees like it's blowing out a candle. The sky is gray, and smoke from fall wildfires curls into the air and sits there, hanging over the town as if waiting to swoop down and asphyxiate us all.
BRYCE	Wildfire safety tips: Do not leave grills, candles, or small children unattended. If you see something, say something—
ELLA	Bryce, I'm trying to build *atmosphere*.
BRYCE	Oh right, right.

(Wind chimes rustle.)

ELLA My name is Ella McIntire, and with me is Bryce Miles. Welcome to episode two of *Lethal Lullaby.*

(Theme music begins. A music box plays; soon the notes grow discordant, and the song falls apart.)

ELLA Where did it begin, a life of sickness, a life of misery? And was it really that miserable? To better understand what happened to Alex Clark, we must get to know his mother.

BRYCE Clarissa Anne Clark made "being a mom" look like an extreme sport—one she wanted to win. Despite raising two kids pretty much on her own, she always had baked goods in the house, which, in hindsight—

ELLA Bryce—

BRYCE I'm just saying, we will never know if I ate a mercury cookie.

ELLA Please don't tell me you've been thinking about this since the news came out.

BRYCE Alex's mom was disorganized! She could've mixed up the batches!

ELLA Okay, she was disorganized. But she was also devoted. Whenever Alex had a medical emergency, she would spring into action—like she was truly becoming alive.

BRYCE Kinda suspicious.

ELLA To me, it sounds like a woman who had a deep sense of what her kid needed—and was willing to advocate for him. Maybe she was "annoying" with doctors. But does "annoying" mean that she was trying to tell them how to diagnose Alex? Or does it mean she was going to bat for him?

BRYCE I don't know.

ELLA You spent years visiting that house, and even you can't tell if Clarissa was devoted or deceiving.

BRYCE Well, I—

ELLA All I'm saying is: We don't have the full story. Police only found mercury in the hospital room, not in their house. And Alex's little brother never got sick. Isn't that weird?

BRYCE I guess—

ELLA There are so many pieces that don't add up. But don't worry, listeners. It's our job, here at *Lethal Lullaby*, to put them together.

Alex had to do something.

He'd thought that episode two would explore his mom's relationship with the truth. He'd stayed out of their way that week, figuring that Bryce and Naomi could handle Ella while they wrote and recorded, and what a mistake that'd been. Ella had twisted every detail he'd given them.

He couldn't let Ella keep warping his story. He spent Saturday morning spinning in circles trying to figure out what to do—and so far he had nothing.

Talk to Naomi? Naomi didn't seem like the type to stand up to Ella. She hadn't even been in this episode, anyway. He couldn't blame her for stuff she hadn't said.

Talk to Bryce? *Hey Bryce, so I want to stop Ella from saying that sketchy stuff on the podcast, because it's not true. What* is *true? Ha ha, I'm glad you asked, because I still can't bring myself to tell you…*

Talk to Ella? Ha.

Alex left the house to try to clear his head, but as he walked along the sidewalk he just wanted to tear his hair out. It was unseasonably warm, and when he turned the corner and spotted the gas station, he slipped inside. The air-conditioning was a relief; he'd worn his Maryland sweatshirt, which was a mistake. The one advantage of dysautonomia was that he didn't sweat—except sweating was a pretty important biological reaction. Sweating kept a person from passing out.

There were a few *Rosé and Decay* posters tacked up by the front counter, advertising an upcoming con. Maybe that would distract Ella from the podcast for a while, though it seemed unlikely.

"These poll options are ridiculous," a girl was saying in the next aisle over. "I mean, saying Clarissa did it because she wanted to flirt with a doctor? Come on."

"Hey, if the guy was anything like Dr. Kim at Campus Health, I can imagine it," another girl said with a giggle.

"Jenna, gross! Do you think they'll let me write my own option—"

"Yes! Look! Okay, put down your theory."

Alex's breath caught in his throat, and he froze in the middle of the snack aisle. Poll options. Flirting with a doctor. Clarissa.

They were talking about the podcast.

Two feelings surfaced at once. The first was wild, unfettered glee: Random people at a gas station were listening to the show! They would hear what he had to say! They might understand his side of the story! The second was raw panic. Why was there a *poll*?

He staggered outside and gripped the edge of a nearby trash can. Breathe, breathe, breathe. There was no reason to freak out. It was just a poll. Just a poll where people could vote on Alex's life.

Option A: Alex was lying the whole time, and he helped his mom mix the doses.

Option B: Alex was lying the whole time, and he poisoned himself so people would feel bad for him.

Option C: Alex was lying the whole time, and—

He pulled out his phone, his thoughts going so fast he couldn't keep track of them. There was no way he was talking to Ella, and texting Bryce would be too weird. Which meant he'd have to try Naomi. Likely to go nowhere, but he had no other option.

Alex: we need to talk about the podcast

Alex: can we meet tomorrow???

Then he added, for good measure: **it'll look bad for your class if the podcast is pushing a conspiracy theory . . . journalistic ethics are a thing, right??**

He sat down on a bench at the park across the street. Within moments, Naomi replied.

Naomi: No can do! I'm at a con this weekend.

Of course Naomi texted with perfect punctuation.

Naomi: Ella and Bryce are going too.
Celebrating all our work from this week.

Alex tensed up. Ella had invited Naomi and Bryce, and shut him out. Again. It wasn't surprising, but it was unsettling.

Naomi: It's for Rosé and Decay!
But I don't have a cosplay yet.

Her texts kept coming—she wasn't sure what to wear, she'd made two petticoats already but the stitching was messed up, would she need to fake an accent, did he know the British accent of the 1800s didn't sound like the one from today, et cetera. He let out a groan. This was unbelievable.

One option would be to try to catch Naomi at school on Monday—but if someone saw them talking, the podcast could be screwed. He'd gotten lucky that day in the library, and it wasn't a good idea to chance it again. If he waited any longer, Ella might have the next episode drafted, and it would be harder for Naomi and Bryce to push against her. They were always down to the wire, recording these things just hours after drafting them.

Alex: maybe we can meet sunday evening or something

Naomi: On a school night????

For crying out loud.

Naomi: I have to go. Ella and I are working on finishing up our costumes. Turning my phone off so I can prep for this thing. See you next week!

Alex barely registered the rest of the message over the buzzing, gnawing realization that Naomi and Ella were becoming *friends.*

He stepped back inside the gas station. A *Rosé and Decay* poster called to him like a siren. It was this weekend, a two-day extravaganza at a hotel and convention center. Maybe he could talk to Naomi there. And somehow not run into Ella.

The tightness in his chest began to ease. He could just...

No way. Tickets were ninety-nine dollars. And it was in freaking *Baltimore.*

But what other option did he have? No. He'd go to this con. Somehow.

He'd just have to find a way to convince his dad.

CHAPTER 15: 66 DAYS TO TRIAL

Convincing his dad to spend a hundred bucks and give up his Sunday would require some craftiness. And probably lies. Lies were bad, of course—but 100 percent essential in this case.

"So," his dad said over dinner. "Did either of you get up to anything fun today? Logan, how's the game going?"

"Yep," Logan said, cutting each of his carrots into smaller and smaller cubes.

Alex wanted to grab Logan by the shoulders and shake him. *Talk to Dad, for crying out loud. He's not like Mom. He actually wants to get to know you.*

His dad watched Logan for a moment and then went back to his food. It was silent and awkward and terrible.

Alex had to get moving. "Soooo," he started. "You know that fandom I'm super into?"

His dad raised an eyebrow. "What's a fandom?"

"Uh, a group of people who really like something."

"The way I like hockey?" His dad's voice was eager, as if he'd answered a trivia question correctly. "I'm in the hockey fandom!"

Logan put his head in his hands. "I can't believe I'm related to you."

"Yeah, sort of like hockey," Alex said. There was no point explaining the nuances of the internet to his father. "Anyway, it's a TV show called *Rosé and Decay*. There's zombies, but also, it's old-timey England? There's Western-style shoot-outs but also cholera."

His dad gave him a look that said, *I am worried about your choice of hobby.*

"Anyway," Alex went on, "I've never gotten to go to a con for it, and it turns out there's one tomorrow—"

"That's great!" His dad's eyes were bright. "Do you want me to take you two?"

Alex cleared his throat. "Well, here's the thing. It's a hundred dollars... and it's in Baltimore."

Baltimore was, optimistically, an hour away by car. The drive often took two hours, and you lost pieces of your sanity with every mile. Alex had witnessed this slow unraveling when his mom had driven him to Baltimore for doctor's appointments, hospitalizations, and surgeries; she'd clutched her scalp so hard it obviously hurt.

"Hmm. I have to be in the office tomorrow," his dad said, rubbing his temples. He worked in IT now that he was stateside, and that meant occasional weekend shifts. "So, I'd have to get up extra early to drive you to Baltimore... spend a hundred dollars... find a sitter for Logan—"

"I don't need a babysitter. Mom left me alone once and I only set the house on fire a *little bit*," Logan protested.

Time for a new tactic. "I know. It's just, I've always wanted to go to one of these cons. And, well..." Alex's voice dropped, and he let his dad fill in the blanks.

His dad ran his hands over his face and let out a groan. "It's a long drive."

"Right." Alex's shoulders fell. He could ask Naomi to meet up after school Monday, but what if Ella noticed them leaving together? Ella already believed he was deranged; who knew what rumor she would spread next.

"Sorry," Alex said. "You're right. It's just that there were never cons in the area, and the one time I could go, I was too sick, and Mom kept saying, *Well, one day when you're better...*"

His dad let out a defeated sigh. And Alex knew he had won.

Jesus, he was a monster.

"All right." His dad pulled his hands away from his face. "You can go. But you need to take Logan."

"*What?*" Alex and Logan demanded in unison.

"I don't want to go to this thing," Logan said. "There's gonna be people *kissing*. It'll be disgusting."

Alex floundered for words. "I don't even know if the show is PG-13—"

"That's final." His dad's voice was firm now. "I can drop you both off in Baltimore. I'm sure a child's ticket is cheaper. It's the only way it'll happen."

No way. Talking to Naomi about the podcast would be near impossible if he was on babysitting duty.

Logan didn't look pleased, either. He didn't touch the rest of his chicken and scurried away from the table without saying another word. Alex poked at his plate, wondering if he should leave the table too, or if that would make things worse.

His dad spoke up first. "Listen, I get this has been hard for you. I'm sorry I wasn't around much."

Whoa, that escalated quickly. Was this about the con? Even if Alex's boo-hoo story about wanting to go all his life had been true, it was just a con. "Dad—"

"I know I wasn't present. It was complicated." His dad didn't make eye contact. "There were a lot of reasons—"

"I know." He knew all the reasons. There were hospital bills.

Deployments paid more than remaining stateside, so his dad went overseas again and again. At first it had been Afghanistan, the stress of which his mom talked about to anyone who would listen. And then his dad had been sent to Germany, and his mom kept telling people he was still in Afghanistan, actually, which was weird now that Alex thought about it—

"Right." His dad set his plate aside. "I forget sometimes, you're not as young as I think you are."

Alex grimaced. "I know you tried."

And the truth was, he did. During his dad's weeks at home, he'd take the kids on outings—to the park or the state fair or wherever he could manage with a chaotic toddler and a kid who might collapse at any moment. Alex remembered those days as happy—watching people ride a bull at the state fair, splitting an enormous turkey leg between the three of them. But the memories were filtered through a gauzy film, as if none of it had ever really happened. Clearly, Logan didn't remember any of it.

"I wanted to come home more," his dad pressed. "Spend more time with you both. Logan was so little in the beginning, he didn't remember me between deployments."

That sounded awful—having to reintroduce yourself to your own son.

"And you"—his dad took a ragged breath—"I thought, every time I left, it could be the last time I saw you. So I tried to make it count."

Hot shame lurched through Alex's blood. He had literally just manipulated his dad into letting him go to some ridiculous convention.

"I know you tried." Alex didn't know what to do besides repeat himself.

"I don't expect Logan to understand," his dad went on. "I just don't know why he's so quiet with me. Your mother used to tell me how wild and rambunctious he was, how much mischief he'd get into at school. His teachers tell me he's still like that, and I see how he is with the other kids when I pick him up. But at home..."

Alex drew his finger along the wood grain in the table, trying to find the right words. "Mom was different with him," he managed.

His dad's forehead creased. "What do you mean?"

"Like..." Memories floated to the surface. Logan showing their mom a monster drawing and being waved off. Logan asking their mom to come to a school play: *Honey, I'm sorry, we have to take Alex to the hospital for a sleep study.* Logan tearing Alex's report cards off the fridge so that Logan's stood alone and proud.

"Mom was busy with me," Alex began carefully. "And she didn't—it was hard to make time for him in the same way."

His dad's expression darkened. "He felt neglected."

"I guess." It was like she was two different people with them, and it was impossible to hold that reality in his hands and not let it shatter to pieces.

His dad shook his head. "If you were getting the attention, why didn't Logan lash out at you? You seem close, despite everything."

Because Alex was the one to admire Logan's drawings, even the ones that gave him nightmares.

Because Alex was the one to research a coding summer camp, knowing Logan would love it.

Because Alex was the one who beta tested the video game (more nightmares), who attempted to learn to cook with him, who tucked him into bed.

Not that Alex could say that. The last thing he wanted was for his dad to feel even guiltier.

"We're close." Alex poked at the food on his plate. "It's not that complicated."

The truth was that Logan *had* lashed out. He would drop to the ground and pretend he'd fainted; he went through a phase where he faked seizures. It'd made Alex furious at the time. It took him years to realize Logan hadn't been trying to make fun of him.

His dad glanced at the stairs. "Well, I'm here now. I don't know how to get him to give me a chance."

"I think he's trying to protect himself." Alex bit the inside of his cheek. "If he shuts you out, it won't hurt if you turn out not to care."

"Is this why he doesn't talk about your mother?" his dad asked. "He acts as if she never existed."

"She didn't." Alex pushed his plate aside. "Not for him, anyway."

Email 4 ★ ⮌ ⋮

My strong son,

I've always loved Halloween with you. I still remember when you were nine, and you wanted to be Santa Claus. Your idea to give out candy to other trick-or-treaters you passed was remarkably thoughtful. And it was so cute that you called them early Christmas presents. It was wonderful, even though pulling you all over town on that sleigh was so much work. Remember—you couldn't walk that year.

It's impossible to picture you changing. Getting too old for trick-or-treating. Getting a driver's license, graduating, getting married. Every time I imagine those things, it stings, because an alternate reality is also lurking: You might not experience any of those moments.

I want you to outlive me. It's the only thing I ever pray for. But I can't live with the fact that I might only see you with a cap and gown in my dreams.

Whatever you do, know this: One day, I want to see you grow taller than me.

There was something strange about the way his mom had written these emails. They were more formal than she usually sounded, for one. Like she had something to prove. Like there was something lingering behind every word.

But even stranger was the fact that she didn't mention her part in the poisoning. She still wouldn't admit it. She acted like she'd never dripped chemicals into the IV bag, like she'd never filled a syringe with water and salts.

Like Alex had never broken open a pill capsule and seen—

No. Don't think about that.

When he'd first come back to school, his teachers had gushed over him: *You look so much better, I'm so glad you're not sick anymore, we're thrilled that you're well!* Sure, his mom had betrayed him, his entire life was a lie, and his family was a wreck, but at least he wasn't *sick*.

As if that was the only thing that mattered. As if his life made perfect sense now, as if everything was great.

As if this was the happy ending, and not the beginning of the real nightmare.

CHAPTER 16: 65 DAYS TO TRIAL

The lobby of the convention center was packed with cosplayers, shiny swords and fake rifles catching the glow of the overhead lights. People in disturbingly realistic dead-person makeup and wigs that must have weighed twenty pounds milled around, taking pictures and waiting for friends. An exhausted-looking security guard kept waving people with prop weapons through the metal detectors.

"Okay." Alex turned to Logan. "Here are the rules. You don't have to hang out with me all day, but you have to stay in touch." Logan, fortunately, had a cell phone—Alex had convinced their mom to give him one last year so he could work on developing his game. "If you're gonna go somewhere, you have to tell me where, and you have to *stay there.*"

Logan groaned. "I'm not a baby."

"We don't need another reason for our family to be in the news," Alex pointed out.

"Relax." A booth with zombie posters caught Logan's eye. "Oh! I wanna check that out. See you later."

Alex walked on, feeling out of place. He hadn't thought to dress up, and he was one of the few attendees in jeans. Normally, his Maryland flag–patterned sweatshirt didn't stand out—in any given place in

Frederick, someone was wearing a Maryland hat or T-shirt—but here it was as if he'd dropped in from another time period.

He had to find Naomi. He scanned the aisles, traversing past dozens of booths, and there, at the end of the third aisle, was a familiar figure.

Naomi was dressed head to toe in *Rosé and Decay* regalia. A deep-pink skirt with a satiny shimmer swished around her ankles, and she'd even gone to the effort of wearing a corset. Her look was complete with a tiny top hat. Alex walked over. "Wow, you really outdid yourself."

"Alex?" Naomi waved a fan covered in cherry blossoms. "I didn't know you were coming. You watch the show?"

"I can't say I've seen more than a couple episodes," Alex admitted. "Cool outfit."

Naomi fanned herself dramatically. "The dress is about ten years off, but it was the best I could do." She looked Alex up and down and drawled, "Wow, your getup is *incredible*."

Alex rubbed the back of his head. "This was kind of a last-minute thing."

"So was mine. I'm missing two petticoats, and the hat is wrong, but at least I made an attempt." Naomi paid for some stickers and started walking, still fanning herself delicately. "Let me guess: You're worried about our podcast numbers. But you shouldn't be! That last episode got tons of downloads. We're starting to climb the ranks!"

This triggered a wave of panic, but Alex fought it back. "Oh, that's... great."

Naomi cast him a sideways glance. "I thought you'd be more excited."

Alex jammed his hands in his pockets. "Well, that episode was a lot. Ella took the details I gave her and twisted them. That's not what I signed up for." He frowned. "Why weren't you in the episode?"

"I had a thing. But I read the script beforehand. Of course, it didn't include all of Bryce's rambles—he's always derailing the narrative—but I thought Ella's approach made sense. And it was nice to have a cohesive draft, instead of the half-baked thing we came up with in the Shitwreck." Naomi ran her fingers over some plushies on display. Her fingernails were painted a deep red, dotted with tiny pink flowers that matched her fan. "We need to get the podcast out to more people."

"But why?" Alex asked. "Your scholarship doesn't depend on the number of listeners, right?"

Naomi winced. "An audience helps."

Of course it did. "But it's not the most important thing. The truth is the most important thing."

"The truth is important, yes." Naomi stopped at a booth with parasols and admired one with horses embroidered around the rim. "You know, Ella can actually be kind of nice. She's intense, but once you get used to it, it's not so bad. You're kind of intense too. No offense." She shrugged.

"Anyway, we're getting tacos with Bryce after the con. My mom couldn't believe it when I told her I had plans this weekend." Naomi was beaming, and it hurt to watch.

Maybe it was a mistake to try to convince her. She may have been the one to bring Alex into this podcast mess, but she had no leverage. "Okay. Enjoy your tacos." He pulled out his phone to check for texts from Logan. Nothing.

Naomi must've read something in his body language. She looked at him, her eyes round and large and ultrasincere, and said, "You should really just talk to Bryce."

Alex swallowed. "It's complicated."

"Yeah, I get it." Naomi's gaze was so full of sympathy, it was hard to make eye contact. "I know what it's like to lose a friend. When I was in middle school, I started getting these... intrusive thoughts. Like, *What if I forgot to turn the oven off after I baked those cupcakes and the house is burning down right now?* They stressed me out so much, but I felt like I couldn't tell anyone. The only person I told was my best friend at the time, Kiera Warren. But it turned out she didn't want to listen. She freaked out and called me crazy and just—" Naomi took a shuddering breath. "That was that."

Alex rubbed his arms. "I'm sorry that happened to you," he said softly.

"You still have a chance with Bryce. I know it," Naomi said. "You should take it."

They'd wandered outside the main exhibit hall and found themselves in front of the entrance to the ballroom next door. Naomi peeked inside, then entered. Alex followed; it wasn't like he had any other plans. Toward the back of the room, a group of people was gathered at an enormous table covered in felt, scissors, and buttons, making last-minute touch-ups on their cosplays.

"There's a competition," Naomi explained. "Bryce is entering, although I don't have much hope for him."

Alex spotted Bryce standing near the table, trying to pin a button back on his three-piece suit. His cosplay was the worst of the bunch—his tails were even lopsided—but, well, he had tried.

"Ella thinks he'll embarrass himself," Naomi whispered. "She's probably right, but I like that he puts himself out there. Ella won't do it unless she's sure she'll win."

Alex took a chair and sat down; all the walking and standing was beginning to make him woozy. *Ella won't do it unless she's sure she'll win*. It almost felt like Naomi was talking about the podcast, not cosplay—like Alex and Ella were competing with each other over which story they'd tell on-air. Except they were supposed to be on the same team. Ella was supposed to be giving him a chance.

"He didn't even style his hair, but whatever! I wish I had that confidence." Naomi sat down beside him and smoothed out her skirt.

Alex turned to her. "I wouldn't have taken you for a person lacking in confidence. You have no problem asking strangers for signatures on your petition."

"I'm a social pariah. It doesn't matter what I do or don't do. I have nothing to lose." Naomi let out a sad half laugh. "That's not the same as confidence."

A social pariah thanks to OCD. It was messed up, how people could take this one little thing—just one part of Naomi, alongside her extensive knowledge of Mandarin Chinese, a longing for international travel, and a fierce hatred for Latin—and blow it up into all they saw when they looked at her. It was a shame that Naomi hadn't had a real friend in her life back when she'd been diagnosed. Someone to stick around, even through the worst of it.

Alex had always had Bryce. Before things got *really*, really bad—back when they were only really bad—Bryce had come over to his house regardless of whatever episode he'd had at school that day. And yet Alex had still pushed him out.

Bryce, who was trying to fix his cravat, looked for all the world like he was in a Halloween costume.

Maybe Alex *could* talk to Bryce. Maybe it wouldn't make him want to burst into flames.

He had to try.

"I'm going to see if Bryce needs help," Alex said. "You're right. It's cool that he's trying." He stood up—slowly—and walked over, trying to seem casual. "Hey. I didn't know you'd gotten into *Rosé and Decay*."

"Hey dude." Bryce grinned at him, and for a second it was like they were back in eighth grade. Maybe this wouldn't be so hard. "I wasn't, but then Ella invited us to the con. And I was like, no way I'm going to a con without knowing anything about the show, so I binged it last night. Man, it's addictive. Viscount Abernathy totally deserved to drown in that tar pit."

Naomi approached them. "Bryce! I can't wait to see you compete."

"Thanks! Although I need to find something that looks like tar. Preferably before three thirty."

"Do you have a minute? I wanted to talk to you about the podcast," Alex said. "Maybe we could walk around before your competition starts."

Bryce looked at him, and then at Naomi. Naomi gave Alex a small, encouraging smile. It was clear she thought he was going to try to smooth things over with Bryce. Maybe even apologize. But he couldn't talk about that in a crowded convention hall. He just needed to get Bryce to side with him on the podcast.

"All right, yeah," Bryce said. The two of them gave Naomi a wave and headed back toward the main hall.

"So listen," Alex began. "I think Ella's approach is getting out of control."

"Is it?" Bryce asked. "Our engagement's looking good."

Alex's shoulders slumped. "Do you really care about that?"

"I dunno." Bryce pulled at a loose thread on his jacket. "It's cool that people are listening. Paying attention. Right?"

They stepped into the main hall, then entered Artist's Alley. Alex caught a glimpse of bright blond hair—Logan, talking to someone at a booth with fan art of the show's monsters.

"Not if Ella is pushing her agenda," Alex protested. "I joined the podcast so I could get my story out. Not so she could lie about me on-air. She said she'd hear me out."

"But you haven't told us much." Bryce looked straight ahead as they headed down an aisle. It was hard to keep up with his long, easy strides. "I mean, a lot of what you've said is stuff I already knew."

Alex took in a slow breath. *What happened is that I had a psychotic break, and if you'd seen me then, you wouldn't be talking to me now. What happened is that Mom was the only person that made me feel like I was tethered to reality. What happened is that she was the one who helped ground me when I was hallucinating, who tried to keep the delusions from tearing me apart. What happened was that I couldn't trust anyone else.*

No. No way.

A slurry of nerves grew in his stomach. He could barely talk to Bryce, and yet in two months, he was supposed to testify before a jury. Just imagining their faces—heads leaning forward with interest, curious eyes watching him—made it hard to breathe.

He needed to get the podcast back under control. He needed to get his story out there. Then he might survive the trial.

Bryce turned to him, his brows lifted slightly, as if he thought now was the moment Alex would spill. He'd gotten even taller over the past year; it was disorienting to have to look up at him.

"I can explain everything to you. But not now. Not here." Alex knew, logically, that no one was watching them. Despite that, he had the creeping sensation that someone was listening to every word, cued in to every sentence. "I need Ella to stop pushing her angle."

"You're pushing one too, you know." Bryce started walking again. "I'm not gonna step on Ella's toes over this. To be honest, it's hard to trust either of you. Sorry, man."

He took a few steps forward, his coattails fluttering in the powerful convention center air-conditioning, and then he was consumed by a sea of people running toward a new merch drop.

Alex knew better than to follow him. Bryce didn't trust him yet, and if Alex was honest with himself, he understood why. Naomi wouldn't help because she didn't want to lose out on a potential new friend. Frustrating, but again—kind of understandable.

Which meant only one thing.

Alex was going to have to talk to Ella.

CHAPTER 17: 65 DAYS TO TRIAL

What a nightmarish day.

Alex roamed the convention hall, adrift like a piece of seaweed. He'd told Logan not to leave Artist's Alley, and Logan had promised he wouldn't, a promise he promptly broke when Alex spotted him heading toward one of the ballrooms. Not that it mattered. It was time to find Ella.

If only he could go home and crawl into bed. Poke at a German crossword puzzle. The nice thing about German was that you never had to dig through hidden meanings, never had to sift through coded phrases to figure out what someone was actually saying. No, in German they just said it: He's got a *Backpfeifengesicht. Backpfeifengesicht* being, of course, a face in need of a fist—a word that needed to exist in English.

Now, where was Ella? Alex poked his head into a room where a panel discussion about zombies in literature was unfolding.

"Zombies represent our fear of mortality, of death," one of the panelists said. "A horde of zombies reminds us that most people who have ever lived are dead..."

A girl nodded along in the front row. Something about the way she was nodding, so vigorously, told Alex everything he needed to know. He stepped into the room and took a seat a few rows behind her. Yep, that was Ella, wearing a British Army officer uniform from the 1800s. She even had authentic-looking military badges on her chest. The outfit, unfortunately, looked really good.

When the panel ended and Ella stood up to leave, Alex moved to intercept her. He plastered on a smile as if he enjoyed Ella's presence. "That was cool, huh?"

"What on earth?" Ella shot him an incredulous look. "What are you doing here? You don't even watch this show."

"Maybe I have some new hobbies," Alex said as they walked out of the lecture room. "I've got more free time, since I'm not dying and all."

Ella frowned. "You didn't dress up."

"Not *that* much free time." He nodded at her cosplay. *Start with something positive.* "Yours looks awesome, though. The shoulder pads are cool. How long did that take?"

Ella half smiled. "Ages, to be honest. I have no idea how to use a sewing machine. But I only stabbed myself a few times." She touched her hair, as if to ensure that the slicked-back bun was still smooth. It looked rock-solid.

Now he had to fix this mess. "We need to talk."

Ella's expression tightened as they stepped back into the main hall. "If this is about the podcast—"

"You told me I'd have a chance to explain things to you," Alex said. "And I thought we were going somewhere when we drafted episode two. But you used a wildly different version when you went to record on Friday."

Ella let out a long-suffering sigh. "Look, making a podcast with Bryce and Naomi is hellish. Bryce derails us all the time. After you left the Shitwreck that day, he went on a ten-minute rant about the health-care system." She shrugged. "So I decided to move the process along. I had already drafted an episode on my own. It just made sense to use it once it was time to record."

"It wasn't anything like what we talked about in the Shitwreck," Alex said.

"I don't agree." Ella ticked off points on her fingers as they walked past people gushing over an autographed poster. "Your mom annoyed the doctors. She leaped into action whenever you were sick. She was disorganized. I mean, that's what you gave us."

Something in Alex's chest burned. "You told me I had a chance to show you the truth."

"I've given you one. But I'm not hearing a coherent story." Ella shrugged, as if that was that.

Alex gritted his teeth. "Listen," he said. "I know why you want the podcast to be the way it is. I get it—"

"No." Ella's voice was hard. "You don't. You don't know what this has been like for me."

"Of course I do," Alex cut in. "People are spreading rumors about both of—"

"No." There was something new in her voice. Something dark. "There's something else. You can't tell anyone, not even Naomi and Bryce. Got it?"

"Okay," Alex said uncertainly.

Ella sat down on the floor and leaned against the wall, and Alex sat beside her. "This situation is kind of... opening old wounds. I've been through this before," she said.

Alex frowned. "What do you—"

"My dad. We don't have a diagnosis, but my mom has always

thought he has bipolar disorder. Or maybe schizophrenia. I dunno." Ella bit her lip. "He'll be fine for weeks, and then he'll vanish for a few days and come back saying he was captured by aliens. Or he'll break all the mirrors in the house because he thinks they're cameras. He'll scream at things that aren't there. He's sick."

"Oh," Alex managed weakly. Despite knowing Ella since elementary school, he'd had no idea.

"It's a psychotic disorder." Ella grimaced. "And you, you have—"

"Yes." Alex's voice was hard-edged. "Yes, I know."

Ella looked away from him. "My dad's gotten into trouble with the police in the past. I think part of it was that he didn't know what was true, but the other part of it was that he didn't care. He made my sister cry constantly. He drove my mom"—Alex knew what the next word would be, but Ella caught herself—"up the wall."

Alex swallowed what he wanted to say. He had to be kind, even if he hated her. No matter what Ella had done to him, she'd grown up in a difficult situation. "I'm sorry it was like that."

"It's not your fault." Ella wrung her hands. "But I appreciate it, I guess."

Alex hesitated. "Is he—"

"Dead? No." Ella shrugged. "He's in prison. Crashed Mom's car into someone's house. He'll be out in January. They've hospitalized him a few times too. But when he comes out, he doesn't take his meds, and it goes to crap all over again."

Instantly Alex felt like he'd been knocked off his feet. *He doesn't take his meds.*

Except Alex had a valid reason for not taking his meds. They could be poisoned! They could make him even sicker! How could he risk it, when he already felt so out of control?

"Alex?" Ella leaned forward. The pins on her chest flashed under the bright convention lights. "Are you okay?"

"Yeah." Alex dug his fingers into the scratchy carpet. "I'm uh, sorry he doesn't take his meds."

It's different for me. Ella's dad's meds would never be poisoned. He'd never open one of them and see—

"Anyway, being home sucked. But then I would go to your house to babysit," Ella continued, "and it was like a breath of fresh air. Your mom was so nice to me. I knew she was exhausted, but she would still smile and hug me and say how grateful she was to see me." Ella played with the shimmery gold buttons on the bottoms of her sleeves. "I loved it."

Alex didn't know what to say. "So you believe her?" he asked. "Because she was nice to you?"

"It's not just that. Your story doesn't add up. For one, I *saw* you messing with your IV line." Alex opened his mouth to protest, but she went on. "Plus, your mom was always losing her car keys, her wallet, her phone. Yet somehow she hid a secret stash of poison? And why did she keep Logan healthy? I just don't buy it."

Alex had never been able to answer the Logan question. His lawyer said these cases were complicated; people with Munchausen syndrome by proxy didn't behave in predictable ways. His dad had said, *Let's not go down that road.*

"I almost want your version of things to be true," Ella was saying. "I want you to convince me. Obviously, it would suck having to take my posts down, but that would be better than dealing with the fact that my ex-friend is a liar. Better than looking at you and thinking about—"

She paused, then shook her head.

"I've seen this before," Ella went on. "What mentally ill people can do. The lying. The way they take advantage of normal—"

Alex choked on a bitter laugh.

"Sorry," Ella said, not seeming particularly sorry. "The way they take advantage of the rest of us. And it's one thing for my dad to do it to my family—we know the drill by now. It's another thing to see you manipulate this town, the whole world."

"Is that what you thought last year, when you saw me?" Alex couldn't keep the harsh undercurrent out of his voice. "You saw me filling my IV and thought, *Holy crap, he's just like my dad*?"

Ella ran her hands over her knees. "I don't know what I thought. I just knew I couldn't be your friend anymore."

"And yet you were my friend before that, despite my . . ." Alex didn't know how to say it. "Psychotic episodes."

"I didn't see them that often." Ella shrugged. "You had maybe, like, one major incident a year. They were easy to excuse. Even that big one, when we were freshmen—it didn't seem that serious. It was freaky, but not scary, like with my dad."

Heat crept up Alex's neck. The memory of his episode in freshman-year Biology was still vivid—a humming from the air vents, whispers he couldn't decipher, the sensation that something was peering into his mind. He'd felt exposed, like pieces of himself had been cut open and displayed on the lab benches. In his memory, the lab faded to the background, hidden behind a heavy fog.

Ella's expression softened. "You remember it."

Alex pulled one knee up. "Of course I do."

"Right." Ella winced, wrinkling her button nose. "What I'm saying is, it didn't happen that often. With my dad, it was constant. And I had a front-row seat. Plus, my mom had to deal with his stuff, so she never had time for me. I guess I just liked that your mom prioritized you. She was patient. Loving."

The pressure in Alex's chest was so high he thought he'd burst. That would be excellent decor for the con: blood vessels streaked across the floor, guts painting the walls, maybe a bit of brains here and there; the fans would love it.

"But if this thing is so triggering for you, why did you push to do a podcast?" Alex asked. "You've gotten what you wanted. Everyone believes you. They think I did it to myself."

"No. Not everyone." Ella drew her jacket in. "The fact is, most people don't."

He wanted to call her out—sure, there were people who didn't trust her, but no way was it *most* people. Although maybe that was just how she saw it. Each person who doubted her would take up enormous space in her mind, just as each person who doubted him took up enormous space in his mind. But his doubters definitely outnumbered hers.

"People hate me for speaking up." Ella's voice wobbled. "I was just trying to tell the truth. But the thing is, you got the first word in, and that counts for a lot."

"What are you talking about?" Alex knew he ought to give up and go find Logan, but he couldn't resist pressing her. "Ella, I was literally—"

"In a coma? Yeah. I know. *You* didn't get the first word, but journalists did, and they fell for your act. I guess it helped that you were so fragile. They went wild over the fact that the doctors thought your heart might stop when they tried to wake you up, how you weighed only a hundred pounds."

A cold wave went through him, making his bones feel hollow. He'd gone back and read a lot of the news coverage, but he'd never come across these details.

"You were the perfect victim, and I looked like the worst person in the world." Ella let out a bitter sigh. "I regret it sometimes, honestly. I think I should've just let you get away with it."

Alex's head was so scrambled he didn't even know where to begin. Ella's dad, jail time, *He doesn't take his meds*...

"Ella," he began, "I think maybe—"

"I meant it when I said you had a chance to prove me wrong," Ella went on. "And you still do. But the more I hear, the more I realize you won't be able to convince me. You can't tell me a coherent story because you don't *have* a coherent story."

Alex wanted to snap, *Do you think it's easy, spilling everything to someone like you?* But he couldn't antagonize her.

He ran his hands through his hair. From down the hall came the sound of cheering; maybe it was another merch drop.

"We can work past this," Alex tried, desperate. "We can come up with something for episode three that has the details you asked for. Like..." He dug into himself, trying to find something that would give Ella what she wanted. He tore through memories: a blur of Christmases, doctors' visits, summer camps, surgery consultations—wait.

"Okay," he said. "We bounced around hospitals a lot. I always thought it was because she didn't like the doctors at the previous hospital. But looking back, the real reason seems more obvious, doesn't it? Spend too much time at one place and the doctors might figure you out."

Ella didn't look impressed. "Or she was looking for someone to take her concerns seriously."

"Yeah, maybe." That was what his mom had told him, but in hindsight, it didn't seem that simple. "We started in Frederick, of course. Then DC, then Baltimore, bouncing back and forth. Ended up back at Frederick Health towards the end." Sometimes Alex wondered if he should've picked up on how strange that was. Sometimes he wondered how much of this was his own fault.

Ella raised an eyebrow. "Okay. That is a little suspicious. But is that it? There are tons of ways to explain that."

Alex thought he would scream. Maybe Ella had never truly meant it when she'd said he could convince her. Maybe it was just a ploy for her to get more details.

"I'll dig into this some more," Ella decided, and when Alex snapped out of his thoughts, he was both relieved and alarmed to find she was writing something down in a notebook. "Maybe we can turn this thread into a storyline for episode three. I'll talk to Bryce and Naomi."

"Yes," Alex said. "Okay. Thanks."

"I can't promise anything," Ella said as she stood up.

Alex watched her go, his mind reeling. He had the disorienting, unsettling feeling that he'd given up too much, like she was going to take this information and use it against him, just as she had in episode two.

Like he'd fallen into a Venus flytrap, and the jaws were about to snap shut.

CHAPTER 18: 59 DAYS TO TRIAL

Lethal Lullaby, Episode 3: "One Dose a Day" (FINAL CUT)

(A music box plays.)

ELLA	A pediatric waiting room, covered in murals of smiling suns and fluffy clouds. An MRI machine, whirring like it's about to take off into space. A hospital ICU, packed with beeping heart monitors and IVs. A child shouldn't be in any of these places.
BRYCE	I mean, the pediatric waiting room doesn't sound so bad. Kids need checkups—
ELLA	Bryce.
BRYCE	And you forgot the most important one! An examination room, with a poster on the wall. The poster is of a kitten hanging from a bar, with the caption, *Hang in there*—

ELLA I already told you that doesn't work!

BRYCE But it's so freaking cute!

ELLA Ugh . . . welcome, listeners, to episode three of *Lethal Lullaby.*

(Theme music begins. A music box plays; soon the notes grow discordant, and the song falls apart.)

ELLA Clarissa Anne Clark was creative in her plans to induce misery. Reports speculate that she used a variety of chemicals on her son, from arsenic to uranium.

(Muffled scream; a music box plays again.)

ELLA Admittedly, I came across the uranium theory in a quiz called "What Would You Poison Your Son With?," so I doubt it's true. I got bath salts, if you're wondering.

BRYCE I feel like anyone who takes that quiz is gonna be put on a watch list.

ELLA It was four a.m. and I was *bored*, okay?

(A hospital monitor beeps.)

ELLA Police detected two distinct substances in the hospital room where Clarissa was arrested: sealed jars of mercury under the bathroom sink, and bags of kosher salt hidden in a duffel.

BRYCE It's important to keep things kosher.

ELLA Your first thought might be, "Wait, salt?" Yes, salt. The same thing you sprinkle over your steak can kill you if you inject it into your veins. Salt poisoning can cause a lot of things: vomiting and diarrhea, which, gross. Thirst, which, duh. And irritability, which, yes, Alex was always a bit of a pain in the butt.

BRYCE You might be wondering why we aren't dramatizing this segment. That's because of the vomiting and diarrhea part. That's weird, bruh.

ELLA The thing is, with the salt poisoning, wouldn't you notice if you were extra thirsty? Wouldn't you question it?

BRYCE Honestly, I haven't drunk water in like two years, so I don't know.

ELLA Mercury, on the other hand, can cause symptoms such as headaches, passing out, problems seeing or hearing, and—this is the interesting part—memory loss.

BRYCE	Ella, where are you going with this?
ELLA	It would explain some inconsistencies. For example, when I used to babysit at their house, sometimes Alex would tell me what hospital they were going to for their appointment. But the name of the hospital changed all the time. Ascension, Johns Hopkins, Frederick Health. As if he couldn't remember which was the right one.
BRYCE	Or as if his mom was purposefully switching hospitals to throw suspicious doctors off the trail.
ELLA	Maybe. Or maybe not. Maybe, there's a simpler explanation.
BRYCE	Uh...
ELLA	What I want to know is this: How much does Alex Clark *really* remember about what happened all those years ago?

Alex stormed over to Ella's house Saturday morning.

They'd drafted a script for episode three in the days after the con, and it'd covered a few topics—mostly the bouncing around from hospital to hospital, how his mom would shuffle them somewhere new once a doctor started asking too many questions. It'd been a good direction.

That draft had had nothing about the questionable side effects of mercury. Nothing about whether Alex's memory might be faulty.

And yet, immediately after agreeing on that draft, Ella—and Bryce!—had recorded this forty-two-minute-long monstrosity.

The situation was infuriating. Loathsome. Hateful. Or, in German: *Hass. Abscheu. Gehässigkeit.* The real word Alex wanted was too big for either language. It was *ITriedToFixThisAndYouShouldHaveListened*; it was *WhyWouldTheySayThat*; it was *IWillBurnEverythingToTheGround IfThisPodcastMakesThingsWorse.*

Ella lived a few neighborhoods over from Alex's house, in a McMansion with an octagonal turret. Alex had hoped the walk would give him time to come up with something coherent to say, but no amount of falling leaves, golden tree canopies, and squirrels hoarding acorns could get him to calm down and focus. At least there weren't any steep hills, so he didn't show up at Ella's house on the verge of passing out.

When he got there, someone else stood outside the front door.

"Naomi?" Alex asked.

Naomi cast him a sideways glance. She looked haggard, bags under her eyes.

Hmm. Naomi hadn't been in this episode—maybe she was upset about it too.

"You okay?" Alex asked.

Naomi clutched her purse to her chest. "I just need to talk to her," she said. "I just need to talk to her, and I can't freaking do it! Every time I reach for the door, all these thoughts spill in, and I can't—I can't—"

She swallowed hard.

"I don't want to lose a friend over this," she said. "But I just keep thinking of all the ways it'll go wrong. All the ways Ella won't get it. All the ways Ella might retaliate."

Alex knocked on the door. "I get it. We'll talk to her and sort this out." Or Ella would kill them. There was no way to know.

The door flew open and Ella stood before them, her dark hair tied back in a loose ponytail. "What are you..."

She trailed off, looking from Naomi to Alex and back again. "What's up? Should I call Bryce?"

"So you can push him into spreading more lies about me?" Alex's voice was cold.

Ella clenched her jaw. "I'm just asking questions. Building intrigue."

"Okay, here's my question." Naomi put her hands on her hips, her stance resolute in a way that implied she'd spent a lot of time practicing it in front of a mirror. "Why did you lie to me? You said you'd use some of my scenes."

So Ella *was* icing Naomi out. That was reassuring, because it meant Ella didn't trust Naomi to go along with her plan—but also unsettling, because it meant she *did* trust Bryce.

Ella glanced up and down the street, as if there could be spies in the bushes. Alex would never sleep again if they reached that point of podcast fame.

"Come inside," she said.

She led them down into the basement, which was littered with fuzzy beanbag chairs, a one-hundred-inch plasma-screen TV, several massive bookcases, and a desk with a computer setup that probably cost thousands of dollars. One of the monitors displayed a Google Doc, but Ella switched off the screen before Alex could get a closer look.

"I'm texting Bryce." Ella tapped at her phone. "If we're having a meeting, I don't want to leave him out."

Naomi let out a harsh laugh. "Oh, how thoughtful of you."

Alex stood by the staircase, trying to ignore the jittery feeling in his chest. He wanted to say something, but what could he say? *Hey Ella, I sincerely hope you get struck by lightning.*

Naomi sat down on the couch and crossed her arms. When no one spoke, she started tearing through her bag. Checking pockets. Zipping and unzipping various pouches.

Ella leaned against a bookshelf. "What do you think you forgot this time?" she asked after a moment.

"Shut up." Naomi's hair was loose and frizzy at the ends, and her T-shirt—emblazoned with Mandarin characters surrounded by flower petals—was wrinkled.

Bryce showed up within ten minutes, looking like he'd just rolled out of bed. At 2 p.m. on a Saturday, which checked out. He glanced at Naomi, then Alex, then Ella, his expression a bit bewildered.

"What's going on?" he asked. He really had no clue what the problem was. That was gut-twisting.

Alex took a breath to calm his nerves. "You and Ella recorded an episode that barely resembled our script."

"Ah." Bryce rubbed the back of his head. "Well, to be honest, Ella's script seemed cooler." He frowned and looked at Naomi. "Ella said she texted you about it."

"She didn't." Naomi's voice was bitter.

"Well, it worked," Ella cut in. "You've seen our stats, haven't you?"

"We have ten thousand plays." Naomi sighed. "We've even got international reach now."

This made Alex want to crumple in on himself.

"Dang, I thought it was higher," Bryce muttered.

"It's high enough!" Alex protested. "Ella, if you keep veering off script, I'm out."

"Wait a second—" Bryce began, just as Naomi said, "Come on!"

"I mean it!" Alex's heart hammered so hard he thought he'd be sick. This would be a great time to pass out, trapped inside Ella's overpriced basement. "Ella, I don't just want to get people talking. I want them to understand."

Ella dropped into a giant leather office chair. "If you want them to understand, then first you need them to talk."

"So you threw out my script?" Naomi snapped.

Bryce watched Naomi and Ella, his eyes wide, like he'd stumbled across a car wreck. "Ella, I wouldn't have been cool with this if I'd known we were going behind Naomi's and Alex's backs."

Ella let out a sigh. "I'm sorry, Naomi."

No *I'm sorry, Alex.*

"You were so . . . *iffy* about my ideas for episode three," Ella went on, looking at Naomi, "and I didn't want you to delay things. Bryce does that enough already. Look, it won't happen again."

Naomi had been iffy about the episode? Maybe Alex hadn't given her enough credit.

Naomi shot Ella a glare. "We're supposed to be collaborators!"

"And Naomi's translations are really helping us in China," Bryce added.

Ella pinched the bridge of her nose. "Come on. I brought this podcast to life. Episode three is finally getting us traction. If you all want to collaborate, what are your ideas for the next few episodes?"

A tense silence hung over the group.

"Besides the draft you trashed?" Naomi snapped.

"Maybe an episode from a doctor's perspective?" Bryce said. "But I'd need like, a medical dictionary."

"Exactly." Ella sat cross-legged in the chair. "You'd flounder without me."

Lightning shot through Alex's veins. "No, you'd flounder without *me*. It's my story! Don't I get a say in how you're telling it?"

Ella looked at him, and there was something familiar in her gaze—so familiar it was jarring. When it clicked, Alex's stomach turned.

Pity. His mom had worn that same expression countless times. When he was hallucinating, when he was delusional. That strange, consolatory look said everything: *He still doesn't get it, does he?*

"Alex." Ella clasped her hands. "Has it occurred to you that your story is all over the internet? In leaked police reports and hospital memos. Sure, those of us with half a brain suspect there's something deeper to it. But your side is already common knowledge. We don't need you."

Alex stiffened, while Naomi and Bryce managed to look at the rug, the bookshelves, the ceiling. Literally anywhere but at him.

No, no, no. If they threw him off the podcast, he was finished.

"Here's the thing." Ella tented her hands. "Naomi, your draft was dull. Boring. You have to think about what the audience wants. True crime junkies aren't in it because they love the fact that young women get murdered every day. They're in it because they love catharsis. Healing. Seeing the bad guy bite it in the end."

The look in Naomi's eyes was furious.

"Isn't your mom's trial coming up?" Bryce said cautiously. He rubbed his arms, his knobby elbows catching the light.

"The trial's not gonna cut it. I mean, I'm sure it'll be juicy." Ella spoke as if Alex wasn't even there. "But the newspapers will cover it. Everyone will know what happens, what the lawyers say. We need something more."

"I don't know." Bryce continued to avoid looking in Alex's direction. "I thought we were just stirring up ideas to get clicks. But to actually come out and say—"

"Think about it." Ella's eyes gleamed. "There are two types of true crime podcasts. The type where everything already happened and the hosts are simply recounting the story, and the type where the story is still in progress. Where the listeners get to investigate alongside the hosts. Where everyone picks apart the story together, until they find the real culprit."

The real culprit.

Alex should've seen this sooner. Ella was never going to let him convince her. She'd never intended to give him a chance. No—she was planning to take *Lethal Lullaby* and spin it into a vortex of lies that would make it seem like Alex had poisoned himself. She was going to tell *her* truth.

Alex took a shuddering breath. "You can't be serious."

"You've given me nothing, Alex." Ella gave him a halfhearted shrug, as if this was just a sad, unfortunate fact and not her stabbing him in the back. "I have to move forward."

Alex's hands clenched. This couldn't be happening. "You know what people expect out of true crime podcasts? The truth."

Ella swept to her feet.

"Fine." She met them all with a gaze that could've leveled cities. "Then get out."

"Uh, what?" Bryce said.

Ella's voice held raw venom. "I'm done with your worthless podcast."

Wait a minute. *Your worthless podcast.* She was kicking *herself* off.

"You can't do this!" Naomi protested. "We have to be in two-person groups for this project. Mrs. Richards isn't going to give me credit if you quit."

Alex had to keep this on track. Without Ella, they could start over.

He could get down his testimony and figure this out for real. "Maybe we can talk to Mrs. Richards?" he said carefully. "I'm sure if she knew the current version of the podcast was slandering another student—"

Ella cut in. "It's not slander if it's true—"

"—then she'd understand." Alex turned to Ella. "You're right that this isn't working. But hey, you could always come on for a special episode, if you still want to share your side of things. We can give you a place to clear the air—"

"Ha. Thanks, but no." Ella took a pile of papers from her desk and tucked them into a folder, but not before Alex caught a glimpse of marked-up printouts of news articles.

She turned to face them, her gaze cold. "I'll be conducting my own investigation."

CHAPTER 19: 52 DAYS TO TRIAL

Email 10 ★ ⮌ ⋮

My precious son,

I feel like it's been years since I could talk to you. I know it's only been a few months, but when you're sick it's like you're a million miles away. I've always felt that distance acutely. When you have a seizure, it's like the boy I love is gone. When you're sedated at the hospital, it's like you're on another planet. And when you're delusional, when you're screaming at things I can't see... it hurts like you wouldn't believe. You're there, but you don't sound like you.

That's how I feel now, if I'm being honest. Like you're light-years away.

Sometimes I think about how much you love stargazing. How you like to take me outside in the dead of night, no matter how cold it is, and point to the heavens: Cassiopeia, Perseus, Lyra. Ursa Major and Ursa Minor. The North Star. You always know what will show up in the sky, and when. You can pick out any star and tell me where it will go, where we can find it again.

Where can I find you again?

I'm sorry this message is so sad. I just wonder, on the days when you're too sick to speak, when you don't wake up, where you are. If I can look to the sky and calculate when you'll arrive on my horizon again.

The emails kept landing in his inbox, one after another, as if they were haunting him. The latest one stuck with him for days. He thought about it in school, tabbing to his inbox every few minutes and reading it over and over again, as if he needed to be able to recite it from memory. He thought about it while walking home in the afternoon. He thought about it in bed at night, feeling like a shadow of the person his mom had described.

He couldn't recognize the constellations anymore, couldn't do the calculations in his head. Part of it was brain fog, but the truth was he'd lost interest in astronomy sometime in middle school. He'd found other hobbies, like dabbling in languages, ultracomplicated board games with Bryce, and hanging out with Logan. The astrolabe sat in the back of his closet, buried under books.

His mom talked about that phase like it was yesterday.

It was like Alex was in stasis in her brain. Trapped as a little boy forever. The emails were supposed to bring him closer to her, but the gulf between them was growing wider.

Alex lay on his back in bed. He glanced at the pills on the nightstand and took slow, steadying breaths.

Phone screen off. Time to stop.

Maybe it didn't matter what his mom said. He wasn't the sick, dying boy anymore. He wasn't the boy who would stay up to watch a lunar eclipse at midnight. He was something else.

The problem was, he had no idea what.

Trial Notes 2: What do you remember about when she was caught?

Nothing. I'd been in a coma for months. When I woke up, she'd already been arrested. Dr. Melvin, the neurologist, told me it went like this:

Nurse sees Mom fiddling with the IV. Nurse tells doctor, who waves it off. Parents always mess with the IV to get the last bits of fluid out, no biggie. Nurse doesn't like that answer, gets a weird vibe, maybe just finished watching an episode of *Law & Order*. Shoos Mom out of room. Apparently gets permission to install cameras—which is not easy, but she's persistent. Less than a day goes by before they catch something on tape.

Crime thwarted, life saved, happy ending!

The problem is, that implies there *is* an ending. In the movies, once they figure out it's Munchausen syndrome by proxy, the story stops.

No one tells you that's when the real shit begins.

CHAPTER 20: 44 DAYS TO TRIAL

The end of October arrived, and the neighborhood transformed overnight, as if a cheesy nightmare had descended upon them. Pumpkins with sloppy, demented grins filled front yards. Skeletons waved from porches like sentinels. Gimmicky plastic graves cropped up in the grass, with names like SIR SINISTER and DEADLY DISMAY.

Alex, sitting next to Logan at the kitchen table, drew stitch marks on Logan's arms for his Frankenstein's monster costume. Logan was rambling about something, but it was impossible to focus.

Alex hadn't spoken to Ella since the showdown in her basement, and he was starting to feel a bit better about the situation. Bryce had helped Naomi talk to the Journalism teacher, who said she could continue the podcast without Ella; her scholarship chances were safe.

The three of them had taken a week to regroup. They'd started drafting the next episode, and the plan was to release it during the first week of November. Meanwhile, Ella seemed to have dropped off the face of the earth. She'd said she would do her own investigation, yes, but what did that mean? Alex had no way of knowing.

He knew he should focus on putting together episode four—and come up with something coherent for his testimony. Something that might help him connect the boy in his mom's emails to the person he was today. Something that might help him face his mom on the stand.

He had no clue what she would say in court. Maybe she'd keep pretending she'd never done anything: *I don't know where those chemicals in the hospital room came from. I only tapped the IV to get him more medicine. I just wanted to help him.*

Maybe she'd drag his mental illness into it: *He says the most unbelievable things when he's delusional. Now he thinks I've poisoned him? Is that what he's telling you?*

Or maybe she'd admit it, but that seemed unlikely. She'd entered a not-guilty plea.

Alex tried to shake his thoughts clear. He sat back after finishing the stitch marks. "All right, you're done. You excited?"

Logan nodded, his hair bouncing. "I'm gonna get *all* the candy." His face turned wistful. "It's sad. I'm almost too old for Halloween now."

"Dude, you're ten."

"I *know,*" said Logan, as if the oldest trick-or-treater in the world was eleven. "Pretty soon I'll have to start doing real Halloween stuff, like TP'ing a house or something."

Alex raised an eyebrow. "When does that start, middle school?"

"Probably," Logan said.

"But I've always gone trick-or-treating with you, nugget." Alex was going to be an elderly wizard: fake beard, purple robe, and pointy hat. The beard was going to be so itchy, but Logan wouldn't dare let Alex trick-or-treat without a costume.

Logan shrugged. "Yeah, well. You're not exactly the leader of the cool-kid gang."

Ouch. Alex, officially uncool according to his ten-year-old brother. Although he was dying to ask what a *cool-kid gang* looked like.

"You two ready?" their dad asked, walking in. "I'll stay here and hold down the candy fort. Can you promise me you'll be back by nine? No, eight thirty."

Logan threw his head back in despair. "The rest of the fourth grade gets to stay out until eleven, Dad."

"That is definitely not true."

Wait a second. This was it. This was their golden opportunity.

"Hey," Alex cut in. "Why don't you two go together?"

Logan balked. "*What?*"

His dad's eyes narrowed. "You're planning to sneak off to some party, aren't you?"

"Honestly, it hurts because it's not true."

Logan stood up. "If anyone's going to a party, it should be me! I need the practice—"

Alex shook his head. "Come on, it'll be fun! Dad has never gone with you. I'll stay here and pass out candy, and when you guys come back we can blast the 'Monster Mash' so loud the neighbors complain." A classic Halloween tradition.

Logan shot Alex a glare, but nope, Alex wasn't going to let it faze him. Nothing was going to change if Logan and his dad never got to spend time together.

His dad looked nervous as he turned to Logan. "How about it, kiddo?"

"Okayyyy." Logan folded his arms over his chest. "*If* you have a costume."

His dad broke into a grin. "Oh, I have a costume."

He jogged upstairs and returned a minute later with a roll of toilet paper, medical tape, and a pack of beaded Mardi Gras necklaces. "All right, TP me."

Logan didn't hesitate. He tossed the roll in the air and began lobbing TP all over their father.

Alex could only stare. "What is happening?"

His dad waved his arms around, toilet paper fluttering in the air like banners waving in the wind. "Logan is Frankenstein's monster. And I'll be the Mummy!"

Great. Their dad was going to wander around the neighborhood covered in toilet paper. Well, at least it'd be a distraction from everything else people were saying about their family. "What's with the necklaces?"

"Mummies had bling, Alex. Read a book." Logan stood on his tiptoes and slung the necklaces over their dad's head.

For a second, Alex was back in the same living room five years ago, putting together a knight costume with his mom, the two of them painting the cardboard to look like metal. *You want to blend the colors, make it look real. It's very important to make it look real.*

In the end, it hadn't looked real in the slightest. The color had been more trash-can gray than armor silver, and the cape was cut out of an old tablecloth. But putting it together had been ridiculously fun.

The memory had come unbidden, the way they always did, a voice in the dark when he least expected it.

"Graaah!" His dad put up his hands in a fighting pose.

"Graaah!" Logan punched the air.

The two of them were out the door without another word.

Alex settled in on the couch with a bag of Reese's Pieces. Now that he knew that his allergies to peanuts, cranberries, strawberries, coconut oil, red meat, and six different types of cheese were all fake, he was letting loose.

He scrolled through social media on a burner account; it helped him stay on top of things. He'd kept tabs on a few true crime fan accounts over the last week, in order to better understand the competition. Murder, murder, murder, kidnapping, murder... they began to blur together.

And then he saw it. A link. For a podcast.

Liar's Dose: Available now on Apple Podcasts.

Shared by the account @EllaMostEnchanted, with over 20,000 likes.

***Liar's Dose,* Episode 1: "A Mother's Love"**

ELLA Let's talk about moms. Most people have one, and most people have some kind of problem with theirs. But let's be honest: Your mom is probably trying her best, under pressure you can't even imagine. We joke that moms never sleep, that they have eyes in the backs of their heads, that they don't know what the words *take a break* mean—we joke, but are they jokes? I think they're truths. I know, because I saw my mother fight for survival in a house that tried to tear her apart.

(Triumphant music.)

ELLA This tenacity, this fierceness, is why cases of abusive mothers rattle us so badly. Mothers who shake their babies to death, mothers who smother them with pillows, mothers who drown their toddlers in bathtubs—we can't stop talking about these women. A mother is one of the only people in the world who we assume will love us unconditionally. When someone like that snaps, the consequences can be deadly.

(Muffled scream.)

ELLA But a mother who explodes in a fit of desperation—that's one thing, right? On some level, we can understand. We've all babysat that one brat who made us want to commit crimes. In some way, we see ourselves in these women, even if we're disturbed. Clarissa Anne Clark, on the other hand? That's a different story.

(Dramatic beat.)

ELLA My name is Ella McIntire, and welcome to the first episode of *Liar's Dose.*

(Voices whisper, resolving into a quiet song, almost like a lullaby.)

ELLA You might know me from a podcast covering the same story, *Lethal Lullaby.* Unfortunately, I've split with the creators of that series over . . . creative differences. Regardless, I think you'll want to stick around for what I have to say. I was close to the Clark family—in fact, I used to babysit their youngest son, Logan.

(Hospital monitor beeps.)

ELLA Clarissa Anne Clark was arrested in my hometown this past May for allegedly poisoning her son Alex over the course of ten years. Alex goes to my school. And yes, for years, this boy was sick. That's not up for debate. I'd see him black out in the middle of class, collapse, and start frothing at the mouth. Sometimes when people tried to talk to him, he'd respond with words that didn't make sense. And sometimes he wouldn't say anything at all—just stare at you as if he'd never seen another human being in his life. So here's one thing I can say with confidence: He was definitely sick.

(Rustling sounds.)

ELLA Was Clarissa sick? The newspapers say she has Munchausen syndrome by proxy. It's the only explanation we can stomach. Because what kind of mother would poison her kid for years?

(Beat.)

ELLA A mother like that has to be messed up. Right?

(Beat.)

ELLA Right?

(Whispered lullaby begins again, fainter than before.)

ELLA Here's the truth: We think we know Clarissa Anne Clark. But all we know is her headline, her mug shot, her eyes looking out at us from the photo at the top of a news article. We think we understand her, but maybe we're looking at Clarissa Anne Clark the wrong way. Maybe we've been looking at her through a fun-house mirror, when actually, we need to break the glass.

(Dramatic music begins in the background, faint and slow.)

ELLA Maybe Clarissa Anne Clark isn't the monster we think she is.

(Dramatic music rises to a crescendo.)

ELLA Maybe the real villain has been with us all along.

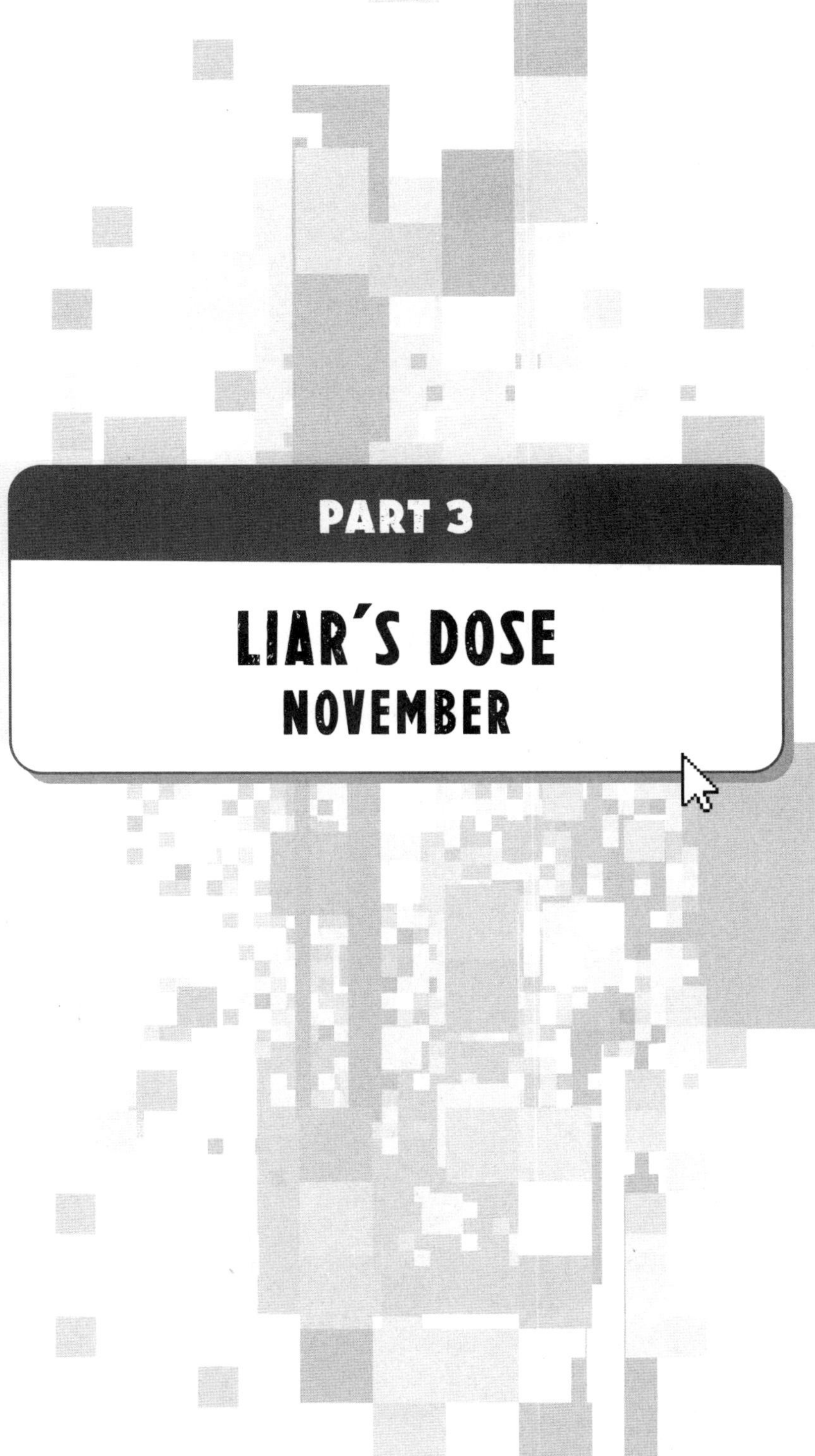

PART 3

LIAR'S DOSE
NOVEMBER

CHAPTER 21: 42 DAYS TO TRIAL

Alex stormed into school on Monday as if he was on fire.

Two days. It'd been two days since Ella's podcast dropped, and it felt like the world had started spinning on a new axis.

Her podcast had been shared on every mainstream social media platform. It had landed on WeChat in China and Vkontakte in Russia—Alex made accounts to check. Lisbeth Carson and Rachel May, the creators of the podcast that spawned the hashtag #StaySlyAndDontGetSlain (people were using both that hashtag and #StaySlyAndDontGetSlayed, but Alex checked: *Slain* was the correct conjugation), had posted about it; soon enough, it was trending.

Alex was going to have to create a new language for this betrayal. A language where words were made of acid, where sentences burned like flames.

Eight o'clock. He had fifteen minutes to talk to Ella before first period. In the hallway, faces came into focus and then grew blurry again. Eyes darting back and forth, gazes meeting his and then snapping away. Mouths were moving, but the words came out scrambled. Was it one person trying to talk to him, or two hundred? Were voices coming from the lockers, from the walls, seeping down from the air vents? The air molecules were speaking now: *Alex, Alex, Alex,* they chanted. *What's the real story? Why haven't you told us the real story?*

His hands were shaking so violently, he knew he couldn't have taken his pills today. He wouldn't have been able to hold them.

He turned a corner. "Alex?" a girl said, or maybe it was the door whispering, *Alex?*

"Hey, can you tell me about—" a boy cut in, or was it the walls? *Hey, can you tell me—*

There she was.

Ella stood at the end of the hall opening her locker, which was covered in *Rosé and Decay* stickers. She was smiling, surrounded by a crowd of people, cheeks flushed as she twisted her hair around her fingers. Not a gleeful, deceiving chess master—just a girl who couldn't believe how quickly her little project had taken off.

One step. All he had to do was confront her. Two steps. All he had to do was—

"Alex!"

The voice came from behind him. Real or fake? He couldn't trust his senses, but also, the voice sort of sounded like—

He turned around and Naomi's eyes locked on to him.

"Alex!" She grabbed him by the arm, and soon Bryce was at his side too, grabbing his other arm. "What are you doing?"

Alex sputtered out, "Have you heard—"

Bryce winced. "I know. It's bad."

"Yes." Naomi met Bryce's grimace with one of her own. "I heard everything."

But their grimaces meant they were sympathetic, right? Bryce and Naomi were on his side. *Just apologize,* a voice in Alex's mind said. *Just apologize and tell Bryce why you disappeared. He won't look at you like Ella does. He won't decide you can't be trusted.*

Instead, Alex blurted out, "I need to talk to her."

"Are you kidding?" Naomi yanked him away from the crowd and began power walking in the opposite direction, his left arm tight in her grip. Bryce flanked Alex to the right. It felt like they were hauling him off to jail.

"That's the last thing you should do," Bryce said.

Alex stammered, "But—"

"Alex." Naomi met him with a fierce look. "If you talk to her, how do you think it's going to look? You're the guy at the center of her podcast. If you confront her in public—"

Aw, hell. "Her podcast will seem more credible."

"Bingo." Bryce's expression was grim.

Alex swallowed hard. "But then how—"

"We don't need to call out her lies." Bryce let go of him. "We just need our story to outshine hers. Crowd her out. Two podcasts about the same crime? They're competing for the same audience. One will get buried."

Alex didn't ask the obvious question: *What if it's ours?*

"Meet us in the Shitwreck at three," Bryce said, and then he and Naomi were gone.

During first period, the guy behind him asked when he planned on fainting that day.

In second, a girl at a nearby lab bench warned him not to sample the formaldehyde.

No one spoke to him in third period.

And in fourth, no one even made eye contact.

The worst part was that at any moment he *could* have an episode—maybe he'd pass out, maybe he'd hallucinate and cause a scene, who knew? His body was a time bomb.

The final bell couldn't come fast enough. At last Alex hurried through the woods. The faint blushes of yellow and gold on the trees had deepened to violent orange and fire-truck red; soon the leaves would scatter in their final act. At least today the leaves weren't whispering to him.

Little victories, his mom said from somewhere far away—

He missed the step before the drop-off to the ravine and crashed through the underbrush, leaves and branches snapping under his weight. At the last moment he threw his leg out, catching on a rock before he could land in the creek. Then again, if he got soaked and froze to death out here, at least he wouldn't have to face tomorrow at school.

In the boat, Naomi's features were illuminated by wavering flashes of light; the camping lantern's battery was threatening to give out. "All right, Bryce, tell him our idea."

"We need to steal the spotlight." Bryce placed a notebook on the floor. "The problem is, Ella was right about a few things. We need drama. Suspense. No one wants to listen to episode after episode about child abuse."

"We need a hero," said Naomi.

No way. Alex, a hero? They couldn't pretend he'd tried to stop his mom. It would be perjury if he took that approach on the stand. A lie to upend his life even further.

"You can't be serious," Alex said. "I don't think I—"

"Hold up. You thought *you* would be the hero?" Bryce grinned. "Aw, Alex. Alex!"

Alex didn't respond, heat creeping up his neck.

"It doesn't make sense for you to be the hero," Naomi said, not unkindly. "I mean, that would imply you *knew* what she was doing. Plus, it'd make it too obvious that we're working with you. We have to be careful, especially since people might've seen us in the hallway this morning."

Alex let out a shaking exhale. "Right."

"Anyway, our plan is better." Naomi rubbed her hands together. "We're going to invent a doctor. Our protagonist!"

"A... doctor," said Alex.

"Someone at the hospital. She'll be the one who gets suspicious and tries to alert the authorities, only to be sidelined. She'll be the one to collect clues, start digging." Naomi looked as if she'd just aced a spelling bee. "I've already drafted her backstory. You wouldn't believe what happened on her vacation to Ecuador in 2002—"

"Naomi," said Bryce, but he was smiling.

"Okay, okay." Naomi cleared her throat. "The important thing is that the listeners will root for her."

Bryce must've caught something in Alex's expression, because his smile faded. "Unless, of course, you have a better idea."

Alex's throat went dry. Bryce would get sick of Alex's delaying soon enough, and then he might run to Ella—but if Alex told him everything now, he might run to Ella anyway. Two options, yet neither was viable. "I'm still... thinking."

"Right." Bryce's expression didn't change. His soccer jersey was so shiny it reflected the glow of the camping lantern; if Alex looked closely enough, he might be able to see himself. He looked away.

Just talk to him. He would, of course he would, soon. Just not yet.

"A doctor, yeah," Alex said. He couldn't use it in his testimony, but this could still help—at the very least, it would divert attention away from Ella. Then he could dig in and mold the podcast into what he needed it to be.

He breathed in, breathed out, ran his hands over his jeans. *Okay. Okay. Okay.*

This could work.

There'd be a compelling narrative to follow. It was way better than years and years of hell, until someone intervened without much fanfare. *Nurse sees Mom fiddling with the IV… Less than a day goes by before they catch something on tape… Crime thwarted, life saved, happy ending!*

Alex straightened his back and said, "I want it to be a nurse."

"Ooh," Naomi said. "More of an underdog! Listeners will love it."

Bryce raised an eyebrow. "Why a nurse?"

"It was a nurse." Alex rubbed the back of his head. "In real life. I mean, it's not like she was on the case for a decade, because she only met me last year, but—it was a nurse who figured everything out. Deirdre Wilson."

Naomi stroked her chin. "Is it plausible for you to have been with the same nurse for several years? So that she has time to get suspicious and begin investigating?"

Alex nodded. "I didn't know Deirdre for more than a few months. But there were a few nurses I'd known for longer. It's not impossible. But…" An ugly possibility grew in his mind. "If we name her on the podcast, people will go after her. They'll break down her door trying to get information. I don't want to do that to her."

He couldn't drag Deirdre into his mess. His legal team knew she was involved, and she would probably testify, but the public didn't know about Deirdre yet.

"We don't want people going after Deirdre," Naomi agreed. "We'll have to keep her anonymous."

"How?" Bryce asked, pulling out his phone. "She must've been in the news reports. Her name's probably already out there."

"I don't think it is," Alex said. "Some of the articles mention that a nurse was involved in catching my mom. But they don't name her."

"We'll tell her story, or some version of her story, without her name," Naomi offered. "Say we're using a fake name to protect her privacy. How about that?"

Going ahead with this—the story of a nurse on the case for years—would mean lying. Digging through the rubble of his past for something he could polish and show off. He was no better than Ella, dredging up fanciful stories and turning them into "facts." But he had no other choice.

"Sweet," Bryce said. It was amazing that he could be calm at a time like this. "I bet Ella doesn't have *this* up her sleeve."

"We're going to get this back under control." Naomi gave Alex a warm smile.

The nurse would be the star. His mom would be the villain.

And he wouldn't matter at all.

"I like it," Alex said. "It puts me on the sidelines. A side character. Nobody important."

"Nobody to worry about," added Bryce.

"Nobody to suspect," Naomi agreed.

Warmth rose in his chest, sparks crackling between his ribs, like a promise coming to life inside his bones.

Maybe that was what hope felt like. It had been so long.

"All right." Alex broke into a grin. "Here we go, episode four."

CHAPTER 22: 42 DAYS TO TRIAL

This time, Alex helped write the script.

It got too cold in the Shitwreck, so they went to Bryce's house, and it was disorienting to be back there. Some things had changed—the carpet looked dingier, and a pile of laundry covered one of the couches, like the house had let out a big sigh and given up—but others were the same. Bryce's soccer gear shoved haphazardly next to the front door so it could be conveniently tripped on. The painting of some Mediterranean villa, one corner of the frame chipped. The end table, covered in dust.

"Mom's not home." Bryce dropped his bag on the floor. "Doing some stuff with the lawyers."

"Geez." Alex stood at the front doormat, overcome by the sense that he couldn't go farther, that he'd somehow crossed a line by coming here. "Still? After a year?"

"Yeah, you'd think when you get divorced, all you have to do is be like, look, I'm out, and then someone takes the rings and you're done. But nope! You have to do paperwork. For months." He did jazz hands. "With the person you hate."

It was the first time Bryce had talked to Alex about the divorce since before. "That's awful," Alex said uselessly.

"Yeah," Bryce said. "It is."

In Bryce's room, Alex and Naomi scribbled ideas in a notebook while Bryce typed away at a keyboard. His fingers moved so fast the cursor could barely keep up.

Naomi: "We should characterize the nurse first. To get people attached to her!"

Bryce: "She could have a dog?"

Alex: "A golden retriever!"

They storyboarded the dramatizations: Naomi would be the nurse, and Bryce would be a random doctor who repeatedly dismissed her concerns due to his own incompetence. Alex sketched out a map of the pediatric ward at Frederick Health so they'd get it right.

Naomi: "I think Clarissa should try another chemical at some point. To keep the doctors on their toes."

Bryce: "Lead?"

Alex: "Right after the lead poisoning test came back clear, so they don't think to check it!"

It was easy to accept the lies now that Alex had decided they were necessary. Besides, once they shoved Ella's podcast to the bottom of the rankings, they could dive back into the real story. And in six weeks—oh God, just six weeks—he'd go on the stand and not feel like disintegrating.

After the sun went down, stars took their places in the deep blue sky beyond Bryce's bedroom window. Alex didn't recognize the constellations anymore. It could be brain fog, memory loss, new hobbies. Who cared?

He wasn't the same boy he was back then. Drafting the podcast, it didn't even feel like he was talking about himself.

His mom watched him the whole time, sitting on the rug by Bryce's bed, her eyes saying one thing.

Tell the truth.

Eventually, their snack cravings grew too powerful. They meandered down to the basement, where Bryce had hidden two huge bags of cheese puffs and a two-liter of soda from his eternally dieting mother, and settled in on the wraparound couch.

"Wow." Naomi kicked her feet up and tossed a cheese puff in her mouth. "This is how I want to live every day."

Alex sat down beside her, throwing a fuzzy blanket over himself. He was always freezing—hooray, circulation disorder. A fun side effect of chronic mercury poisoning.

"Want to watch something? I've got a bajillion apocalypse movies." Bryce grabbed a remote.

"Everyone does, Bryce, it's called Netflix." Naomi poured soda into a plastic cup.

"No, my dad legit bought them and everything. He doesn't believe in the internet." Bryce dug through DVDs in a bin.

Naomi frowned. "What do you mean he doesn't *believe* in—"

"How about *Zombie Raid at the Zoo*? Nah, the elephant twist at the end is too weird. Oh! *The Communist Plague in the White House*? Nah, that was mostly propaganda—"

"Why is there a virus on the cover?" Naomi asked when Bryce held up the DVD.

"Oh, it was a literal plague. Spread by communists."

Bryce landed on another plague movie, this time caused by zombies. "Let's do this one. It's wild."

They settled in. After three people were eaten by the horde (one was eaten from the inside out, which was logistically impressive), Naomi grabbed a blanket for herself and wrapped it around her shoulders.

"My friend Kiera loved weird, scary movies," she said. "When she slept over, she always made me watch these things, even the R-rated ones."

"Did they freak you out?" Alex asked.

Naomi smiled, but there was something sad behind it. "The benefit of having a brain with constant intrusive thoughts is that not much else can scare you."

"My dad would quiz me after watching movies like this." Bryce didn't make eye contact, but there was something wistful in his voice. "Ask me what I'd do if a plague broke out, or if there was a coup resulting in the 'total breakdown of civil society.' "

"Did you do well?" Alex asked.

Bryce gave him a sideways grin. "Always failed 'em."

There was a long silence. Alex's mind wandered to horror movie nights with his mom. They'd watch giant dodos emerge from a frozen pit and terrorize New York, or people get infected with brain worms that gave them a hunger for human bone marrow. The special effects were so bad it was possible to see the actors' wigs—but the movies had scared his mom so much, she'd have to watch rom-coms the next day.

"My dad is a jerk," Bryce said at last, jolting Alex out of his thoughts.

"Yeah, Kiera turned out to be a pretty bad friend," Naomi said.

Alex didn't say anything.

"But I miss him." Bryce's shoulders fell. "Is that weird?"

Naomi pulled her blanket tighter. "I hope not."

Alex tried to ignore the pit in his chest.

"No," he said. "It isn't weird at all."

Trial Notes 3: What did your mom tell you about the "medicine" she gave you?

Her excuses were always different:

"Dr. Leonard prescribed it; I picked it up at the pharmacy this morning. Don't try to pronounce the name, it's a mouthful."

"These are painkillers. I know you've been having terrible migraines. No, they don't look like Daddy's, but your migraines are much worse, aren't they?"

"I went to a natural healer in Takoma Park for this one. You take it with tea. Maybe it'll help with your night sweats. You don't want to look like you've wet the bed, do you?"

"Antonia gave me this; she said it's the only thing that works for her boy, but of course it's not legal in Maryland yet. It doesn't look like regular marijuana because—well, you're only ten. Why do you think you know what marijuana looks like, young man?"

"It's a new electrolyte mix. I'll just put it in the IV. Don't tell Dr. Melvin, you know how he gets. Let's keep it our secret."

It'll be our secret.

CHAPTER 23: 38 DAYS TO TRIAL

"NOOOOO!" Logan screamed in rage.

The screen flashed GAME OVER. Alex tapped his controller, but there was no escape from mortality in *Road Rage Apocalypse 9,000: Radioactive Drift.*

Logan threw his controller to the side. "Ugh. I can't make my own video game and now I can't even *play* a video game. I should just launch myself into the sun."

"Lighten up, nugget." Alex ruffled his hair. "It's not like you have a deadline."

"I want to finish it before I graduate elementary school." Logan pouted. Outside the living room window, leaves fluttered off trees, leaving them bare and exposed. "Why do you call me *nugget*, anyway? I don't look like a chicken nugget. I even googled human-shaped chicken nuggets, and I don't look like those, either."

"It's from Halloween when we were little." Alex leaned back and stretched out his legs. "I dressed up as an astronaut and Mom made you a big round planet costume. It was so round you could barely walk, so you had to roll around the living room. It was hilarious."

"Embarrassing." Logan turned red.

"But then all the rolling messed up the costume," Alex said, "and made it lumpy. The name *nugget* just seemed to fit." Alex tried not to think about the fact that he got to be the astronaut while Logan had to be a lumpy orb.

"You can never tell anyone that." Logan cringed. "Or else I *will* launch myself into the sun."

"Sworn to secrecy."

"This Halloween was weird." Logan slid against the beanbag. "Dad is awkward."

Alex laughed. It was like Logan had discovered the color purple. "Yeah, kinda."

"He kept trying to get me to talk to other kids in the neighborhood. And most of them were like, six," Logan said. "He'd be like, 'Oh Logan, that boy in the dinosaur costume looks creative! Maybe you guys should be friends!'" He threw his hands up. "Then he started questioning some lady who was giving out apples because he'd heard something about razors in them. I told him I didn't want apples anyway, and then they *both* got upset."

Alex bit back another laugh. "That's brutal."

"He's annoying."

Oof. "Hey, he's trying."

"I know." Logan twisted around. "He wants to go fishing next weekend."

"That could be fun," Alex tried.

Logan gagged. "No! Don't you have to go *outside* to go fishing?"

"Well, yes."

"Disgusting."

"Maybe you guys should do something else," Alex offered. "Didn't you have fun at your friend's laser tag party last year? Why don't you guys do that?"

Logan frowned, his brow furrowing. "He'd destroy me at laser tag. He's ex-military."

"He was in comms. I don't think he shot any guns."

Logan let out air through his teeth. "So, what? I should ask him to play laser tag with me?"

"Yeah, why not?"

"What if he says no?"

"He won't say no," Alex said. "I promise."

Lethal Lullaby, Episode 4: "The Case Against Clarissa" (FINAL CUT)

(A music box plays.)

BRYCE	It happened over several years. One dose a night, then two, then four. One doctor's visit a month, then every couple weeks, then once a week. Soon they were visiting specialists more often than the playground. Soon they were regulars at the hospital instead of at Chuck E. Cheese.

(Chuck E. Cheese commercial plays in the background, faded out.)

BRYCE	That last part might not be so bad. Chuck E. Cheese is the worst.
NAOMI	You'd seriously rather be in an ER than an indoor fun park?

BRYCE Look into that rat's eyes, Naomi! He is the denizen of nightmares!

(Children's laughter can be heard, but it's distant.)

NAOMI I'll never understand you, Bryce. Welcome, listeners, to episode four of *Lethal Lullaby.*

(Theme music begins. A music box plays; soon the notes grow discordant, and the song falls apart.)

BRYCE Some villains get away with their crimes while no one suspects a thing. Some monsters hunt in the dark for decades before anyone sees them there. This wasn't the case for Clarissa. Someone sensed a problem early on, and we're going to share their story. We're changing this person's name to protect their privacy—we don't want the public breaking down their door.

(A hospital monitor beeps.)

NAOMI *(In an extreme New York accent.)*
Sorry I'm late, boss. The dog kept me up again.

BRYCE *(In an overly gruff voice.)*
Now, Deonna. We're understaffed. Your patients need you to show up at eight.

NAOMI I know. But the dog ate my son's papier-mâché project, and she was pooping out glitter all night.

BRYCE Uh-huh.

NAOMI She's a golden retriever, by the way.

BRYCE Well, one patient needs you right now: eight-year-old Alex Clark. He was admitted last night with seizures, back pain, and weirdly colored veins.

NAOMI Weirdly colored veins, you say? That sounds... suspicious.

(Voices resolve into murmurs and whispers.)

BRYCE *(In his normal voice.)*
Deonna Williams, thirty-six, grew up here in Frederick County. When she finished high school, it seemed like everyone in her life was joining the army. But Deonna never wanted to be in the military.

NAOMI I'm scared of guns!

BRYCE Instead, she moved to New York, planning to become an artist.

NAOMI I lived there for just over a year, but I still can't shake the accent.

BRYCE The artist dream didn't work out, either.

NAOMI Apparently my portraits were "too scary."

(Wheely cart rolls through a hallway.)

BRYCE *(Back in his doctor's voice.)*
I wouldn't worry about the veins, Deonna. One time, I drank a pint of Tabasco sauce, and my veins were orange for a week.

NAOMI You should get yourself checked out, doc.

BRYCE Negative. Duty calls, Deonna!

(Sound of tiny wheels rolling down the floor. The doctor wears Heelys.)

BRYCE *(In his normal voice.)*
Deonna Williams wasn't convinced. Alex had come in and out of her hospital regularly over the past year: sometimes for seizures, sometimes for difficulty breathing, sometimes for temporary paralysis. The medical team had run hundreds of tests. Unfortunately, we can't access Alex's records due to something called HIPAA—

NAOMI *(In her normal voice.)*
The Health Insurance Portability and Accountability Act. It protects patient privacy.

BRYCE I called two hospitals, six doctors' offices, two neurologists, and one kidney specialist. No one would tell me anything.

NAOMI Bryce, I don't know if you should be saying . . .

BRYCE But we know there were lots of tests. And Deonna always felt there was something off about Alex's case. A clean MRI, yet excruciating back pain. Superhigh sodium levels in his blood, despite eating standard hospital food. An anxious, worried mother, halfway to tears most of the time—except when she spoke directly to the doctors.

NAOMI	**Clarissa was very, very calm when she spoke to doctors.**
BRYCE	**Something didn't add up.**

(A hospital monitor beeps.)

NAOMI	*(Back in her New York accent.)* **And I'm gonna find out what.**

A hero turned out to be exactly what they needed.

The podcast surpassed 100,000 plays within twenty-four hours; after two days, it was over 200,000. Alex spent that Sunday afternoon holed up in his room, scrolling through comments, reaction videos, and forum posts. People gushed over Deonna's dog (Bryce had circulated a stock photo of a golden retriever on social media) and complimented her art (Naomi whipped up a few truly atrocious paintings soon after they released the episode).

The episode dug into Deonna's growing suspicions about his mom, how she was waved off by the doctors, with enough real details about the hospital and a typical nurse's workday there that it was obvious the podcast had a real scoop. It ended with a bang: Alex's mom had moved him to another hospital for a few years, then came back to Frederick

Health when he was a teenager, which was when Deonna uncovered the truth. *Bam*—a heroic showdown, years in the making.

Bryce and Naomi made it clear that "Deonna" had chosen anonymity to avoid possible harassment from the public—and retaliation by Alex's mom.

That sent the internet *wild.*

What does she think Clarissa would do? someone posted. *I thought she only targeted her family.*

She'd totally poison Deonna if she got out on bail, a person replied.

OMG Clarissa would know EXACTLY what to use so that NO ONE would FIND OUT!!!!!!!!!!

Alex scrolled and scrolled, but no one was talking about him. Or Ella's podcast.

Bryce and Naomi had been right; all it'd taken was a hero.

That night, Alex slept like he hadn't in years, dreaming of a world where no one knew his name.

WHO IS DEONNA WILLIAMS, HERO NURSE OF MONSTER MOMMY CASE?

With less than six weeks to go until Maryland's infamous "Monster Mommy" case goes to trial, residents of Frederick have been watching with bated breath, desperate to see whether friend, neighbor, and local mom Clarissa Anne Clark will be convicted of poisoning her teenage son. Clarissa Clark has lived in Frederick for over two decades, and was deeply connected to the community through her work with the PTA and a network of military spouses. Although she did not seem to have close friends, many people considered her to be a kind and thoughtful neighbor.

New details about the case emerged Friday night, thanks to an episode of the podcast *Lethal Lullaby.* A longtime nurse at Frederick Health Hospital is alleged to be a central figure in the case—according to the podcast, she suspected Clarissa's actions for years.

The podcast did not provide her real name, using the pseudonym Deonna Williams to protect her privacy. No current or former nurses at the hospital could be reached for comment.

In the past, so-called evidence shared on *Lethal Lullaby* has not been independently verified. However, details from the latest episode were confirmed by our team of fact-checkers, from the names of the victim's various doctors to the locations of specialists within the hospital. Furthermore, the hosts went into surprising detail on the nature of the victim's medical results, details which were corroborated by an anonymous source at Frederick Health.

However, most medical professionals in Frederick County are less willing to speak on this active investigation. Neurologist Dr. Melvin provided only the following comment: "Isn't this a major HIPAA violation? Can you tell me who spoke to you?"

We do not give out the names of our anonymous sources.

HERE'S ONE FOR THE TRUE CRIME JUNKIES—SOMEONE WAS ON THE CASE LONGER THAN ANY OF US

Have you been listening to the podcast *Lethal Lullaby*? Shut up, don't lie to us here at *Total Crime Media.* We know you've been bingeing it.

The rumors about this case are out in full force. Initially, followers suspected that "victim" Alex Clark was involved, faking his illness to get attention. This theory was compounded by rival podcast *Liar's Dose*, which argues that Clarissa was innocent and the poison found in Alex's hospital room was planted.

But the latest episode of *Lethal Lullaby* introduces a new figure onto the scene: Deonna Williams.

It's exciting to have more details in this case, and we here at *Total Crime Media* are just as thrilled as you are to dig into this story. Allegedly, Deonna Williams suspected Clarissa for years—pulling together abnormal blood test results, inconsistent scans, and Clarissa's pattern of behavior into a shocking theory. Deonna has already become a fan favorite, with her paintings racking up thousands of likes in just a few hours.

While many questions remain about the Clark family, Deonna seems squeaky clean. We just have one question: Where *did* she adopt that adorable golden retriever? Lacey is so cute, it's a crime!

CHAPTER 24: 35 DAYS TO TRIAL

The Monday after episode four dropped, Alex walked into school feeling like a new person.

It was the most beautifully unremarkable morning he'd had in months. One girl asked if Deonna had ever confronted his mom, but he waved her off. A few kids wanted to know if he'd ever met Deonna's dog. He said she'd showed him pictures.

Who cared if he was lying? No one was whispering. No one was watching him with narrowed eyes. For once, he felt normal.

Alex closed his locker, turned to go to class—

And met Ella's gaze; she was watching from down the hall. If she was capable of killing people with a glance, she would've incinerated him where he stood.

They'd thrown her off guard. According to her social media posts, she had intended to release an episode every week, but she hadn't posted anything after the latest *Lethal Lullaby* dropped. It had been nine days since the first episode of *Liar's Dose.* Alex almost wanted to smile and wave, as if it was last year and she was off to babysit Logan. But instead he stood frozen in place as she walked past.

"Cute story." Ella's voice was casual; only her eyes betrayed her fury. "I think you'll like my next episode. Some nostalgia for you. It's about stargazing, actually—tiny Alex and his obsession with the constellations."

It was only after Ella stepped into a classroom that Alex thought, *I never told her about that.*

CHAPTER 25: 32 DAYS TO TRIAL

Liar's Dose, Episode 2: "Vital Signs, Star Signs"

ELLA Munchausen syndrome by proxy is a disorder shrouded in mystery. Despite all the movies, TV shows, and novels relying on it as a plot device, no one knows much about it. In fact, few people even know the correct terminology. The condition is called *factitious disorder imposed on another*. Read the DSM, folks.

(Little jingle plays. Children sing: "Go to your local library!")

ELLA And welcome to episode two of *Liar's Dose*.

(Whispered voices, resolving into a quiet song, almost like a lullaby.)

ELLA There aren't many statistics for this rare disorder, but its victims tend to fit the following criteria: They're often young children, too little to speak or advocate for themselves. If the victims are older, they are usually elderly, infirm, or disabled—in other words, similarly unable to tell doctors what they're experiencing.

(Doctor in the background asking, "Can you describe your symptoms?")

ELLA Teenage victims are rare, since they can talk about what's happening to them.

(Someone saying, "Shhh!")

ELLA They're so rare, in fact, that I decided to do some digging.

(Papers rustle.)

ELLA Clarissa knew her son had an impeccable memory—she was proud of it. She gushed about how he could remember constellations with ease; how even in elementary school, he could tell her which stars would show up and when. Perseus, Lyra. Ursa Major and Ursa Minor. The North Star. He didn't even need an astrolabe.

(Wind blows.)

ELLA How could a boy with a mind like that not know what was going on?

Alex listened to the latest episode of *Liar's Dose* on his walk home from school. It had dropped on a Thursday instead of a Saturday—Ella had posted that she was changing up her release schedule to improve engagement. Nothing to do with *Lethal Lullaby*, of course.

The episode finished as Alex reached a crosswalk a few blocks from his street. He yanked out his earbuds and came to a halting stop.

What the *hell*?

He had to give Ella credit: Her information about the disorder was correct, and she'd even used the proper terminology, which he was bitter about because now he couldn't hold it against her. But the rest—her comments about teenage victims, the constellations—rattled him.

Sometimes I think about how much you love stargazing...

His mom's email, back in October.

How you like to take me outside in the dead of night, no matter how cold it is, and point to the heavens: Cassiopeia, Perseus, Lyra. Ursa Major and Ursa Minor. The North Star.

Ella had listed those exact same constellations.

You always know what will show up in the sky, and when. You can pick out any star and tell me where it will go, where we can find it again.

Exactly how Ella had described it.

But how? They hadn't become friends until high school, when he was already pretty much over astronomy. It had never been a hobby he shared with other kids, anyway. Just something he did on his own—and with his mom's encouragement. No way was it in the police reports. Maybe his mom had told Ella about it at some point, like when she came over to babysit? But that seemed unlikely. His mom had always been in such a hurry, focused on getting Alex to his next appointment.

The constellation stuff was from their shared life. It was *his*.

And Ella had gotten her freaking hands on it.

A horn blared, tearing through his thoughts. Alex found he was still standing in the crosswalk.

"You going to talk to yourself all day, kid?" a guy shouted from his car.

Had he been talking to himself? That wasn't good.

Alex crossed the street. He took out his daily pills, dumped them in a drainage ditch—*no one will look there!*—and hurried home. He couldn't talk to Bryce and Naomi about the *Liar's Dose* episode without telling them about his mom's emails, and that felt too raw. Besides, they were focused on managing *Lethal Lullaby*'s newfound fame.

They needed their next episode to build on the gains of episode four. They'd perfected the script, and the episode was almost done—scenes describing Deonna sneaking around, gathering evidence. It would be great, but Alex knew it wouldn't compare to what Ella was doing. The case she was building.

After dinner, Alex settled onto the couch and read through his mom's October email again. It wasn't like his love of stargazing was supposed to be a secret. Still, it was weird and nerve-racking that Ella had dredged it up and blasted it on-air.

"Hey, kiddo." His dad sat next to him.

Alex almost dropped his phone. "Oh hey, uh, sorry. I'll do the dishes in a minute."

He couldn't let his dad see the email. And he definitely couldn't let his dad find out about the podcasts. Luckily, his dad wasn't on any social media—he'd deleted everything, just like Alex, after the arrest.

"I'm not here to ask you to do the dishes." His dad hesitated. "I wanted to ask if you've been... okay, lately."

Alex was fine—well, maybe not, but he was better than he had been. It was just this latest episode getting to him. And the emails.

Would his dad have answers? He probably knew his mom better than most. Maybe he'd have some idea of what she was trying to do. Why she was sending the emails, if not to tell Alex the truth.

Alex just had to get answers without tipping his dad off.

"Dad," he began. "Did Mom ever . . . write emails to you? When you were abroad?"

"No," his dad answered. "Never emails. She was old-fashioned, you know. Wrote letters like it was 1942 and I was off to the front."

That sounded like her. "What did she talk about?"

"Well, she talked about you," he said. "She was very . . . detailed. To be honest, I didn't want to know all of it. I was too far away to be useful—I just wanted to know if you were okay, if you were happy, what kind of things you got up to that didn't involve a hospital." He met Alex's eyes with a grimace. "Occasionally she would mention a school play you were in, or the summer camp you went to. But it was mostly hospitals, doctors, test results."

Alex wrung his hands. He wanted to ask if his mom had ever mentioned Logan, but he suspected he knew the answer.

"I should have seen the signs," his dad admitted. "Looking back, it feels so obvious. She never wanted me to take care of you, even for a day. She said I wouldn't know how." He scrubbed a hand over his face. "I thought she was so dedicated, so selfless. I was *proud* of her!"

Alex couldn't believe he'd thought bringing this up was a good idea. Staring this level of guilt in the face was overwhelming.

His dad caught himself and winced. "Sorry, kiddo. I shouldn't be unloading on you. I hope this won't come as a surprise, but I'm filing for divorce. I'm just waiting until after the trial to start the process."

It was strange to imagine, though Alex didn't know what he'd expected. Of course their marriage was over.

"What matters now is getting through the trial," his dad went on. "Making sure you and Logan are safe."

"Right." Alex's throat was dry. His "testimony" remained a disjointed, useless collection of notes.

His mom had probably figured out what she would say by now. It was easy to envision: She'd sit down, meet the lawyer with a shy and nervous smile, tap her lip in that way she did when she was puzzling over a question. *It's hard to remember some of the details. It was such an overwhelming time. I was so scared he wouldn't make it.*

"I know preparing for your testimony has been challenging," his dad said. "I want you to know that I'm here for you. I want to support you." He gave Alex a worried smile. "You've seemed a little . . . off."

Alex's gaze wandered to a collection of fish that floated along the corner between the ceiling and the wall. Just a handful of them, twisting and turning, as if they were exploring the house on a guided tour. Striped blue fish and ruby-red fish and fish in radiant gold, reflecting the lamplight and splashing shadows of themselves across the walls.

It didn't matter if they were real or not.

"Right," Alex whispered.

"Have you been working on your trial notes?" His dad squeezed his shoulder. "I think that'll help you sort out your thoughts."

Alex wanted his dad to be right, to believe that there was an easy solution. Hell, he wanted to blurt out everything right now—to tell his dad about spilling their family's secrets on-air, being threatened by Ella, seeing visions of his mom around every corner. He wanted to tell someone, anyone, about the white-hot shame that burned in his throat. If his mom had been here, he could've told her. He could've told her every last word.

Alex let out a slow breath. "I'll work on my notes."

Maybe this time they would actually mean something.

Trial Notes 4: When did you start to suspect something was wrong?

Never.

CHAPTER 26: 25 DAYS TO TRIAL

Liar's Dose, Episode 3: "Mind Over Matter"

ELLA The brain is a strange, complicated thing. It allows us to dream and wonder, it fills us with hope and dread. It's the organ we understand the least, yet it controls our perception of reality. Which means most of our perception of the world is an enigma.

(Wind chimes rustle, but far away.)

ELLA I might see one thing, and you might see something completely different. Isn't that beautiful? The world is full of messy, conflicting, nuanced perspectives. But I hope that right now, we're all hearing the same thing. Welcome, listeners, to episode three of *Liar's Dose*.

(Whispered voices, resolving into a quiet song, almost like a lullaby.)

ELLA Some of you might remember me from a few interviews I did back in June—explaining what I saw when I was at Alex Clark's house, what I still believe to this day. Some of you think of me as a truth teller. Others call me a vicious gossip. Either way, I hope you'll keep listening.

(Faint, melancholy music plays in the background.)

ELLA One thing that we should all agree on is that Alex Clark is mentally unwell. It's impossible to know if he's always been like that, or if he became unwell after he started poisoning himself, or if he had to be unwell to poison himself to begin with—I don't know. And I don't care. Because I've seen this playbook before.

(Door slamming.)

ELLA It starts with an honest mistake. Something you could call a white lie, just a stretch of the imagination. Maybe the person says you left the door unlocked, but you didn't. Maybe they tell you they studied abroad in Australia in college, and then you find out they've never been out of the country. It's harmless—who really cares?

(Music picks up again.)

ELLA Except then it starts to escalate. They tell you they got a huge bonus at work, and it'll come in soon, so they buy a new car—but the bonus never arrives. They tell you they can't come to your school play because the aliens have gotten in touch, but not to worry, they'll be there next time! They disappear for days, and when they come back, they don't look fully present.

(Music darkens.)

ELLA I've seen this story before, within my own family. I just never expected it to play out with a former friend.

(Sound of children laughing.)

ELLA Yes, Alex and I were friends. I knew he had issues, but I tried not to think about it. I didn't want to assume Alex was like my dad. Wouldn't that be stereotyping? Anyway, it seemed like he was mostly in touch with reality, mostly there. It took years for me to notice the ways he wasn't.

(Laughter is cut short.)

ELLA You don't have to take my word for it. Like I said, everyone's perception of the world is different. With that in mind, I've gathered numerous accounts about life in the Clark family. On our next episode, I'll take you back to Halloween seven years ago, when Alex dressed up as Santa Claus and his doting mother pulled him all over town in a sleigh. Why? Because he couldn't walk. At least, that's what he wants you to think. But I'm getting ahead of myself.

(Gentle pitter-patter of footsteps.)

ELLA The point is, I know how to read the signs. I should have seen it: the lying, the erratic behavior, the way he didn't seem quite there. I just wanted to believe it was different. I wanted to believe *he* was different.

(Music grows ominous and low.)

ELLA But that's the problem with belief: It doesn't make things true.

Alex knew Ella would eventually go there. She'd been hinting at this, implying that he couldn't be trusted because he was sick, because he had a psychotic disorder. He'd known it was coming. And yet.

After finishing the full episode, he headed for the Shitwreck, texting Bryce and Naomi to meet him there. It was a Thursday, and he didn't know if either of them would even be available. But they had to meet up. They had to deal with this.

Because Ella had brought up a detail that she couldn't possibly know. Halloween when Alex was nine: when he couldn't walk, when his mom had pulled him on that sleigh. Alex and Ella hadn't been friends back then, and Alex knew his mom had never posted photos of that Halloween; he and Naomi had already scoured his mom's Facebook account. Yet somehow Ella knew about it.

Unless... had he been Ella's friend in third grade? Was his memory playing tricks on him? His mom had warned him about this. *It's okay that you don't remember that year we went to Chicago. It's fine that you think we went to New York instead—you're sick, sweetie, it happens. Maybe you should just be careful about what you say in public.*

He stepped into the boat and leaned against the wall. Breathe. They'd find a way to fix this in the next episode. They had to.

Their latest episode—episode five—had been fine, covering more of Deonna's sleuthing around. But it didn't land with the same force as episode four had. And here Ella was, claiming she had some anonymous sources, racking up listeners like they were moths pulled to a flame.

Fifteen endless minutes later, Bryce strolled into the boat in that easy, casual way he had, expanding to fill a space. Naomi followed him in with purpose, and it brought Alex back to when they'd met in the park. Immediately, she sat down next to the camping lantern and pulled out what looked like a tangle of yarn.

"I crochet when I'm stressed," she said matter-of-factly when Bryce glanced at it.

"Cute frog," Bryce offered.

"It's *supposed* to be a salamander."

"Listen, we have to talk," Alex said. The holes in the boat couldn't keep out the mid-November cold, and he couldn't stop shivering; he'd already lost feeling in his toes. "I don't understand how Ella knows anything about that Halloween."

Naomi cast a glance at Bryce, then at Alex. "I thought you'd be more concerned about what she was implying about your... sanity."

Alex shook his head. "Everyone already believes that about me. But there's a bigger problem with that episode. She had so many details that she shouldn't have, like about the sleigh. There's no way she could've known about that."

"I wondered how she knew about that," Naomi admitted. "You didn't know her back then?"

Alex paced the hull, running his fingers along the seams in the wood, in case there were cameras. Maybe Ella was spying on him. "No."

"Maybe she found photos," Bryce said. "Like on Facebook?"

Naomi frowned. "But we already went through Clarissa's entire profile."

"Could a friend have posted something?" Bryce tried.

Except Ella also had those details about the constellations, about how he used to track them, back in episode two. That definitely wasn't on Facebook.

Had she hacked his email account? That was a level of stalker-y obsession that seemed unlikely, even for her. Then again, how else could she know this stuff? Alex paced the hull again and flashed his phone light into the cracks in the ceiling.

Bryce leaned against the wall. "I guess we need to look more closely at your mom's online friends."

"Maybe Ella can access deleted posts?" Naomi said.

Alex shone the light through cobwebs, twisting it this way and that. Something flashed—a reflection? A recording device? Or just sunlight, breaking through a gap in the hull?

Wait a second.

There was also a sound, so faint he could barely make it out. A tiny beeping. Like a low-battery alert, or a recording device glitching. Did they beep?

He froze. *Beep, beep, beep.* There it was.

Although it also sort of sounded like a hospital monitor: *beep, beep, beep.*

What was happening, what was happening, what was happening—

"Alex?"

He turned around to find Bryce and Naomi watching him with puzzled, uncertain looks.

"Uh..." Bryce trailed off. "You okay?"

"Do you guys hear anything?" Alex blurted out.

"Just you pacing around for the millionth time," Naomi said.

"You sure you're okay?" Bryce's voice softened. "We can put the podcast on hold for a while, if you need a break."

That was the last thing Alex needed. He had to get his side of things out there, and they'd wasted time with the first few episodes. "I just—there was this beeping..."

"A beeping?" Bryce raised an eyebrow.

Alex forced in a breath and glanced back up at the planks crossing the ceiling. The light was gone. "Like a tiny *beep, beep, beep.* A ticking." Naomi and Bryce met him with identical blank looks, so Alex threw his hands up. "I thought I heard it! Maybe I was wrong. You guys are right. Facebook. Facebook makes sense."

Bryce and Naomi exchanged a glance.

"Alex," Bryce said. "Have you felt... okay, the past few days?"

"What?" Alex shoved his phone in his pocket—what if Ella was outside, looking through the walls right now?—and stepped away from the wall. "I'm good."

"Right," Bryce said in a flat tone. "Except you've kind of been... how do I put this..."

"Talking to yourself," said Naomi.

The world heaved off-balance.

"I'm okay. I'm great." Alex forced a smile. "I'm sorry. This Ella stuff, it's been getting to my head. Working on one podcast was tricky enough, but trying to get ahead of Ella's—it's enough to make everything feel inside out. Trying to guess what she'll say is like trying to read someone's mind. It's so... screwed up."

That was the truth, and it felt good to say aloud.

Bryce's worried expression faded. "Hey, we got this. I'll go through your mom's Facebook posts again to see if there are any details we could add to our podcast. Maybe there are posts from her friends! We'll drop some new content to drown out Ella's episode. Like maybe—"

"Wait." Naomi set her salamander down and got to her feet, her expression troubled. "Bryce, you had a good point earlier. Maybe we should stop for a bit."

That felt like a punch to Alex's ribs. *"What?"*

"Think about it!" Naomi put her hands up. "We take a strategic hiatus. Instead of releasing a new episode tomorrow, we tell viewers we're on break for a few weeks—maybe two, maybe three—because we've landed on a bombshell, and we need time to investigate. We could even hint that we got an interview with Deonna."

Alex fumbled for words. "But..."

"And then," Naomi said, "we release a new episode in late November, or early December. The speculation will build while people wait. Our last episode got mainstream news coverage. Imagine what the suspense for this one will do."

It didn't make sense. They had no bombshell, no explosive reveal.

Alex raked a hand through his hair. "We don't have anything to investigate."

"This is genius!" Bryce pumped his fist. "We just need to come up with something—"

"And we'd have three weeks to do it!" Naomi finished.

The two met each other's gazes, eyes blazing, all light and fire and terrible, terrible plans.

Alex shook his head. "You don't get it. I can't just 'come up' with something."

"We'll do some digging." Naomi waved a hand in the air. "And if not, we can spin something. Ella's being so annoying in Journalism—she keeps hinting at having new intel—and it's driving me up the wall. But if I could tell her *we've* got new information..." She let out a dreamy sigh. "I would die to see her face."

Alex had forgotten about the school-project part. "She says she has new intel?"

"She's just trying to psych us out." Naomi shrugged. "But if we go on hiatus and hint that we've got major info, she'll freak."

This wasn't the way to fix this. It wasn't.

Was it?

"But..." Alex could barely get out the words. "Ella could—Ella could retaliate. What if she tells people *I'm* on *Lethal Lullaby*? That I'm working with you guys? She could tank the podcast's credibility."

"I don't think she'll do that," Bryce said. "If she does, people will ask why she was willing to work with you on *Lethal Lullaby* too. It'd make her look bad—she's doing all this work to discredit you, and yet she was on a podcast with you for weeks."

"Exactly! We need to move forward. We need to generate buzz." Naomi rubbed her hands together. "No matter what Ella drops next, people will be waiting for *our* next episode, waiting for the bigger scoop."

"Why would they think ours'll be bigger?" Alex asked, voice faint.

"We'll drop hints!" Bryce punched the air.

Alex dug his fingers into his scalp. "About *what?*"

This was followed by a long silence.

"Well," Naomi said, "we can make something up. Like...oh! Maybe we can say Deonna tried to sabotage Clarissa a couple years back—"

"Yeah!" Bryce snapped his fingers and turned to Alex. "And then your mom took you to some other hospital—"

"But Deonna told some doctors, and Clarissa—what if Clarissa tried to poison one of the doctors? Oh, that would be so dramatic!" Naomi rubbed her hands together, then frowned. "Although probably not believable, hmm."

"We'll workshop it," said Bryce.

Alex couldn't speak.

"Anyway, we can make something up," Naomi said breezily. "Would that be so bad?"

Was it so bad? The podcast was already full of lies. The story of the bumbling doctor, the nurse on the case for years, the bright-eyed golden retriever. Still, those things were rooted in the truth. They had grounding in reality.

What Bryce and Naomi were suggesting—it felt different.

And yet.

There was Ella, spewing lies on her podcast. Hinting that his mom was framed. That there was some big cover-up. That he'd been the one—

No.

"Let's do this," said Alex.

CHAPTER 27: 23 DAYS TO TRIAL

@LethalLullabyOfficial, Saturday, 12:05 a.m.

Hi dutiful followers! Loyal fans! Lethal . . . legion? We've got to come up with a good name.

It's me: your host, Bryce! You might be wondering why we didn't post a new episode tonight. We've landed on a gold mine of intel . . . and it could change everything.

So while we hate to disappoint our fantastic, non-factitious listeners, we've decided to put the show on hiatus for a few weeks as we sort through this information and figure out what it means. We owe it to you to get the truth. With Clarissa in jail, so many questions remain: How did she get away with it for so long? What tricks did she pull to fool the doctors? And *how* did she maintain those curls? Oh yeah, listeners, I've been keeping up with your comments.

We might have answers to some of these soon (not the curls one, though: sorry, Cindy from Dallas), and you're gonna be hella psyched to hear our new episode when it drops in early December.

Stay gold! But don't inject it in your veins. That's bad.

Alex didn't watch to see if Bryce's post would take off. Instead, he completed an online German lesson for the first time in months, and, in a moment of put-togetherness that shocked even him, changed his email password on the off chance Ella had hacked into his account. Then, he scrolled videos until the travel vloggers, dance challenges, and cooking tutorials all blurred together.

When he woke up, noon light poured through the slatted window blinds, sending rectangular streaks across his blankets. Aching pain traveled down his spine, radiating through his shoulders and deep into his nerves. Opening his eyes felt like moving two-ton bricks. It wasn't a normal sort of tired, an I-want-to-stay-in-bed-all-day kind of tired. It was an I-feel-practically-paralyzed kind of tired. It was an I-don't-think-I-can-even-speak kind of tired.

Hooray. The other fun side of dysautonomia: unpredictable, uncontrollable, crushing fatigue.

It made sense. He hadn't given himself a break since getting into the *Liar's Dose* mess. He should've known it'd catch up with him. There was always a price.

Alex closed his eyes, ignoring his phone buzzing on the nightstand.

When he opened his eyes again, the room was awash in a pink-gold glow. It would've been beautiful, except the light sent pain lancing through his neurons, and he squeezed his eyes shut.

"Hey there, kiddo, easy." The bed sank where his dad sat down. "It's almost six p.m. Are you going to get up today?"

"Nghhh," Alex answered. He wasn't capable of saying more.

It was incredible that people believed he'd chosen this, that he'd actively caused this condition for himself. *I wish* I *could get a day off from school*, classmates would say, and it made him want to scream. It wasn't like he was lying in bed playing video games. He was unable to move and usually unable to sleep, trying not to throw up while it felt like acid was dripping down his spine.

Great day off.

"Mmm." His dad smoothed his hair back. It was strange to experience that kind of tenderness from someone other than his mom. Alex wanted to relax into it, to tell himself it was okay, that he could trust this person. He wanted to. But trying was like opening his mouth underwater and trusting he'd breathe. He couldn't risk it.

"You need to drink something," his dad was saying. "Hold on."

His dad wrapped an arm around Alex's back and helped him sit up. Stars exploded in his vision, the room vanishing into a sea of sparkling white. Everything went cold, as if he'd dropped through ice—

"Whoa, whoa." Back on the bed, back on the pillow, and it was such a relief, because if he sat up any longer he would've puked. "Okay. Maybe we'll try that again later."

Alex made a noncommittal noise that was supposed to be *sure* and came out as *sghh*.

"Your eyes did that thing—they rolled almost all the way back," his dad said. "I hate it when that happens."

I think Mom freaking loved it, Alex wanted to say, but instead he managed, "Uh-huh."

"I'm leaving your medicine on the nightstand. When you feel well enough, be sure to take it, all right?"

Freaking hell.

Sometime past midnight, if his alarm clock was to be believed, Alex woke up again.

The pain and fatigue lingered, but he could move his hands, so that was a win. Maybe this would only take him out for a few days, instead of the weeks-long flare-ups he was used to. He managed to grab his phone from the nightstand.

There were over one hundred new text messages in the group chat with Bryce and Naomi. The first one was from 11:08 p.m. the night before. It seemed likely that Bryce and Naomi hadn't slept.

Bryce: Okay. Our post is picking up!

Naomi: I sent it to Total Crime Media.
Do you think they'll put it on their front page?

Bryce: Deonna's dog got a feature last week,
so who knows?

Naomi: I hope the stock photo agency doesn't find out.

Sitting up was difficult but doable. Skimming the group chat, it looked like there'd been no news from Ella or *Liar's Dose*. Maybe they'd gotten her to back off—or at least to stay quiet for a while.

The hiatus on *Lethal Lullaby* meant something else too. It was time for Alex to put together his testimony. No more scripting fake scenes, no more posts hyping up intel that didn't exist. He had less than a month now, and his trial notes were half-baked sentences on scraps of paper.

The truth is, I was the only person in the world who really knew her, and look how much good that did me.

They'd want dates, details, drama. They didn't want the slimy, screwed-up mess of his thoughts.

The truth is, she promised she'd keep me tethered to reality, and I'm still waiting for her to reel me back in.

It wouldn't fit the narrative. It wouldn't fit the story.

The truth is, none of this has ever felt real.

Email 17 ★ ↺ ⋮

My lovely boy,

Things are hard. There's never a break from your illness. Of course, that's motherhood, isn't it? There's never a break from that, either.

But I don't want to dump my problems on you. You're still so young. I love taking you to the park. The big, winding one a few miles north of here, with the trails and rolling hills. Every time we go, it's different: White flowers bloom on the dogwood trees in spring, and in summer, the forest is alive with birdcalls and buzzing insects. I used to think that in fall the trees turned from yellow to orange to red, but it touched me one year when you pointed out there was a missing step—before they turned orange, they turned gold. I haven't forgotten that.

During winter, the park is so quiet. The trees seem dead, but they're still alive.

When you're sick, I have to remember that: Things are quiet. But you're still here.

Here are the things that are hard for me: When I'm in the grocery store, looking through the kids' snack aisle, and I realize there's no point in getting anything because you're intubated. When I find a new movie to watch and realize you won't be able to watch it with me, because the light from the screen has started giving you migraines.

Sometimes I try to connect with your brother in the same way. Take him outside, go for walks. Your brother...I love him, I do. But he's not you. He's off in his own world.

You were always part of mine.

Notes 1: Things That Don't Add Up

- How did Mom write these emails in the space of just a few days?
    - That's seventeen freaking emails so far.
    - Each email is . . . long? How long? I'm not sure. I should do a word count.
    - Theory: She wrote some of the messages in jail.
        - Do they let you keep your phone in jail??
        - Why would they let you do that???
        - I need to ask Bryce about this, he would know.
- Why is Mom writing as if I'm still sick?
    - I am sick but not intubated-in-a-hospital sick. But she writes as if I'm still intubated-in-a-hospital sick. She writes as if she wasn't the one causing it.
- Or am I reading these emails all wrong?
    - What if the emails are normal, but I'm seeing something else?
        - Is that possible with psychosis?
            - No idea.
        - Could I take the pills and check?
            - Can't risk it.
        - Could I ask someone?
            - Absolutely freaking never.
- Was she so mentally ill she couldn't see reality?
    - Am I so mentally ill I can't see reality?

CHAPTER 28: 17 DAYS TO TRIAL

Liar's Dose, Episode 4: "Pick Your Poison"

ELLA

Welcome back, my lovely fans. I've spent some time digging through records, uncovering documents, and searching for the subtlest of clues—all for you, listeners.

(Papers rustle.)

ELLA

But before I begin, I have some exciting news: *Liar's Dose* has a merch store! Right now, we're only selling buttons, but wow, do we have a lot of buttons! We've got buttons of a home laboratory (I even figured out what color mercury is!), crime scene tape in a hospital room (spooky!), and Clarissa in a variety of fabulous hairstyles (thanks for the suggestion, Cindy from Dallas!). I even tried to do a button of an EKG, but I got a complaint from a local cardiac health society that it looked too much like their logo. Boo, Cardiac Society of Western Maryland!

(Voices saying, "Boooo!")

ELLA Anyway, you've been waiting long enough. Welcome to episode four of *Liar's Dose.*

(Whispered voices, resolving into a quiet song, almost like a lullaby.)

ELLA In episode two I mentioned my doubts about the official story of Alex and Clarissa Anne Clark. Cases of factitious disorder imposed on another where the victim is an older child are rare; cases where the victim is a child who is verbal are even rarer.

(Hospital cart rolls down a hall.)

ELLA So why did this illness begin when Alex was six?

(Children laugh, but the sound is distant.)

ELLA I went to school with this kid, and he was fine in kindergarten. He seemed smart. You could tell he always knew the answers in class, even though most of the time he didn't bother to participate. He loved running around the schoolyard—or more accurately, running away from teachers to explore the woods by himself. The teachers hated that. No one wants a five-year-old going off into the forest alone. But even back then, Alex Clark was full of secrets.

(Leaves rustle.)

ELLA The woods had a hold on him, through every season. He loved how the landscape felt alive in summer, and when the leaves changed in the fall. Gold was his favorite—just before the leaves turned orange.

(Wind blows, almost whistling.)

ELLA Cute, huh? But also interesting. Gold is the color of wealth, of riches, of power. It's also a heavy metal—although, unlike mercury, I doubt Alex ever tried poisoning himself with gold.

(Leaves rustle again; footsteps can be heard, though faint.)

ELLA The same year that five-year-old Alex was running loose on school grounds, items started going missing from the nurse's office. Little things at first—tongue depressors and cough drops, which were found scattered throughout the school. Kids passed them around like tokens.

(Kid laughs, saying, "Look what I found!")

ELLA The school couldn't find the culprit, though they investigated for weeks. Soon more items started vanishing. The nurse had a medicine cabinet where she kept prescriptions for certain kids and staff. Inhalers, EpiPens, antibiotics. Those things began disappearing next.

(Pills bounce around in a plastic bottle.)

ELLA Eventually someone got into the secure lockbox for controlled substances. Codeine, anticonvulsants, Xanax. OxyContin. The works.

(Phone rings.)

ELLA No one ever got caught. And the pills were never found.

(Line goes dead.)

ELLA A few months later, Alex started getting sick—though most of us weren't aware until years had passed.

(Dramatic beat.)

ELLA Alex, the same boy who wandered the woods alone, the boy who could spend hours studying the stars in silence, the boy who disappeared without his teachers noticing. The boy who, maybe, decided to take a few pills. The boy who just wanted to see what would happen.

(Another dramatic beat.)

ELLA The boy who had his own illness already. Factitious disorder, self-inflicted. Period. Full stop.

(Dramatic beat.)

ELLA The media loves factitious disorder imposed on another but doesn't pay attention to its more common counterpart—factitious disorder by itself. When you have factitious disorder, you want the attention that comes with being a sick person.

(Papers flipping.)

ELLA Patients fake symptoms, complaining of vague aches and pains, nothing doctors can verify. Sometimes they interfere more directly—cutting their finger to drip blood on hospital sheets, or slipping chemicals into urine tests to cause altered lab results.

(Voice saying, "Can you pee into this cup, please?")

ELLA In the most extreme cases, they can even poison themselves.

(Mysterious dripping sound.)

ELLA These people aren't victims. They're just sick.

(Music begins in the background.)

ELLA Our school never found out who was stealing the pills—but we do know the last time something went missing. It was October thirtieth, 2019. The day before Halloween, back when Alex was nine years old.

(Music swells.)

ELLA Let's just say, I think I know where those missing pills went.

Gold. The leaves were gold.

After Alex listened to the episode, all he could think was: *Gold was his favorite.*

He loved how the landscape felt alive in summer, and when the leaves changed in the fall. Gold was his favorite—just before the leaves turned orange.

And from his mom's email: *I used to think that in fall the trees turned from yellow to orange to red, but it touched me one year when you pointed out there was a missing step—before they turned orange, they turned gold.*

Alex lay sprawled across his bed, his mind reeling.

This was the third time Ella had shared a disturbingly intimate detail on *Liar's Dose*. At this point, the only explanation was that Ella had spoken to his mom, but that couldn't be. His mom was in jail.

His phone buzzed.

Email 18 ★ ↩ ⋮

My sweet boy,

Do you remember when you were small, and someone started stealing things from the nurse's office at your elementary school? Maybe you don't—you were busy getting up to your own mischief, running off at recess.

Sometimes, when you're really sick, I think about the kid who raided the office. When the doctor is proposing another surgery, or putting you on an IV drip, or talking about an experimental drug from Norway . . . I think about that kid. I wonder what they were hoping for, breaking into the nurse's office, picking the lock to the cabinet. If they knew someone who needed the cough drops, EpiPens, or OxyContin they poured into their bag. If, as they riffled through the boxes and tensed up at every sound, their hands shook with desperation.

I wonder. Because I understand that kid, wherever they are.

If there was some magic pill that would fix you, I would steal it in a heartbeat. I would trespass, I would break in, I would hoard millions of dollars' worth of the stuff. I'd go to prison. Maybe I'd never see you again.

But you'd be okay.

Here are the things that are hard for me: When the doctors start talking about odds and statistics and chances, like I'm in a gambling ring, placing bets on my family. When it's late at night, and I wonder if you're still breathing upstairs. When I come across a baby monitor at the store and think: I could use this. I would know right away when you have a seizure at night. But then I feel horrible, like I'd be spying on you—like I'd be taking away one of the few pieces of privacy you have left.

Here are the things that are hard for me: when I miss you.

I miss you.

CHAPTER 29: 17 DAYS TO TRIAL

He had a panic attack.

It was impossible to know how long it lasted, how long Alex lay there feeling like he couldn't breathe. It was a vortex that sucked him in and clung tight. Blood rushed in his ears, the world pulsed at the edges, and all around him there was the sense that he was going to tip into an infinite blackness and never come back.

Nothing made sense. Nothing made sense. Nothing made sense.

The email: *cough drops, EpiPens, OxyContin.* Ella's podcast: *cough drops, EpiPens, OxyContin.*

Nothing made sense.

The email: *There was a missing step—before they turned orange, they turned gold.* Ella's podcast: *Gold was his favorite.*

Eventually the panic attack subsided. His skin was clammy. He sat up slowly, feeling strange and heavy.

The email: *How you like to take me outside in the dead of night, no matter how cold it is, and point to the heavens: Cassiopeia, Perseus, Lyra. Ursa Major and Ursa Minor. The North Star.*

The podcast: *She gushed about how he could remember constellations with ease; how even in elementary school, he could tell her which stars would show up and when. Perseus, Lyra. Ursa Major and Ursa Minor. The North Star.*

There was only one way to fix this.

Alex burst out of the house without telling his dad. It was early afternoon, and he thundered through the forest, climbing over fallen branches and crashing through piles of leaves.

There. The Shitwreck.

He stormed inside, stepping up onto an overturned crate Bryce had left behind, and inspected the ceiling of the small cabin. Ella had probably bugged it using some state-of-the-art camera, with a battery that could last years. A device that could get access to Alex's phone, read every email, interpret the electromagnetic waves emanating from the device and decode them into messages. Maybe it could even see into the email server itself, see which emails were scheduled to arrive before Alex received them.

That had to be it—Ella was loaded, and rich people had things normal people didn't know about.

Crap. There was nothing here.

But the ceiling was full of cracks…

Was there a storage space on the boat? Of course there was; no one would ever think to check up there. The problem was, there was no easy way to get up onto the second level—the only accessible entrance to the boat was the gash in the hull.

Ella must've gotten it up there somehow.

Oh boy, this was going to hurt.

Alex tore off his sweater—he could barely feel his hands in the cold—balled up a fist inside the fabric, and—

It took several punches to break through the rotten wood, before pieces of the ceiling rained down from above. Alex's legs gave out, and he crumpled to the floor in a cloud of wooden dust.

Blood poured from his hand, forming thin rivers, dripping onto the floor.

And in the blood: something shimmering. Silvery. Almost like…

"Alex?"

Alex jolted. Bryce and Naomi stood in the hull's entryway, wearing matching expressions of concern.

Aha! So they'd figured out that Ella'd bugged the place too!

He scrambled to his feet, bracing his bloody hand against the wall to avoid any incidents. "I'm sorry. I'm still looking. I think if we get up there—"

"Alex," Bryce cut in. "What the *hell*?"

The atmosphere in the boat became charged.

Bryce's gaze flickered from Alex to the blood on the wall and back again. "What are you *doing*?"

Maybe they hadn't figured it out yet. "Ella's podcast has too many authentic details," Alex explained. "It's too specific. It's obvious: She's got this place bugged. And somehow, she has access to my phone."

Bryce stared at him.

Naomi pursed her lips. "So that's what you were doing last time we were here. Flashing the phone light at the ceiling, looking all over the place like a…"

Like a crazy person hung in the air, though she didn't say it.

A wave of dread passed through him like a phantom. *Nonononono*, they couldn't bring up his psychosis now. He *wasn't* in the throes of a psychotic episode. Oh sure, the visions of his mom he'd been seeing, those were hallucinations, he could admit that. But this? This was cold, hard reality.

It had to be.

"What do you mean, her podcast has too many details?" Bryce ventured, taking a step forward. "Like what?"

Alex couldn't explain this without explaining the emails, and he didn't want anyone to know about them. It was bad enough that Ella had read them. Those messages were meant for him. They were *his*.

He couldn't let them get snatched away too. It would be like pulling the wrong brick out of a Jenga tower. There'd be nothing left.

Alex choked out, "Ella talked about... the nurse's office thief..."

Bryce nodded. "Right. But we were all here when that happened. So Ella took that and used it to fit her story. Same thing we're doing. That's not enough to explain why *you*"—he leveled his gaze on Alex—"seem to think she knows something she shouldn't."

Alex folded his arms over his chest and—yep, blood on his shirt. He'd forgotten about his hand. "I can't explain it. I just need you to trust me, and I'll tell you everything later. Maybe we can—"

And for what might've been the first time in his life, Bryce yelled.

"No!" He took a step forward. "No, dude, I won't trust you. You're talking to yourself, disappearing for days, and then coming back acting like Ella's sent spies after you. You keep telling us you'll explain what happened to you if we just wait, but we've been waiting for months, and you've given us nothing. How are we supposed to make a freaking podcast when you're out here acting like Ella's going to murder you in your sleep?"

Oh. Oh no.

"You don't understand!" Pain spiraled up Alex's arm, but he didn't care. "She knows things she doesn't have any right to know. I need to figure out where she got her intel!"

"Her intel about the *school nurse*?" Bryce shook his head. "We all lived through that. What's next? Are you going to shake me up, demand where I got the name of the local hospital?"

"Guys..." Naomi began.

"She's not making it up!" Alex shot back. "That thing about the stars. About gold leaves—"

"What are you *talking about*?" Bryce demanded, getting right in Alex's face.

"Hey!" Naomi stepped between them and pushed the two apart. "Can we sit down? Alex, your hand looks kinda—"

"What aren't you telling us?" Bryce's stare was like a knife in the stomach.

Alex bit back the urge to deny everything. "It's complicated—"

"Don't you get it?" Bryce dug his fingers into his scalp. "If you're hiding something from us, and Ella finds out before we can get ahead of it on the podcast—"

"This isn't about the podcast!" Alex pushed past Naomi and got back in Bryce's face. He'd never been in a fight before, but standing there, heart crashing in his chest, it seemed like today might be the day. Although Bryce didn't have any right to be three inches taller than him.

"Of course it isn't, because it never was!" Bryce threw his hands in the air. "You don't give a crap about the podcast!"

"That's not true—"

"Naomi and I, we've been working our butts off, while you wander off and talk to walls—"

"HEY!" Naomi elbowed into the fray. She shot Alex a look that seemed intended to knock him unconscious, then did the same to Bryce. "Do we have to do this silly boy thing where you puff up your chests? Or can you both chill out?"

Bryce took a step back, his soccer T-shirt rising and falling with each heaving breath.

Alex backed away too, though his legs felt hollow.

"I thought you were pissed at me." There was a ragged edge to Bryce's voice. "I figured I messed up when you were sick—I should've visited you in the hospital more, or invited you to play *Minecraft*, or whatever. I didn't know what to do to fix things after you woke up from the coma. How do you go back to being friends with someone after what you went through?" The words were spilling out of him, like he'd held on to them for months. "But then you showed up in the Shitwreck, and you didn't seem to hate me. I thought okay, maybe we can talk it out. Little did I know we'd be playing a freaking mind game. It's like I don't really know you. Like I never knew you."

Alex's stomach turned. In a way, he'd been hoping that if the podcast went well enough, he and Bryce could just forget what had happened—that he'd show Bryce he hadn't meant to abandon him without having to say it.

"I..." Alex had no response.

Naomi watched them, her expression like she was witnessing surgery, guts and gore everywhere.

"Listen, you seem sick, okay?" Bryce exhaled. "And not in the cool way. I mean in the I-think-you-need-to-get-help way."

Sick like...

He wasn't talking about the blackout spells.

Looking all over the place. Talking to yourself. Disappearing for days.

There was a big difference between being mentally ill in the past—*if you took shots of arsenic, it would mess you up*—and being mentally ill in the present. They were going to discredit him, write him off.

Naomi spoke up. "We're not your enemy, Alex. I promise."

"Have you like, talked to your dad about any of this?" Bryce asked.

"Yeah!" Naomi's voice softened. "Maybe you can change your medication or something. My symptoms were a lot worse before I switched meds. I could barely finish tests because I kept checking my answers over and over again. It's still a thing, but it's better." She gave him a weak shrug. "You should think about it."

"That has nothing to do with why I'm here," Alex managed to say.

This wasn't about his mental state. This was about Ella's podcast, and her somehow cutting to the truth of his life story. This was about taking her down. This was about making things right.

"Fine." Alex's voice came out like ice. "If you won't help me, I'll fix this myself."

He stormed out of the boat without looking back.

CHAPTER 30: 17 DAYS TO TRIAL

Alex had no other option. He went to Ella's house.

By the time he got there, the sun was starting to go down, and the late November wind bit at his skin. He'd wrapped his hand in an old napkin, which was now crusty with dried blood. He stood on Ella's front step and rolled his shoulders back. Three. Two—

The door flew open.

"What are you doing here?" Ella stood before him, squinting as if he was a piece of dirt on her shoe.

"How did you know I was coming?" Alex demanded.

She held up her phone. "Virtual doorbell app."

Well. Alex took a breath. "Where are you getting your information?"

Ella frowned and glanced out onto the street, as if checking to see if the coast was clear, before grabbing Alex's arm and dragging him into the house.

Once they were down in the basement, Ella turned to face him. "I don't want my mom overhearing. She's not a big true crime person, after all my dad's encounters with law enforcement. Anyway, what are you talking about?"

Alex exhaled. "The constellations. Gold leaves. All of it. How could you possibly know—"

Ella's lips turned up at the corners. "So it's true."

This he hadn't expected. He took a step back. "You used all of that and didn't even know if it was *true*?"

"Well, I—"

"Is this some kind of game to you?" Alex snapped.

Ella balked. "Of course it's not—"

"Because I could do the same thing!" He was a runaway train now, careening off the rails, unable to slam the brakes. "I could start my own podcast. Let's see . . . maybe *Pretender by Proxy: How One Girl Ruined Her Own Life, and Several Others, Just to Get Attention*—"

"First of all, screw you—"

"Or, *True Slime: The Real Story Behind a Podcaster's Shattered Family*—"

"Shut UP!" Ella grabbed him by the shoulders, and he almost fell over. Wow, he needed to gain some weight so stuff like this wouldn't happen. "You're the one who pointed me toward the blog. Ages ago. Remember?"

Blog? Alex blinked a few times.

Ella waved her hand in the air as if conjuring the words. "'*Being a parent, becoming a mother, it changes something inside you. Hardwires something so that the only thing that matters is your child.*' You said that to me. In the Shitwreck. You told me *she* said it."

That didn't explain anything. What blog was she talking—

"It seemed weird to me that you'd remember a direct quote like that, even though you're supposed to have memory issues," Ella said. "I thought maybe it was from a book or something. So I googled it."

She'd googled it. But what could that possibly . . . ?

No. No way. Someone had hacked his email account. Someone had posted every email on a blog. Someone had taken the only private thing he had left and put it on display as if he was a zoo exhibit.

Alex collapsed onto the couch.

"The way she wrote..." Ella's voice sounded distant. "The way she talked about you, it was beautiful: *You always know what will show up in the sky, and when. You can pick out any star and tell me where it will go, where we can find it again.*"

Something shuddered in Alex's ribs. He was a rag doll, Ella tugging on the thread, undoing the stitches.

"There was one line that stuck with me. At the end. *Where can I find you again?*" Ella looked at Alex. "And I realized that Clarissa and I, we understood each other."

Alex doubled over, his elbows on his knees. Something still didn't add up.

Email 21: disappearing into the woods, someone stealing medication from the nurse's office. All those details had landed in *Liar's Dose,* episode four. Except her episode had come out *before* Alex got the email.

If someone had hacked his email and posted the messages online, if that was where Ella had gotten her information—how could that person have shared an email that hadn't even been sent?

"You're lying," Alex blurted out.

Ella blinked. And then her jaw dropped.

"Oh no." She took a step back. "You don't know?"

"Know *what?*" Alex demanded.

Ella looked like she was about to break bad news to a dying patient.

"Your mom wrote about you online." Her words came out soft and gentle. "Clarissa had a blog."

PART 4

STARLIGHT MOMMY
NOVEMBER

CHAPTER 31: 17 DAYS TO TRIAL

BLOG ENTRY 1: FOR YOU

When you were first born, you were so small. I could carry you with one hand.

Can you imagine that? Imagine carrying a creature in the palm of your hand. But not a hamster or a gerbil—a tiny human, with preemie-pink skin and dark eyes like your father's. You were unlike anything I'd ever seen.

You probably don't understand this, but being a parent, becoming a mother, it changes something inside you. Hardwires something so that the only thing that matters is your child. You were a star, my whole universe. You still are.

But you don't need to hear my platitudes. What I want to tell you is that everything I've done, I've done for you.

I've always done it for you.

Email number one. Blog post number one.

They were the same.

Alex had walled himself up in his room after he got home from Ella's. He had to pretend he was sick to get his dad to leave him alone, and while there was probably something messed up about the fact that his first instinct was to fake illness, he was desperate.

Everything I've done, I've done for you.

I've always done it for you.

Her blog was called *Starlight Mommy.*

He found it after googling a single line from the email. One line, and it was the top result.

The site's background was an elegant midnight blue, tiny stars twinkling against the darkness, as if waving. Everything about it was sleek and tidy: The home page had an *About This Blog* section, and a sidebar in dark blue and glimmering silver led to different pages: *Sister Blogs, Resources, Posts. Contact Me.*

Alex let his cursor hover over that last button, wondering, wondering.

It was strange. His mom had always been so disorganized, flying from one thing to the next, the house in disarray as she shuttled her kids back and forth from school to extracurriculars to—well, the doctor, in Alex's case. He'd always assumed it was because she was too tired to pull things together, and who could blame her? But this blog was meticulous.

ABOUT THIS BLOG

Hi! My name's Claire. I'm a mom from the good old USA! I guess I want to get my thoughts out and connect with other moms out there. Life can be hard when you have a sick kid. This blog is a collection of letters written to my critically ill son—things I wish I could say when life gets difficult. But I wouldn't trade being a mom for the world♥ Please leave a comment!

Claire. Ha.

He googled a dozen different passages. Every time, it led him back to starlightmommy.blogreal.com. Every single email, except for the opening section of the first one, was lifted from the blog.

It'd never been real. The heartfelt messages, the promises that all would be explained. He'd thought she was reliving memories—summers in the park, long nights in the backyard—and in reality, she'd posted them to her blog right after they'd happened, basking in the attention of who knew how many internet strangers.

He ran his hands over his face, trying to stop shaking. *Why?* If she wanted him to know her, why not just point him to the blog?

Alex stood up and peeked into the hallway. It was 11 p.m., and the crack under his dad's door was dark.

He crept down the stairs to the dining room and riffled around in the drawers of the sideboard, where his dad kept paperwork. The police had confiscated his mom's computer right away, but they'd copied the contents of her hard drive and returned the laptop months ago. It had to be around here somewhere.

He found it buried under a massive pile of insurance forms. When he pulled it free and popped it open, it sputtered and wheezed, but miraculously, it had a sliver of battery life left.

The cursor in the password box blinked at him. He tried a couple of random combinations—*farmlife*, *starlightmommy*, *password*—and then reluctantly tried *alexander*, which worked. Ugh.

Her email was still logged in. He ignored the dozens of promotional and spam emails she'd received since May and went to the sent box. There: eighteen emails, all set to schedule send between September and November. No...not eighteen emails. *Thirty* emails, with twelve more scheduled to land between now and the end of December.

Alex took a shaky breath. The idea of new emails in his inbox, each one more confusing than the last, making him feel less and less tethered to reality—

Breathe. Breathe.

Two clicks brought him to her internet history. He half expected to find something like *mercury poisoning side effects on children* or *how to trigger a seizure*, but there was nothing damning. By the time she was arrested, she knew what to do.

Her browser history was simple. She'd switched back and forth from *Starlight Mommy* to her email account dozens of times on May 11.

Alex braced himself as he opened a new tab and searched: *Clarissa Clark arrest date*. Sure enough, May 11.

There it was.

She must've known the nurse was suspicious—must've sensed something in the air, even if she didn't know there were cameras installed. And yet she couldn't keep herself from poisoning him one last time.

She knew she was on the edge of being found out, and she still couldn't stop herself.

Explain it to me, Alex wanted to scream at the computer screen. *Explain it to me.*

He tabbed back to his mom's email account. Twelve emails, waiting to land in his inbox.

He opened the first one.

My dear son, I know you don't like theme parks, but last time wasn't so bad...

On the blog: *My dear son, I know you don't like theme parks, but last time wasn't so bad...*

The next email: *My kind son, I wish you had more of an appetite, as I've found this new brownie recipe...*

The blog: *My kind son, I wish you had more of an appetite...*

The emails weren't even in order—they jumped around in time, and there was no obvious pattern connecting them all.

He wanted to scream, but instead he scrolled to the last email.

Email 30 / Blog Entry #132: "Scavenger Hunts" ★ ↺ ⋮

My sweet boy,

I'll never forget the scavenger hunt we did for your ninth birthday. I felt like I'd finally done something right. I based it on the constellations: following Delphinus's tail, chasing after Cygnus, riding with Pegasus. It took me weeks to get it straight. I hope you liked the surprise at the end. To be honest, I hope you still remember it.

That's the most brutal part of your illness. It doesn't just hurt you physically. It does things to your memory, your thoughts, your mind. I've watched it tear you open and reconfigure your reality. The day after the scavenger hunt, you unraveled again: You insisted the stars

★ ⮌ ⋮

were following you, that Cygnus was staring at you from the windows, that you needed to hide in the basement to stay away from them. I couldn't believe my beautiful surprise had been twisted by your mind.

I worry about so many things, but underneath it all, my deepest worry is this: that one day you'll look at me and you'll only see a monster.

The thing was, he did remember the scavenger hunt: an evening spent under moonlight, following the stars. How thrilling it had been to stay up past his bedtime. At the end, they'd gone to a twenty-four-hour ice cream shop an hour away. Double chocolate chunk ice cream with rainbow sprinkles and M&M's at midnight. It'd been perfect. Like a dream.

One day you'll look at me and you'll only see a monster.

When she wrote that, she must've known that her ruse would be exposed.

Or maybe it meant something else.

You'll only see a monster.

On the blog: 302 comments.

Alex's chest constricted.

Was this what she'd done it for?

No. That couldn't be the reason she'd loaded up the syringes, why she'd swapped the IV bags.

His phone buzzed, vibrating next to him on the floor.

Bryce: Did you get home? Please don't tell me you're wandering a highway somewhere

Bryce: I mean, not to like, stereotype or anything. But are you wandering a highway somewhere? That's dangerous dude

A third time, and Alex was about to turn it off—but no.

It was Ella.

Ella: I know you hate me, but you have to know something.

A second later, his phone lit up with an incoming call from her. Oh God.

Who *called* people these days? The thought of speaking to someone else on the line, having no time to formulate a response, having to actually *sound* like a stable, well-adjusted person—it was enough to make him explode. He'd expect this sort of betrayal from an adult, like his dad. But Ella? *Ella?*

It rang again. Holy crap, she was trying to torture him.

Alex tapped the green circle. "What do you want?"

Something rustled over the line, as if Ella was walking around. Outside, stars twinkled in the velvety evening as if spying on him from their perches in the sky. Alex tugged the blinds shut.

"Hey," Ella said, "I need to warn you about something. The last episode of my podcast is going to drop tonight at midnight."

Alex's free hand clenched and unclenched. "You just released one—"

"Today, I know. I just…I need to get this over with. You don't know what it's done to me, digging into the lies, it—it brings so much back. I want to be done with it." There was a pause before she spoke again. "But I wanted to tell you. The next episode is about Logan."

Rage bubbled in Alex's gut. He fought the urge to scream. "Is this supposed to make me hate you *less*?"

"I'm trying to help by warning you." There was no smugness in her voice now, only resignation, as if she was dreading this as much as he was.

Alex hissed through his teeth. "Thanks, Mother Teresa."

"Listen," Ella said. "I know what it's like for him. To be overshadowed by a family member and their tragedy. To have your entire family focused on someone else."

Nothing was computing. If she could relate to Logan, then she would know better than to drag him into the podcast. A cold feeling grew in Alex's chest.

There was a long pause, in which a million worst-case scenarios cascaded through his brain. Ella said quietly, "I'm just going off her blog."

Alex shook his head. "I don't—"

And then it clicked.

At some point, the blog had mentioned Logan.

Alex hung up before Ella could get in another word. He scrolled through years of blog entries in a chaotic blur of words and photos—that was *his* hospital bracelet, his IV line digging into skin—and searched his own name and Logan's, but of course, his mom hadn't used their names. He flew through entries as if the blog was a life raft and he was drowning.

Of course it was the last post. Dated April 27 of this year.

I fear, it read, *that this disease will soon strike my youngest.*

CHAPTER 32: 17 DAYS TO TRIAL

It didn't make sense.

Logan had always been the healthy one. He'd faked a handful of seizures, yes, but for attention. He'd never had medical issues. But this...

Alex jumped to his feet. He yanked open a drawer so hard that a sea of papers and folders tumbled free, like an avalanche in slow motion. Alex froze, but there was no sound from upstairs. Clear. For now.

The first chunk of pages in the stack were Alex's medical records. There were MRI results, prescriptions, an email from a nephrologist (*if this progresses another year or two, we may be looking at catastrophic kidney failure—we need to start preparing for the possibility of dialysis and transplants*), and Alex pushed them aside. He tore through the other papers. There were school counselors' notes (*teachers say he forgets everything in class, we may need a specialized plan to manage*), and then: bingo. Something about Logan.

There was a report card (*child is restless and easily agitated, constantly disrupts and vies for teacher's attention*) and finally, papers documenting an emergency room visit.

May 10. Child admitted with signs of generalized tonic-clonic seizure, blue color to fingers and lips, trouble breathing. Keppra administered intravenously.

Alex looked again at the name at the top of the ER paperwork. Even though he knew.

LOGAN CLARK, it read, bolded like an accusation.

Alex took slow, heaving breaths, crumpling the edge of the paper between his fingers.

I fear that this disease will soon strike my youngest...

This had always been the worst-case scenario. But Alex had no idea how close it'd come to reality.

The same "disease" would've struck Logan, while Alex lay comatose under the hospital lights. It would've been Logan whose days were counted out in pill capsules, Logan whose eyes darted from hallucinations to reality and back, Logan who crumpled like a puppet with the strings cut. It would've been Logan who had two concussions in a month, Logan who lost time in the spaces eaten by memory loss, Logan whom she held at night saying, *Breathe for me, sweetheart*, as if reciting lines from a play she'd already starred in.

Alex would've just been lying there, comatose. Or more likely, he would've died before he could learn the truth and pull Logan out.

He wanted to vomit.

Why had Logan never told him? Did Logan remember the ER? Or had it simply passed him by, Logan settling back into his routine of school, robotics club, and video games as if the whole thing was a weird, unfortunate accident?

May 10.

Logan must've been the real reason their mom got caught. He was the ultimate red flag—Deirdre probably got the cameras installed after Logan's ER visit.

Alex knew he and Logan had been lucky. The doctors might've assumed the problem was genetic. Deirdre could've been out sick that day. Logan had already become the next target—and his mom had almost pulled it off.

It was easy to imagine. Logan sprawled across a hospital bed, his thin arm hooked up to an IV, his breath coming fast and shaky. It made Alex recoil, like the image had actually burned him.

I fear that this disease will soon strike my youngest rang in his head, her voice sweet and sad, and for a second he could've sworn she was there, brushing his hair back and giving him a faint smile.

Air, he needed air, he needed *air*—

He powered through the kitchen and flung the back door open. The night breeze sent a chill into his lungs, and water soaked into his socks. Water, because the ground was covered in snow.

Snowflakes swirled through the air with a whimsical, dreamlike quality. In some ways, psychosis felt like a never-ending dream. You could talk to a wall in your dream and be certain it was your long-dead grandma, even if you couldn't see her. Half the time he spoke to his mom, when she appeared in the woods or at Bryce's house, he didn't *really* see her—he just knew she was there with an unshakable certainty.

He was losing feeling in his toes.

Alex needed to get as far away from the house as possible. He strode toward the edge of the yard, where the grass sloped down into the trees. Above the silhouette of the woods, Cetus, Pisces, and Pegasus formed an orderly line, as if marching.

Which stars do you think we'll see tonight? she asked—

He grabbed a clump of snow and hurled it into the shadowy woods. Maybe she was the real reason he'd drifted away from astronomy. It was too tied up with her, too tied up in their life together.

Alex fumbled for his phone. He could text someone, though he didn't know who. He unlocked the screen, only to be hit with a notification that landed like a punch to the jaw.

🔊 Liar's Dose: Episode 5.

His thumb tapped the notification, pulling up the episode. The play icon beckoned, a hand reaching out from the past, about to drag him back under. But before he could let it, a low, crackling sound rolled out from the woods.

Probably just an animal, or a tree rustling in the wind. Maybe.

Unless someone was watching him.

Alex's feet moved before he could think. He jammed his phone into the pocket of his pajama pants and stormed down the hillside. At the bottom, in a clump of bushes where he'd heard the sound, he threw his arms forward. Shoved the branches aside. Bit back a yelp as thorns tore at his shirt—

There she was.

She sat on a tree stump, her curly hair tumbling over her shoulders. Snowflakes landed on her eyelashes as she looked down, fiddling with her phone. The case was familiar—a midnight blue with colorful butterflies adorning the shell. Monarch, morpho, swallowtail. Orange and iridescent blue and white, endless white, like a snowstorm that never ended.

"Look at you," she said, tilting her head to face him.

Alex studied her, cataloging every change like he'd done when his dad had returned. Tiny wrinkles lined the corners of her eyes. Something in her gaze had dimmed, and there was an ashen tint to her skin. On her phone screen, Alex could see the latest episode of *Lethal Lullaby*.

"What's all this?" she asked.

A hollow feeling tunneled through his bones. "I..."

She was supposed to be in jail—and yet she was sitting in the forest like they were having a picnic.

The podcast started playing. Bryce's voice: *It happened over several years...*

"What a strange little project," she said.

Alex pulled at the neckline of his T-shirt. Where was the air, where was the *air*?

"I—" he sputtered out.

"Tell me, Alex." Her eyes could've shot a hole through him. It was like he'd been obliterated into dust, vaporized into ash and snowflakes. "Is this what you wanted?"

She wasn't here just to listen to his podcast. This close to the trial date, she would only have one goal: to prove her innocence. And what better way than to show that Alex was still sick? There was only one way that this would all make sense.

She was poisoning him again.

Fear lanced through Alex like a blade. He tore at his arms, clawed at his skin, picking and tearing until he drew blood. "Get it out!"

His mom stared as if he'd lost his mind. "What are you doing?"

"Get it *out!*" Alex screamed again. He pulled at the gashes in his arms, too cold to feel the pain. Dark color appeared under his fingernails, and blood smeared across his palms.

"Alex." She swept to her feet. "Why don't you sit down? You're looking pale."

Alex shook his head. "So you can rush me off to some hospital and pretend—"

"Pretend what?" Her eyes narrowed, but there was no anger in her voice. "That you're psychotic? That you did this to yourself because you're delusional? That you believe in a lie?"

The accusation was a bullet piercing his lungs.

"This podcast." His mom shook her head. "It's cute, I'll give you that. But I don't understand why there's two of them."

Alex's vision blurred, blackness clouding the edges. Blood dripped onto his pajama pants, splatters of red against the green plaid.

"I guess I thought..." His mom trailed off. "I thought you cared about the truth."

No, no, no. She couldn't force him to talk about it. She couldn't.

His mom looked up to the sky. "I thought it mattered to you, what actually happened. You seemed awfully worked up about it in January."

The memory burned in his veins. He swayed, legs going weak.

"Like you would care." Alex's voice shook. "You were never telling the truth."

His mom met him with a wounded look. "Neither were you."

And the world evaporated into a brilliant, beautiful nothing.

CHAPTER 33: 16 DAYS TO TRIAL

Ella's voice came to him first, her words layered atop faint, melancholy music. *The leaves fall off the trees. Frost creeps across the ground. And a cold settles into the air, heavy and deep…*

Liar's Dose, episode five. Playing from his phone, which was somewhere in the snow beside him. He must've tapped play when he collapsed. Alex tried to move his hand, to shut the freaking thing off, but he couldn't feel his limbs.

"Alex!"

Another voice came, from a million miles away. Honestly, it felt like it was coming from another dimension.

"Alex, hey, wake up!" His dad's face came into focus above him, everything else a sea of black. So it was still nighttime. "What did you do?"

His voice wasn't angry. It wasn't even disappointed. Instead a single note of fear rang through every word.

Then there were arms underneath him and he was up in the air, the backyard pulsing in and out like a bad dream, his ears ringing so loudly it drowned out his dad's voice. He could barely make out *so late at night* and *how did you hurt yourself* and *the woods, the woods, really?* Above, the stars had settled into unfamiliar patterns.

His mom was right, wasn't she?

He was still sick. He still had a psychotic disorder. He was still the boy who talked to walls, the boy who was his own most unreliable witness.

It would be impossible to testify against her. It would be impossible to testify at all. How could he? He couldn't even pin down what year it was.

Alex squeezed his eyes shut.

"Easy, kiddo." The kitchen door creaked and then they were inside, a cloud of warmth enveloping him. His dad set Alex down on the couch.

Two things became clear at once: One, his dad had brought his phone inside. Two, *Liar's Dose* was still playing.

"Clarissa's blog, Starlight Mommy, *provides a haunting account of the ordeal. Her final blog post, posted just weeks before she was arrested, is one sentence:* I fear that this disease will soon strike my youngest."

Alex's hand twitched, but the rest of his body was unresponsive. No no *no*, his dad couldn't hear it—

"Clarissa had no idea what Alex was capable of. She couldn't have."

Ella's crappy music rose in the background, swelling to a crescendo—

"But Alex was close with his younger brother."

His dad's brown eyes went wide.

"... and I think he taught Logan everything he knew."

His dad stood there, bandages in one hand, antibiotic cream in the other. His mouth opened and closed, but nothing came out.

Ella was still talking, her voice grating. She described his mom messaging her—*no need to come watch Logan today, he's not feeling well*—and then finding out about the ER visit later, from Logan no less.

"It seemed like it wasn't a big deal to him. Almost as if he, or Alex, had planned it. At that point, I knew my suspicions were true—"

"Alex," his dad said. "What is this?"

Alex closed his eyes. He couldn't believe he'd let it get this out of control.

Oh no. It was so clear what he had to do.

"Dad?" He could hardly get the words out. "I…I need to tell you something."

While Alex spoke, his phone wouldn't stop buzzing.

Naomi: Why is Ella talking about a blog?

Bryce: Uh, I'm not saying you should see how many plays that episode has, but you should see how many plays that episode has.

Alex didn't tell his dad everything. He didn't know how. Instead, he started with early summer, waking up from the coma. Being told by doctors she'd been arrested. HARROWING NEW DETAILS IN "MONSTER MOMMY" CASE.

Naomi: Is the site really your mom's?

Bryce: You gotta check this out: 22 OF THE MOST CHILLING QUOTES FROM "MONSTER MOMMY" BLOG THAT WILL MAKE YOU FEEL BETTER ABOUT YOUR OWN PARENTS.

Alex told his dad about the creation of *Lethal Lullaby*, about Ella splitting off from the group in search of a more dramatic truth. He told his dad about *Liar's Dose*.

He kept Bryce's and Naomi's names out of it; they didn't need to get in trouble. Meanwhile, his dad bandaged his arms with a delicate, almost surgical precision, and he didn't say a word.

Shame rose in Alex's throat.

"I'm sorry." His voice trembled. "I know. I really, really fu— I really screwed up."

His dad met him with a warning look.

"I..." Alex inhaled through his teeth. "It was bad enough when it was just me. But this can't get Logan too. It can't."

His dad nodded, his mouth thinned into a narrow line. "We'll do whatever we can." He sighed. "Alex, why did you think exploiting yourself would fix this?"

Alex dug his fingers into the couch cushions, though nothing eased the tightness in his gut.

How had he not seen this parallel? His mom had thrived on turning the most private moments of his life into content for likes. And here he was, turning the most private moments of his life into a podcast for—well, if not likes, then something similar. Sure, even if most of it was fake, there was truth behind it. His heart, beating behind the recording.

Alex buried his head in his hands. "I don't know."

"I'm going to send some emails. Make some calls. Get this podcast taken down, if I can." His dad scratched his chin. "And then—"

"Wait." A cold dread settled in Alex's chest. "Take which podcast down?"

"Both of them." His dad's voice was resolute. "*Liar's Dose*. And *Lethal Lullaby*."

CHAPTER 34: 16 DAYS TO TRIAL

"You can't!" Alex scrambled to stand up, but a wave of dizziness crashed over him, and he fell back onto the couch. "I mean, *Liar's Dose,* fine. But *Lethal Lullaby*—"

It was horrible. It was a mess. And it was Alex's one way out of this.

"What about it?" His dad threw his hands in the air. "Do you even understand what you've done here?"

"But—"

"It doesn't matter that half of it is fake." His dad rose to his feet. "It's drawing attention to the case. What if the jury hears the podcast beforehand and becomes biased? What if the defense tries to use the podcast as evidence? What if the defense finds out *you* were on the podcast, and tries to paint you as unreliable?"

Alex hadn't considered that. But he couldn't give up on *Lethal Lullaby* now. It was the only way to string together his testimony. Every day he felt more and more untethered from reality—the sea of his mom's emails beckoning him to the past, Ella giving him ever-increasing reasons to be paranoid.

He couldn't admit to all that, though, so he settled on, "People have already downloaded—"

"It doesn't matter!" His dad's voice was a crackling flame. "Taking it down will stop the spread."

"But I—"

"No. No *I*. This is about *us*. This podcast"—his dad spat out the word as if it was toxic—"affects me and Logan too."

He was right, as much as Alex hated to admit it. *Liar's Dose* would never have gone after Logan if *Lethal Lullaby* didn't exist.

His dad set a hand on Alex's shoulder. "I know you didn't do this by yourself. Why don't you tell me who else is involved? I can talk to their parents—"

"No." Bryce and Naomi weren't going down for this.

His dad took a deep breath, his eyes lingering on the bandages wrapped around Alex's forearms. "Is the podcast why you . . . were you trying to . . ."

Alex swallowed hard. "I wasn't trying to hurt myself. Not intentionally. I promise."

"Did you see something?" his dad asked cautiously. "In the woods?"

Yes. "No."

A pause. "Maybe you heard something?"

Definitely. "I didn't."

"Hmm." It was clear from his dad's tone that he didn't buy it. He smoothed over the bandages, as if without them Alex would fall apart. "Listen, Dr. Melvin told me that you were lucky for coming out as unscathed as you did. The thing is, your medication ought to be working by now. You shouldn't be having symptoms like this so frequently. But . . . more and more each day, it's like you're looking for something to jump out at you. And Logan says you talk to yourself sometimes."

This couldn't be happening.

"Not to mention . . ." His dad waved a hand toward the dining room.

Oh.

The papers. The computer.

Alex had left everything lying there.

"I don't understand." His dad stood up and began to pace. "The pills should've brought this under control."

"Uh-huh," Alex croaked, as if the words had been forced out of him.

"You *have* been taking them, right?" his dad asked.

Of course waited on the tip of Alex's tongue. Saying it was the only thing that could make this better. And yet—

He hesitated too long, and his dad's expression crumbled. *"Alex."*

Crap, crap, crap. "I was going to—"

"Alexander. Matthew. Clark." There it was, the middle-name drop. "You know better than this. You *have* to know better than this!"

"I know," Alex stammered. "I know, I just—"

"What did you think would happen?" His dad's voice rose, confusion tumbling into anger, the situation slipping out of control. "That your symptoms would go away without any treatment, that you'd never have an episode again?"

Of course his dad knew exactly what had happened in the woods, even if Alex hadn't said it out loud. "That's not what I—"

"Then *what*?" His dad paced around the room with heavy, angry steps, a vein popping on his neck. "What were you thinking?"

"I was trying to keep it from getting worse, okay?" Alex shot back before he could stop himself. "I was trying to keep it from getting worse!"

His dad spun to face him. "What could possibly make it worse? Did you think I was..." His voice trailed off.

"Wait." There had to be something Alex could do to rein this in. "Wait, Dad, listen. I trust you. I know you wouldn't..."

There was nothing to say.

Of course he knew, logically, that his dad would never tamper with his medicine. It was as absurd as believing his mom had escaped from jail in the middle of the night. And yet the thought grabbed hold of him, sank claws into his brain, and reeled him in, like it was the most natural thing in the world.

Even now, he could tell the thought was a delusion. And even now, it felt intoxicatingly real.

"You think they're poisoned," his dad said, a strain in his voice like a cord pulled too tight.

I know they're not poisoned, Alex wanted to say, but he also wanted to say, *Mom showed up in the backyard tonight.*

His dad dug his fingers into his scalp, tilting his head to the ceiling.

Guilt twisted up Alex's insides. He trusted his dad enough to let himself be carried back into the house, to let his wounds be bandaged. And yet it wasn't enough, and it was impossible to say why.

His mom's words echoed in his head. *Look in there, it's got the white medicine like normal…I promised I'd always tell you if you were seeing things—*

"I'm sorry," Alex managed. "I know you wouldn't do that."

It took his dad a long time to speak. "Then *why*, Alex."

Alex closed his eyes. He'd never felt so spent in his life. Well, that wasn't true. But this still felt like so many flavors of bad all at once.

"I can't explain it," he said. "I try, I swear. I take them to school and I look at them and I will myself to do it. But then I twist them open and—" *And too many thoughts rush in and I can't.*

His dad looked so worn out. "We should really get both you and Logan in therapy."

"I'm sorry," Alex repeated, but the words felt empty.

His dad's shoulders fell and his posture slumped. "Kiddo. This isn't safe."

"I—"

"I mean it," his dad said, though Alex had known he did. "What if I wasn't home? What if you'd been out there for longer?" He was pacing again. "What if..."

What if you have an episode at school? his mom had asked. *Stay home with me, sweetheart. What if you hurt yourself? What if you fall in front of all your classmates?*

"Listen." His dad sat down beside him. "We'll figure out the medicine. We'll figure out the podcasts."

Alex ran his hands over his knees. "I have to tell you about her blog," he said.

The expression on his dad's face was hard to read. Something knowing, something sad—and then it clicked. His dad already knew about the blog.

Alex swallowed hard. "You knew about it?"

"The police found it when they searched her computer." His dad's expression was pained. "It's considered evidence. But it didn't feel right to tell you. You were already going through so much." He squeezed Alex's shoulder. "Don't worry about that right now. What's important is to deal with these podcasts, and make sure you and Logan are safe and healthy. Don't repeat the past, kiddo. You're better than that."

You're better than that. Ha.

At that moment Alex doubted it.

CHAPTER 35: 16 DAYS TO TRIAL

Sometime after 2 a.m., Alex texted Bryce and Naomi—ignoring his 236 unread messages.

Alex: dad found out.

Bryce: DUDE WHAT

Alex: ok i told him

Alex: i'm sorry

Alex: he saw my phone

There was a long pause. Typing ellipses from Bryce, from Naomi, then nothing. Alex lay on his bed and daydreamed about the empty nothingness of being in the coma.

Naomi: Let me guess. He heard Ella's episode about Logan?

Alex: bingo

Alex: dad wants them both taken down

Again with the ellipses. If Bryce and Naomi never spoke to him again, he couldn't blame them.

Bryce: Do you want them taken down?

Yes. No.

Alex: it doesn't matter

Alex: he's going to contact the streaming platforms or something

Alex: he'll probably say they have too much personal info

Alex: like doxing or something

Bryce: Your dad knows what doxing is??? Dude mine was still running Windows Vista

Alex: we should take LL down

Alex: before your parents find out too

Months of effort, and it was all meaningless. He was no better than Ella, tearing apart someone's hard work, turning their life into rubble. Maybe he and his mom were more similar than he'd thought.

Neither of them texted back. By 3 a.m., *Lethal Lullaby* was off the internet. Alex buried his head in his pillow, but he didn't sleep.

On Monday, *Liar's Dose* was still up.

"I appreciate that you and your friends took down the podcast," his dad said as Alex poked at his toast that morning. Tiny snowflakes fluttered down in the gray sky. "That was a difficult move, I'm sure. I'm proud of you."

Alex forked the toast in half. His mind was overcome with an endless, empty droning.

"I put in a support ticket with Spotify and Apple, and hopefully the other podcast will be shut down soon." His dad massaged his forehead. "We'll talk about the medication with your psychiatrist this week."

The psychiatrist that Alex had been lying to for several months? None of it mattered.

Alex drifted into school Monday, his insides scooped out and hollow, like every emotion that had coursed through him Friday night had been torn out of his chest and spilled in his backyard. He welcomed the strange emptiness. It was better than feeling it all, so much better than feeling anything.

He daydreamed about closing his eyes and waking up in the hospital room, his mom leaning over him: *I thought you'd never wake up*... He could tell her about the horrible nightmare he'd had, this world that was so much messier than being sick.

Alex passed a group of kids chatting by the posters in the front lobby. They went quiet, their gazes following him—

He turned down a hallway. But as he passed the lockers, it happened again: eyes tracking him, smiles turning into strange, contorted grimaces, conversations fading to nothing—

Alex inhaled. Thinking everyone was watching you was a sign of psychosis.

Things were normal. Everything was normal.

And yet.

Kids turned to each other and whispered, but Alex couldn't make out their words; were they saying *Alex* or *let's*? They tapped at phone screens, leaned close to each other to share a pair of headphones…

Their eyes were watching, watching. The school building felt like a fun house, as if the walls were moving. No, he couldn't let this happen. He went to his locker. Spun the combination. Pulled the lock—

A sea of confetti tumbled out.

What was this? *Congratulations on your podcast getting taken down?*

Voices whispered behind him. Alex kicked some of the confetti away, and a piece caught the light.

He hesitated. The voices grew louder. No, he couldn't pick it up. *Don't do it. Don't do it. Don't—*

He picked it up.

It was a slip of paper.

Entry 130: On bad days, I watch you beg for more medicine. I have to hold myself back, but what kind of mother could let her baby boy wail like that?

Alex took a ragged breath, his heart shuddering.

He snatched up another one—

Entry 112: I feel so guilty about this. I know you're eleven. You're growing up. You shouldn't have to deal with this kind of surveillance. But I've put a monitor in your room. The seizures have become so dangerous…

Alex fell to his knees and scooped up the confetti in a mad scramble. Pieces slipped out of his hands and scattered across the floor, and adrenaline shot through his veins.

Entry 82: The doctors say the EEG results are unlike anything they've ever seen.

Entry 98: Do you ever think about how hard it is for me too?

He leaped to his feet, papers fluttering from his hands—

And then a shoulder rammed into his own.

"Don't come for my podcast," Ella hissed, then vanished into a classroom.

Alex had to drag his feet to get to class. At last he reached his desk and sank into the seat like dust floating down to earth.

A boy turned around to face him. "You gonna puke blood today? I don't want to get any on my backpack."

Right. Ella's podcast had told everyone about *Starlight Mommy*. It'd been all over her episode, the source material for her work. The source material for his entire freaking life.

"Hey," another guy said, leaning close. "We're taking bets to see how many posts your mom can go without mentioning you crying. Craig says seven. I say four. What's your pick?"

Everything was blurring together. The podcast was bad enough. A brutal clipping of the worst parts of his life, cut and rearranged to make a story he didn't recognize. But the blog was something else.

His mom had shared the story of his slow-motion descent like it was a tabloid magazine, like she would receive an award for putting up with him. Like his illness was hers to share just because she was his caretaker. When he'd met other disabled kids in hospitals over the years, he'd been disturbed by the parents who posted their whole lives online. It was like they shared the most gutting parts of their children's stories to get a trophy for not abandoning them.

—You wouldn't believe how bad Maia's last seizure was! She frightened a neighborhood boy so badly he ran away in tears.

—Sorry I'm so tired. Arthur wet himself again. I think the urethral surgery will really help!

At the time, he'd been grateful, because he'd thought, *At least Mom doesn't do* that.

But how could he judge her? He'd been furious about all the true crime articles, the news sites gushing about his family like they were hot gossip. And then he'd gone and done the exact same thing.

The two of them, they were so alike.

All day, he checked his phone, on high alert for the vibration that meant Bryce or Naomi had texted the group chat. Maybe a *hey man, you all right?* from Bryce, or an inspirational quote in Mandarin from Naomi.

There was nothing.

He clicked to *Liar's Dose*. Still up.

After last period, he went home, and sank down, down, down.

Two days later, Alex's dad told him that he had a new prescription.

A new prescription wouldn't help things. The problem wasn't that the old drugs didn't work; he'd just never taken them. But his dad explained what he and the psychiatrist had come up with. *We're going to try something that doesn't come in a capsule. Something no one can tamper with. How about that?* Alex was torn between relief at his dad's understanding and humiliation at his own relentless paranoia.

After Alex picked up the medicine from the pharmacy counter—his dad let him do it himself, an act of trust Alex wasn't sure he deserved—he slipped back into the car and stared resolutely at the dashboard.

"Thank you." It was impossible to look at his dad.

"Of course," his dad said. "You keep them wherever you want. I don't need to see them. I don't need to touch them. I just need to know you're taking them."

"I'll take them," Alex mumbled.

His dad turned the key in the ignition. "Glad to hear it."

"I know you're not like her," Alex cut in before they could pull out of the parking space. "I mean it. I know you would never... I know you would never poison them."

His dad watched him, but it was hard to interpret the look in his eyes. "Alex," he said, "let me tell you something."

Alex stiffened as his dad turned the car off.

"Remember when I was in Afghanistan? One day in my office, I heard gunfire outside the window. It was common in the area, but it had never been so close before, so I dropped to the ground. Your radios guy does not get a rifle inside his office." He took a breath. "One round went clear through the windowpane, shattered all the glass. Nothing else hit. And you know what? You'd think after that I'd be scared of windows. But I wasn't. It was corners. In my office, my desk was in the corner, and when I heard the rounds go off that's where I was, back against the wall. I panicked. After that, I moved my desk away from the corner. Even now, you know that recliner in the corner of the living room, the one I used to sit in to read to you when you were little? I can't even go near it."

Alex stared at him.

He'd been living with his dad for months, sharing the cluttered living room, early-morning drives to school and hastily made breakfasts, and somehow he hadn't noticed this. If his dad had been bouncing from place to place, unable to settle down, unable to linger in corners without immediately leaping to his feet—well, Alex hadn't caught on to any of it.

He wouldn't let himself miss something again. He wouldn't.

"It doesn't have to make sense." His dad squeezed his hand. "Just take your medicine."

CHAPTER 36: 10 DAYS TO TRIAL

The next two days started and ended with vomiting. The medicine created a whirlpool in Alex's stomach no matter how hard he tried to keep it down, and when he didn't feel like he was being thrown around in a storm, he was wiped out. He slept sixteen hours on Thursday and barely got out of bed the next day. Forget school. Every part of him was stiff and wooden, as if he was a marionette. Someone would have to tie his limbs to strings to get him to stand.

Bryce and Naomi didn't get in touch. Alex couldn't blame them.

Ella's podcast was off the internet by Friday; his dad had gotten through to someone at Spotify or Apple. Not that it mattered.

Meanwhile, his mom's words lingered whenever he was on the edge of consciousness, her voice floating in from a foggy nowhere. *I thought you cared about the truth... I thought it mattered to you, what actually happened.*

Like you would care, Alex had said. *You were never telling the truth.*

A raw, clear anger coursed through him in a way he'd never felt before.

Even when he was too weak to move, he felt it. The anger was perhaps the first moment of clarity he'd had in months. It was like putting on glasses for the first time and seeing leaves on trees, shingles on houses, raindrops in the sky. She was a betrayal, a secret exposed, a promise unkept.

During those days when he couldn't sit up, anger was the only thing that made him feel real.

But he couldn't deny that she was right. *You were never telling the truth*, Alex had said in the backyard, and she'd looked at him and answered, *Neither were you.*

She was right. She was right. She was right.

His phone sat on the nightstand, inert and lifeless. Bryce and Naomi couldn't make another episode for him. And even if they could, it would be a lie. Just another story.

Everyone had their own version.

Bryce and Naomi—*Lethal Lullaby*—had the tragic story about a boy poisoned nearly to death by his mentally ill mother.

Ella and *Liar's Dose* leaned hard on the Clarissa-was-innocent angle, implying Alex had factitious disorder and had poisoned himself.

And *Starlight Mommy* pretended that no one had ever poisoned anyone. That it was all a tragic mistake of fate.

Three stories. All wrong.

He glanced at his phone. His mind wandered to the day he'd spoken with Naomi in the library, and she'd mentioned how being honest about her OCD had backfired on her. *Sacrificing oneself for the pursuit of truth.* And yet she didn't seem to regret it.

He grabbed a notebook.

Telling the real story on the stand might wreck everything for good. But he had to do this.

He began to write.

Trial Notes 4: When did you start to suspect something was wrong?

I had a feeling that something was up after a few years. It was the way she talked about the doctors: "Dr. Melvin doesn't know what's good for you, he's not a mother, he doesn't understand." Or, "Nurse Lucilla thinks she knows best how to approach your treatment, but you scream so much at night, and I can't take it." After a while it became, "I got this new medicine for you. I think it'll really do something. Don't tell the doctors."

Don't tell the doctors.

I don't remember exactly when she first started saying that. But that's when I knew something was off.

The thing is, I never told anyone.

Trial Notes 4 (Take 2): When did you start to suspect something was wrong?

okay, scratch that last one.

Something you have to know about Mom is that she's disorganized. You have to give her credit, keeping up this ruse for so long. I would've expected that a week in, she'd accidentally take the mercury herself.

It's no surprise that between the constant specialist visits, the merry-go-round of the ER and the peds unit, things got tricky for her. I'm sure shuttling poison back and forth, hiding it in toiletry kits or purses or whatever nooks and crannies she could find in the hospital room—I'm sure all that got complicated. By the time I was in middle school, I noticed how she would mess with the IV. How she would add things—extra painkillers, she said. She'd sneak me food when the nurses told her not to. She'd brew these homeopathic teas.

At some point, it became obvious.

The thing was, by the time I figured it out, I was too sick to do anything about it.

Trial Notes 4 (Take 3): When did you start to suspect something was wrong?

Ugh, that's not true, either.

I could say this is hard because my memories from back then are crap. Which is true.

I could say this is hard because I don't want to hurt Logan and Dad. That's also true.

I could say this is hard because of school, and the two podcasts, and the whole I'll-probably-never-get-better thing, so what's the point. And that's also true.

But.

It feels like my mom is two different people sometimes. Well, all the time. But honestly, I feel like two different people too.

The thing is, this isn't going to work if I'm not completely honest.

The real truth is this: I knew everything by the time I was eight.

PART 5

THE REAL STORY
DECEMBER

CHAPTER 37: 9 DAYS TO TRIAL

By Saturday afternoon, the side effects of the medication had settled down, and Alex could stand up without getting dizzy. It was the kind of victory his mom would've celebrated with a balloon (*savor the little moments!*), but his dad just dropped a packet of papers on his desk.

"Got this from school," he said. "Homework assignments."

Alex screamed into his pillow.

He had more important things to do than homework. As soon as he could stand for more than two seconds, he went to Bryce's house. Bryce lived at the end of a long, winding street, and by the time Alex got there the edges of his vision were twinkling in and out.

It was possible Bryce wouldn't want to see him. It was possible Bryce would slam the door as soon as Alex opened his mouth. Maybe Bryce's mom would get involved, warning him off: *Don't get close to that boy, I think he's deranged…*

Nerves fluttered through his chest. Whatever was going to happen would be painful. But he needed to do it.

Alex stood on the front step and rang the bell.

The door swung open. Bryce's curls were frazzled, shadows lining his eyes. "Alex? You look like crap."

A greeting for their times. "I could say the same for you."

Bryce shuffled his feet and didn't respond.

"Hey." Alex jammed his hands in his pockets. "I want to apologize. You and Naomi were right. I was... I *am* sick, and I should've been taking medication to control it, but I wasn't, and things spiraled. You shouldn't have had to see all that. The talking-to-walls thing. The... episodes."

Bryce blinked a few times, opened his mouth, and then closed it.

"I know it was scary," Alex said. "I'm sorry."

"It wasn't scary," Bryce said at last. "I was just worried about you."

Alex fidgeted with the edge of his sleeve. "I, uh, I had a talk with my dad. And I'm on new medication now. But I am sorry."

There was more to say, and Alex wanted to hold on to it and put it off and hope that maybe, maybe, there'd be a more convenient time—except Bryce deserved better than that.

"And listen." Alex rubbed his arms. "You didn't screw up. Last year, before the coma. That's not why I vanished."

Bryce stiffened, but he didn't move to turn away.

"I was really sick." Alex swallowed. "Kinda like this, but different. I didn't know how to be normal around you. I knew my perspective of reality was off, I knew my own thoughts were lying to me, and I—I thought it would blow up in my face. That you'd see it and shut me out. I couldn't take that, so I had to shut you out first."

The look in Bryce's eyes didn't change.

"But you..." It was so hard to speak. "You were dealing with a lot, and I should've been there. At least to like, work on the RPG or something. Distract you. I shouldn't have left you to deal with your family alone. I'm sorry."

Alex hadn't expected the adage to be true—that it would feel like a weight had been lifted—but it *did* feel like that, and he was annoyed at himself for waiting so long. It would've been so much easier to hang out with Bryce and Naomi, work on the podcast, and be a person again if he'd said something sooner.

"Hey." Bryce's stance relaxed. "I should've reached out too. I was overwhelmed with..." He waved his hand around the house. "And it freaking sucked, and I couldn't think about anything else. But I'm sorry."

Alex let out a breath. "You're all right."

"I thought about calling you when you got out of the hospital." Bryce rubbed the back of his head. "But I figured you'd be pissed at me for not being there in the first place. And then things got weird. Ella was going around saying you were a liar, and reporters actually showed up at *my* house because people knew we'd been friends. I didn't know how to get past all that."

"Yeah." Alex couldn't blame Bryce for this. "I thought about trying to talk to you too. I missed hanging out and having things be normal, you know? But I was sure you hated me."

Bryce gave him a halfhearted smile. "I thought you hated me too."

"Well, I don't," Alex said. "And I'm sorry for not telling you much of anything."

Bryce's voice softened. "It's okay."

It felt like the energy around them changed. Maybe they could just be two people again. Two friends.

It could be that simple.

Bryce glanced to the side. "You want to talk to Naomi too?"

Alex perked up. "Is she here?"

"Yeah. We were thinking of making a new podcast. You interested?" Bryce waved Alex into the house. "You know a lot about poisons, so, like? Your expertise might be helpful."

The invitation, the welcoming hand—warmth bloomed in Alex's

chest. Bryce still wanted Alex as a friend. Bryce still wanted Alex around, period.

"Actually"—Alex stepped inside—"I have an idea."

Naomi was in the den, with so many tabs open on her laptop that the fan was wheezing. The screen cast a blue glow upon her skin. Alex managed a slightly more coherent apology to her, and it was accepted on the condition that he buy her ten spools of yarn for her next crochet project.

"Man." Bryce dropped into a beanbag chair. "Say goodbye to your life savings."

Naomi threw a pillow at him. "Hey, Mrs. Richards said that if I start a new journalism project before January, I can still apply for the scholarship. You remember the Zodiac Killer? The one who tried to copy the original Zodiac Killer, but used the Chinese zodiac instead?"

"Um," said Alex.

"He wasn't Chinese," Naomi added helpfully.

"Actually, I need your help with something." Alex sat down. "But first, you guys have to promise not to kill me."

"Done," Bryce replied, just as Naomi said, "Oh, wouldn't that make an excellent reunion episode?"

"You know how Ella's podcast had those details? Well, she was getting them from the blog, which you know now, yay," Alex said with a sigh. "I didn't know about the blog. But for the past few months my mom has been...emailing me the entries."

Bryce's jaw dropped. "Dude, from *jail*?"

"Well—"

"Holy crap, I had no idea they gave you Wi-Fi in jail."

"I—"

"Just think of how much time you'd have to play video games! No wonder so many people get arrested."

"Bryce," Naomi snapped.

"Right, right, sorry."

"She didn't send them from jail. She set them up to schedule send, back in May." Alex rubbed his temples. "Right before she got arrested. Which is superbizarre? She knew she could get arrested, and yet instead of like, I dunno, hiding the evidence, she sent all these emails. I don't get it." He took a long breath. "They're word-for-word copied from her blog. It's email after email about how sad she is that I'm sick, how worried she is that I'm losing my grip on reality, et cetera…but she *knew* she was poisoning me, she *knew* why I was sick, and yet she still…"

He trailed off. He didn't know how to explain the thoughts churning in his mind.

Bryce leaned forward. "How many of these emails are we talking about?"

"Eighteen so far," Alex said. "Twelve more to come. I looked at her computer."

"Jesus," Bryce muttered.

"You should block her," Naomi said.

Alex rubbed his forehead. "It seems kinda messed up to block your own parent."

"Dude, she tried to kill you," Bryce said.

"Can I see them?" Naomi asked. "If that's okay with you?"

Alex hesitated. It felt so personal, so raw—but at the same time, it was from the blog. Those fragments of his life were already public.

He passed his phone to Naomi. For a few minutes there was silence as she read the emails he'd received.

"I'm wondering about something," Naomi mused. "But I've never poisoned my own child in an escalating ten-year-long medical saga, so take everything I'm saying with a grain of salt—"

Alex snorted.

"—or not." Naomi rolled her eyes. "The blog has hundreds of entries. Your mom only sent thirty. Have you wondered why she chose these?"

It hadn't occurred to Alex to think about this. "What do you mean?"

"These emails insist you're still sick." Naomi's expression brought Alex back to the day they'd met in the park, when she'd gotten him to sign her petition, the look in her eyes blazing with something righteous. "She's sending you reminders that you're mentally ill. Right?"

"Well, yes—"

"And you have a trial coming up," Naomi said. "Where you have to prove your side of things. You're testifying, right?"

Alex's palms went clammy. "I don't really know if I can—"

"Her biggest advantage is that everyone thinks you're off your rocker." Naomi said it without judgment. "If you go up on the stand and no one trusts you, it doesn't matter what you say. But it's even better for her if *you* don't trust you. If *you* don't fully believe what you're going to say. The jury will be able to tell, when you're on the stand, if you seem unsure. And her lawyer will eat that up."

"But what does that have to do with—"

"The emails are meant to make you seem unstable. To make it so you don't trust your thoughts. Your mind." Naomi passed Alex's phone back to him. "She picked posts about how sick you were in order to mess with you. Her goal is to make you question yourself, until you no longer trust what you're going to say." Naomi met Bryce's gaze, and he nodded in agreement. "That's her endgame."

I promised I'd always tell you if you were seeing things...

I couldn't believe my beautiful surprise had been twisted by your mind.

My deepest worry is this: that one day, you'll look at me, and you'll only see a monster.

Alex's throat tightened. "That can't be it."

"Think about it." Naomi sounded confident. "If you doubt everything that happened, you'll look unreliable on the stand, and the defense will be able to take advantage of that. They're probably already betting on it. Your mom planted the seed."

Alex had to take a moment to unravel this. He knew his mom had poisoned him and lied to him and broadcast it to the world, but the fact that she had her hands in his mind even now, that her fingernails were digging into his skull, trying to rearrange his thoughts, was too much to fathom.

"People have tried to do this to me too." Naomi's voice was soft. "*Naomi, it's not a big deal, you're being so OCD about it all. Don't listen to the OCD, listen to me. Chill out, it's just your OCD talking.* On and on and on."

Alex couldn't meet her gaze. "Was it ever your OCD?"

"No." Naomi's voice went tight. "Not when I told the girls in Gym to stop putting random shit in my bag to mess with me. Not when I told people to stop copying my homework. Not when I told Kiera to stop going around telling people I was crazy."

"That's messed up," Alex said softly.

She shrugged. "It's messed up what happened to you too."

"*Are* you testifying?" Bryce asked.

"I don't know," Alex managed. "She has a point. I don't have the best grip on things sometimes, and even what I do remember could be wrong. I have to swear on the stand that it's real, and I just—" He shuddered. "I have notes. That's it."

In his backpack, the notebook of chicken-scratch handwriting felt heavy. Opening the notebook would feel like dropping an atom bomb—and what he was about to propose would be much, much worse.

"I don't know if I can go on the stand," he said. "Which is kinda why I'm here."

Naomi leaned forward. Worry lingered in Bryce's eyes.

"You said something a few months ago, in the library," Alex said. "*Sacrificing oneself for the pursuit of truth.* And I realized—"

"I have to be honest with you," Naomi cut in. "The actual translation isn't *truth*, it's dharma. And also, I found it on the internet, so who knows if it really—" She frowned. "Oh wait, I get where this is going, sorry. Go ahead."

"The thing is," Alex went on, "I haven't been fully honest. *Lethal Lullaby* tells one story. And *Liar's Dose* tells another. But both are wrong."

Bryce looked like he was trying to work out a math problem. Naomi's expression didn't change.

Alex let out a breath. "I want to record the truth. All of it."

Naomi watched Alex. "What truth?"

"Have you forgotten we don't have a podcast anymore?" Bryce asked.

"I know we don't have a podcast," Alex said. "But I need to record it anyway, even if it's just for me. For us. I need to get it out before the trial. And if I can do it here... maybe I can do it on the stand."

"You want to practice." Naomi folded her arms over her chest and leaned back.

Alex couldn't speak. He thought, *I want to tell you. I want to tell you both. I want to tell someone, anyone, before I have to do it in court.*

"I'm not following." Bryce balanced his elbows on his knees. "Why now? After all this time?"

Because Ella had targeted Logan. Because the jury could easily believe her version of the truth.

Most of all: because his mom could choose to tell the truth too.

Alex met Bryce's gaze. "I can't live my life inside a lie. Not like she did."

Admitting it felt like coming up for air. They were similar, the two of them. But he was going to draw a line.

Bryce stroked his chin and said, "Okay."

Naomi nodded. "I like it."

This was possible. This was really possible.

They got out the recording equipment—the microphone, the headphones. They booted up the audio software. As the sky began to darken outside, Naomi hit the button to record. And Alex closed his eyes and began to speak.

CHAPTER 38: 4 DAYS TO TRIAL

It took three days and an agonizing number of takes, but at last the recording was complete. Alex had known that recording a podcast took a lot of work—speaking slowly and evenly, varying your tone to maintain interest, not hacking up a lung in the process—but Bryce and Naomi were brutal with their critiques. "Your voice is shaking," Bryce said after the fourteenth take, and after the twenty-seventh, Naomi blurted out, "Drink some water, won't you? You sound like my grandma."

Finally they were done. Naomi cut the takes into something cohesive. They had the truth, recorded as an audio file, which Bryce and Naomi presented to Alex as a kind of backup plan.

"If you can't say it out loud in court," Bryce told him, "then you can play this. It could be, like, your testimony."

Alex was simultaneously moved by the offering and skeptical. "I don't know if they'd let me do that."

"What if you, like, snuck it into the courtroom? Don't give them a chance to say no," Bryce tried.

"You won't need it," Naomi said, lifting her chin. "You told us. You can tell everyone else too."

Alex wanted so, so desperately to believe her. He wanted to feel it in his bones the way she did. But instead, he thanked them and brought the flash drive home.

The trial was in four days. Four days until a jury decided which truth they wanted to believe. Four days until he self-destructed.

At school, people whispered as he passed through the halls, weird notes appeared in his locker—*Gonna fake an aneurysm today?*—and there was still that look, the way they watched him, like they were peeling off his skin. But none of it felt real.

The real world was beating at his bedroom door, tearing at the hinges, about to rip it off the frame.

"I think you'll do great," his mom told him that night. Or maybe he only dreamed it.

Trial Notes 5: Did she ever tell you where she was getting her "medicine"?

Yes. No. Yes.

Yes: from a homeopathic remedies store, from a natural healer upstate, from a specialist who shipped it out of California.

No: from a broken mercury thermometer, from a gallon of wholesale salt from the grocery store, from the lab she used to work at when I was little.

Yes.

Trial Notes 6: How did she talk about your illness?

She's sad, and she's frustrated, and she's terrified every extra night that a doctor wants to keep me for "observation." She's pacing. She's wringing her hands. She's typing away on her phone—texting Dad, she says—and she's pulling her hair, and she's saying it'll be fine, it'll be fine, though I don't think she means it.

Later, she'll load up another syringe.

But what do I know? I was always the crazy one.

Trial Notes 7: Did Logan ever get sick?

No. Not at all. Never.

Well. Except once.

I read every entry on the blog, hoping I'd find something that could explain it all. But there is so much I still need answered. So much I still want to talk about. And so much I'll never know.

CHAPTER 39: TRIAL DAY

The day of the trial arrived. Their dad dropped Logan off at school—no one wanted to put a ten-year-old on the stand—and then it was off to the courthouse.

Twelve steps up the front stairs into the building. A left, thirty-six steps down the hall, a right, into a big gallery, and then one more turn to the left, eighty-two steps in total. Not enough steps, not enough steps.

They were placed in a side room; his dad explained that the lawyers didn't want Alex—or any other witness—to hear another witness's testimony before he testified. Something about not wanting his own testimony to be "tainted" by what he heard from other people. So he wouldn't see the beginning of the trial. This rattled him. Not the fact that he'd miss part of the trial, but the fact that even their own lawyer didn't trust him to tell the real story.

"It's not personal," his dad explained. "They're doing it for me too."

"Okay." Alex's voice sounded strange to his ears.

"You're gonna be all right." His dad rubbed his shoulder, his face looking haggard, almost haunted. "Whatever happens in there, you're gonna be all right. I'm so proud of you for doing this. Do you know that? So proud."

Alex's body tensed up. He'd told the lawyer everything, even sent him the recording, but he hadn't had the strength to tell his dad. And now... well, once his dad knew the truth, Alex would be lucky if the man ever wanted to speak to him again.

"Do you mean that?" A part of him just wanted to hear his dad say it, to relish in that faith. To hold on to it for one more second.

Alex wanted more too. He wanted them to talk about things that weren't related to the trial, his mom, the nightmare of the past ten years. For them to have other memories together aside from him watching his dad get on a military bus and leave. For his dad to be impressed by Alex's knowledge of German verb tenses, for him to think, *You learned all that just because I was in Germany,* and be touched by it.

"I mean it," his dad said softly. "I know you can do this."

That made one of them.

Soon enough, his dad was summoned. And then it was just Alex.

He balanced his elbows on his knees, fighting to ignore the torrent of his own thoughts. There was no clock in this room; for all he knew, time had literally stopped. It could've been five minutes. It could've been five years. He just knew that his dad was testifying, and that at some point his doctors and Deirdre had testified too. But that was it.

He took a slow breath. Naomi had been teaching him some Mandarin, and he went over the tones in his head to try to calm himself. Two million years later, someone came and escorted him inside. It was time.

The courtroom was packed with dozens, maybe even hundreds, of people. Some had notepads—reporters—but a lot of them looked like Frederick locals here for the spectacle. They were whispering to each other, contributing to a relentless drone of sound that filled the room. Voices moved out of sync with people's mouths, eyes watched without breaking away, and it felt like a veritable dissection.

There were so many voices.

Alex found himself on the witness stand, though he couldn't feel anything—couldn't feel the chair underneath him, couldn't feel his own feet on the floor. It was like he'd been disconnected from his own body. His dad sat behind the prosecutor's table, giving Alex an encouraging nod.

Alex allowed his eyes to drift to the right, toward the defendant's table.

It was hard to know what he'd find there. Maybe she'd look just like the woman who used to wake him from nightmares and hold him when he hallucinated, and he might not be able to go through with it. Or maybe she'd look like a monster, eyes cold and calculating, and he'd panic and run.

He had to look.

She didn't seem a day older than the last time he remembered seeing her, at home back in January. Her long, curly brown hair was drawn up into a loose bun, hair the exact same color as Alex's, and she wore a baby-blue blouse with a perfectly pleated neckline.

For a second it could've been just the two of them in the courtroom, her holding his shoulder to steady him, *Breathe for me, all right?*

Her eyes shone bright, and she gave him a soothing, familiar smile.

A smile like an old friend. A smile like a relative you hadn't seen in years. Or a smile like an accomplice.

For a second, he didn't know if he'd be able to do it. Maybe he'd have to call the prosecuting lawyer and tell him to use the recording as his testimony, that way Alex could hide in another room and promptly have a panic attack. But Alex had told the lawyer that he would give his testimony in person—and he could do it—he could do it—he had to do it. Breathe: in, out. *I have to do this for Logan.*

And then the judge called on Alex to begin.

CHAPTER 40: TRIAL DAY

"Please raise your right hand," the bailiff said. "Do you swear to tell the truth, the whole truth, and nothing but the truth?"

There were a thousand different versions of the story he knew, but only one he could tell.

"I do," Alex said.

Mr. Evans, his lawyer, stepped forward. "Let's start at the beginning, Alex," he said. "When did you start to suspect something was wrong?"

Trial Notes 4: When did you start to suspect something was wrong?

The lawyer stood with a placid expression on his face, though his brow was a bit furrowed. All an act, Alex knew. If he appeared thoughtful and pensive, the jury would listen more carefully. Which was what they needed.

All an act…

Alex couldn't help it. He turned.

His mom had folded her hands under her chin as if watching a show. And yet there was still that look in her eyes, almost like…

I promised I'd always tell you if you were seeing things, she'd said—

It brought him back, just for a second. To a sunny morning when he was eight, one of those days when the sky was so bright the whole world seemed to glow. He'd opened his pillbox and taken out the capsules, like every other morning. But this time they slipped, and when he went to pick one up he accidentally stepped on the second pill.

And a beautiful, delicate marble of mercury rolled out onto the kitchen floor.

Even at eight, he knew what it was, thanks to an accident with an old-fashioned thermometer a few years earlier. He just didn't know what it was doing in his pill capsule.

Maybe the doctors had messed up the medicine. Maybe someone had made a mistake. Or maybe it was a new drug that *looked* like mercury?

He picked up the blob.

Rolled it in his palm.

Watched as it reflected the light from the windows, like a little star.

When his mom walked in, she didn't seem shocked. She didn't even seem concerned. She just frowned and asked, "Are you all right?"

Alex turned it over in his hands. Was it dangerous to hold this thing? Who knew, but it was too beautiful to put down. "Is this...?" There was no way. It didn't make any sense. He picked up the pill capsule and looked inside again, as if there'd be more mercury waiting there, but now it was empty. "Why is there...?"

She took the pill from him, examined it closely. Looked into the empty capsule.

She said, "Alex, it's got the white medicine like normal."

He dropped the blob of mercury onto the floor.

She said, "I know the hallucinations have been getting more intense."

She said, "But remember, I promised I'd always tell you if you were seeing things."

She said, "Why don't you take your medicine before it gets worse?"

Remember, I promised I'd always tell you if you were seeing things.

That was what her eyes were saying, here in the courtroom. Her eyes were saying, *Anything you remember, it's going to be fake.* Her eyes were saying, *There are records of you having a psychotic disorder, so no one will believe you.* Her eyes were saying, *Take the medicine and don't ask questions.*

That glowing morning, he'd taken the empty capsule, and it had been the first day he'd felt well and truly out of his mind.

Trial Notes 4: The real truth is this: I knew everything by the time I was eight.

Except he didn't. Except he did. Except he didn't.

Except—

Alex exhaled and said, "I learned the truth eight years ago."

EIGHT YEARS AGO

It began with the split pill capsule, the blob of mercury. He started checking every capsule—finding mercury one time, what looked like lead another—and then realized there wasn't a single thing he could do about it.

He was sick, that much he knew even by second grade. Shadows jumped from the ceiling in class and swirled at his feet; voices tumbled from the woods as if being set free from a curse. The other students kept their distance. The teachers whispered, *I've never seen schizophrenia present this early…*

He couldn't pronounce the thing they said he had. But he knew he was sick.

Three or four times, he took the loaded pills to school, thinking he'd ask somebody what they saw inside. But the what-if scenarios were like a monster waiting in the dark.

A student: *I only see white dust. Are you okay? You're looking kinda twitchy.*

Another classmate: *Hey Alex, that's a normal pill. What did you think was gonna be in there? Candy? You're so weird.*

Or worse, a teacher: *Sweetie, I think we should call your mom.*

No. No. Never.

For a long time, it didn't occur to him that *she* might've been the one loading the pills. The contents of the capsules were strange and glossy, beautiful and shimmery, and they never seemed like a real threat. Sure, some of it was probably mercury. Maybe some of it was lead. Was that bad in small doses? Or was it some new, fancy treatment for his growing number of problems?

Was it even there in the first place?

He never told anyone. But he did begin to notice something: Whenever he was sick, she was gentler with him. Sweeter. Softer. It wasn't that she was cruel when he was well—she was like any other mom—but when he was sick, she tucked him into bed, and she brushed his hair back, and she told him stories late into the night, well past his bedtime.

And he kind of liked it.

NOW

"Did you ever ask her about it again?" Mr. Evans, the lawyer, asked. "Or anyone else?"

Alex had to force himself to look past Mr. Evans, past his dad, past his mom. Beyond the public benches to a crack in the wall on the far side of the courtroom.

"Not exactly," he said.

"What happened next?" Mr. Evans asked.

SIX YEARS AGO

They talked about it in code.

Mom: *I got some new medicine from a clinic; your doctor wouldn't okay it, but it has special healing properties…*

Alex never asked, *Why didn't they okay it?* He never asked, *What clinic?*

Mom, dripping something into the IV: *I know the doctors hate when I do this, but you thrash in your sleep, and I can't bear to see you in so much pain. It'll be our secret.*

Our secret, Alex had agreed—

And then it transformed into something different. She kept him home from school, even when he felt fine. She shuttled him to the doctor and gave instructions: *Act a little woozier in front of the specialist, all right? He won't believe us otherwise.*

What do we want him to believe? Alex had asked, but she never answered.

What do you want me to believe? Alex wanted to ask, but he never did.

NOW

"You knew," said Mr. Evans.

"I knew," said Alex.

Mr. Evans's expression was neutral, but his mouth was pinched.

Alex couldn't look at the jury. And he definitely couldn't look at his dad.

"You said you never really talked about it," Mr. Evans said. "At what point did that change?"

FOUR YEARS AGO

At some point he knew it was poison, and he knew why he was sick.

And yet.

She was so *different* when he was ill.

They entered into a strange dance—medication mixed with poison mixed with love. Doctors' visits mixed with school events mixed with the ICU. He checked his medicine in advance to see what it would be the next day. A normal day of classes, or would he leave school in an ambulance? A nice afternoon at the park, or would he black out?

Can't I just pretend? he asked his mom one night, after checking the pillbox and seeing what was in store for tomorrow.

She hmm'd, wrapping a blanket around his shoulders as they sat together on the couch. When she held him close, it felt like nothing could get him. She was an anchor.

Becoming untethered would be like going overboard. It would be like drowning, drowning, drowning.

She turned on the TV. *You're no good at pretending.*

NOW

"But you never told anyone," said Mr. Evans. "Not your dad. Not a teacher. Not a doctor, at any of those appointments."

Of course he hadn't.

Alex managed to look up then, to meet his dad's gaze. His hands were clasped, a muscle in his jaw clenched. Something uncertain lingered in his eyes. Like his son's mask was coming off, and underneath was a monster.

Maybe that was how the world would look at him now.

"I never told anyone," Alex said.

There were so many reasons.

TWO YEARS AGO

You think anyone at school will believe you? she'd asked. *You talk to walls.*

It was a good point, though a discouraging one. People would interpret anything he said as the ravings of a sick, delusional boy.

If they take me away from you, she said, *your father will have to return from his deployment to take care of you and Logan. He'll have to find a new job. Maybe he won't find one, and then you'll become homeless.*

Alex accepted that one as truth. She was the adult, after all.

If they take me away from you, she said, *you'll realize that you're still sick. What will you do then? Who will take care of you?*

No one else knew what helped when he hallucinated, what he needed after seizures, what would make him stop vomiting in the middle of the night. She was the only one.

I worry about Logan sometimes, she said one evening, watching eight-year-old Logan draw monsters in the living room.

Alex stopped asking after that.

NOW

"Is there anything else?" Mr. Evans asked.

There was more. Some things Alex had no idea how to say.

"No," he answered.

EIGHTEEN MONTHS AGO

The something else:

There was one more reason he never told anyone.

Deep down, a sick part of him started to like it.

CHAPTER 41: TRIAL DAY

After Alex gave his testimony, he wanted to dissolve into a puddle. He sat behind the prosecutor's table with his dad—now that Alex had testified, he was allowed to stay in the courtroom. And he wanted to hear what his mom would say. He needed to.

The truth was there was more, so much more, he could say about the past few years. About the way it ended. But he didn't know how to speak about the rest of it. And maybe it didn't matter: He'd said what he needed to say. It had to be enough to get the verdict.

They called up his mom. She walked to the witness stand so casually, it was as if she was wandering around the house in her sweatpants on a weekend afternoon. *Why does Logan always leave his sketches on the floor? Don't you boys ever clean?*

She didn't look at Alex. But he cataloged her every move. The slow walk to the bench. The way she sat down. The way she glanced at his dad, as if saying, *Look what your son was capable of, all along.*

His dad hadn't said a word since Alex's testimony. No *hey, it'll be okay.* No *breathe, kiddo.* Nothing.

Behind them, in the public benches, there were so many voices, so many whispers, and it was impossible to know if they were real or not.

"Clarissa," Mr. Garton, the defense attorney, said after she was sworn in. "Let's start by talking about your family. What were the children like when they were young?"

"They're still young," his mom said with a wry smile. "They're both so imaginative."

It sounded like sweet nostalgia. But it felt like an accusation.

"Logan has been working on a video game for years, crafting all kinds of creatures to fill this universe in his head," she continued. "And Alex—we used to make up stories together in the hospital. We would look out at the street and talk about the people we saw. 'This woman is feeding pigeons because her husband turned into one long ago, and she's trying to lure them close so she can bring him back.' Raising those boys was a joy."

She had to be leading to something more.

"With that kind of imagination, do you think the boy could have made this up?" Mr. Garton's voice was relaxed. Matching her casual tone.

"Oh, I don't know," she answered with a sigh. "We're so close. Were so close, maybe. But what motive would he have? It wasn't fun for him to be sick for years."

"No, not Alex," Mr. Garton said. "Logan. Regarding the hospital visit in May."

So this was her strategy.

She couldn't throw Alex under the bus—he'd already done that—so it would have to be Logan. Logan, the one whose hospital visit had tipped off the doctors, the one who had unintentionally exposed the act. Logan would be the one she let the court devour. He wasn't even here, had no way to defend himself. The injustice shook something awake inside Alex.

I worry about Logan sometimes. He'd always been collateral damage.

"Hmm," his mom said. "I don't know. He pretended to be sick a lot when he was younger. Of course, he wanted attention. He didn't understand how overwhelmed I was, shuttling Alex to appointments and consults, quitting my job, running the house on my own while my husband was abroad." She sat back. "He would do that in school too, disrupt to get attention."

"Yes." Mr. Garton looked so punchably smug. "The school counselor's notes confirm that."

His questioning went on for some time, but after a while the initial examination was over. Mr. Evans, the prosecuting attorney, rose to his feet. "Clarissa," Mr. Evans said, "I'd like to talk about a recording your son made a few days ago."

Her eyebrows lifted slightly. "Oh?"

Mr. Evans took out a laptop and set it down on the plaintiff's table. Oh no, was he actually going to *play* it? The file was only supposed to be a backup plan—but it seemed Mr. Evans intended to use it, even though Alex had testified. Alex wasn't sure that he was ready to hear all of it. What went down in January. The way things had ended.

"Your son's testimony indicates that he knew what you were doing, and didn't see a way out," Mr. Evans said. "Was that your understanding of the situation?"

Her voice didn't waver. "Not for a second."

"So you believed he really was sick, and you were doing all you could to take care of him and Logan while your husband was deployed." Mr. Evans reached for the laptop.

"Yes," she said.

Mr. Evans hit play.

Alex's voice filtered through the room, the pitch slightly wrong, the tone slightly off. It was strange to think that was what other people heard when they listened to him.

"What's all this?" his mom asked over the recording.

Look at you, she'd said, that snowy night in the woods. *What's all this?*

Alex clenched his hands. He'd given Mr. Evans permission to use it, but the audio unfurling from the speaker and spreading through the room felt like a noxious gas.

"It's a podcast." Mr. Evans hit pause. "It seems that Alex and his friends had been working on it for several months. The first few episodes took some creative license. But Alex has confirmed that this final episode contains the truth, under oath."

"Hmm," she said, her expression unreadable. "What a strange little project."

What a strange little project, she'd said in the woods—

Alex knew her, he knew her not. It was like ripping petals off a flower, but at the end there would be nothing but a vortex, a collapsing black hole.

Mr. Evans hit play.

***Lethal Lullaby*, Episode 6: "The Real Story" (FINAL CUT)**

ALEX	**It went on for years, this dangerous balance between us. There were doses in breakfast cereal, injections late at night, and, of course, the loaded pills. Taking them felt like playing Russian roulette. Eventually I stopped checking, stopped guessing. There was no point.**

(Beat.)

ALEX It felt like I was a planet trapped in her orbit. Spinning around her with nothing to break the hold. But there was something unsteady about it. Like any second, I'd wobble and slip out of her grasp.

(Wind rustling.)

ALEX When a planet slips out of a star's gravity, two things can happen. The first is that it breaks free and flies off into the void, gone forever. The second? It crashes into the star and self-destructs.

(Sound of fire crackling.)

ALEX I did the latter.

(Beat.)

ALEX It was in high school that things really got weird. We started making deals. She figured out that sugar triggered my seizures, so I'd switch my water for Sprite before class, and she'd take me to see an eclipse late at night as a reward. I never asked why the pills felt heavier than normal, and when I woke up feeling like my head had been bashed in, she'd be extra nice.

(Beat.)

ALEX

But if I'm being honest, I knew what would happen if I tried to put an end to it. The real price was always Logan. It would be so easy for her to slip something into Logan's food, so easy for her to watch him collapse, so easy for her to replace me. No one would question it. Doctors would think the issue was genetic. I couldn't let Mom do that.

(Beat.)

ALEX

People ask me why I didn't freak out as I got sicker and sicker. I guess it's because I didn't see it happening. It went on so slowly. When I was younger, I'd have an episode once every month or two. Then once every two weeks, then once a week, then so often Mom started discussing those fall helmets. But it happened gradually, and my memory was faulty. It felt like it had always been this way. It was hard to wake up in the morning, barely able to sit up, and remember I used to be able to walk.

(Long beat.)

ALEX

Eventually I realized how this would end. It was early sophomore year. I missed classes all the time, but my brain was so foggy I couldn't remember why that mattered. Everything felt surreal. Except I began to notice something.

(Leaves blowing.)

ALEX Other students were getting driver's licenses. Applying to summer internships. Going on cross-country road trips, traveling overseas, growing up. And I couldn't do any of those things.

(Faint music plays in the background.)

ALEX I realized I might never do any of those things.

(Beat.)

ALEX After the holidays, in January, I told myself, *It's time to put an end to this.*

CHAPTER 42: TRIAL DAY

Mr. Evans hit pause. "Clarissa, did Alex confront you in January?"

Alex's mom sat with her fingers tented on the railing of the witness stand, watching Mr. Evans like he was going to methodically rip her apart. Alex knew the feeling too well.

"I don't remember speaking with him about it." She was controlling her tone, avoiding looking at the jury.

Maybe Alex was the only one who noticed. But it felt like a siren.

Mr. Evans said, "I think we ought to keep going."

Lethal Lullaby, Episode 6:
"The Real Story" (FINAL CUT)

ALEX	**I sat down with her and laid it out. We'd been doing this thing for years. I was old enough to realize it was . . . fraud is one way to put it, but fucked-up is another. We sat down at the kitchen table. I had an idea, a compromise—and it was brilliant.**

(*Glasses clink together.*)

ALEX It went like this. We'd go away for a month or two, claim I was doing some experimental treatment. Maybe we'd take Logan, maybe we'd leave him with a babysitter. Afterwards . . . I wouldn't be better; I knew by then I'd never get one hundred percent better. But I'd be well enough to go back to school. I'd be well enough to go back into real life, one way or another.

(*Beat.*)

ALEX We never fought. We talked around things. Orbiting the black hole of our dilemma. She kept proposing other ideas: Maybe we'd homeschool, maybe we'd move, maybe, maybe, maybe.

(*Wind rustling.*)

ALEX I told her none of that would work. And she said, "Are you going to tell people what you think?"

(*Beat.*)

ALEX That was always how she talked about it. *What you think. What you believe.* Sometimes she called it a delusion, paranoia. Sometimes I believed her. It's impossible to describe what that was like. Half the time, I was certain I knew what was going on—and the other half, I knew my perception of reality was screwed up. It was like stumbling on a balance beam, never getting even.

(Beat.)

ALEX How could I prove it? Even if I could, she would say I was in on it. We were in too deep.

(Liquid pouring.)

ALEX It came close to a fight that day in January, the kind fought with hushed voices and half-truths. She made us some tea. It always calmed me down. I know what you're thinking—and I thought the same thing. I asked her what she'd dosed it with.

(Teacups rattle.)

ALEX She seemed hurt, something in her face crashing down. She said, "You really think I'd do that right now?"

(Beat.)

ALEX And she switched our cups.

(Cups slide across wood.)

ALEX I know. It was ridiculous. It was foolish. It was naive. But she switched the cups, and I was so freaking sure it was safe. It never occurred to me that she'd preempt me. It never occurred to me that she knew I'd ask.

(Beat.)

ALEX **Yeah, I drank it.**

(Long pause.)

ALEX **She already had her out. She always had.**

"That was the night Alex was hospitalized, correct? In January?" Mr. Evans asked.

Alex's mom stared straight ahead.

"He was admitted to the emergency room in a state of status epilepticus," Mr. Evans said.

She said nothing.

"Dr. Melvin said he had to be induced into a controlled coma," Mr. Evans went on.

Her expression was so empty, so vacant.

Maybe she was dissociating, unable to piece together the reality she knew—a sick son, a deployed husband, a family in shambles—with the reality in the courtroom. Maybe she was desperately jamming the puzzle pieces together, wondering why they wouldn't fit. Alex knew how that felt.

But for Alex, the world seemed so much clearer. Ella had yammered on and on about the fact that police hadn't found poison in the house, but of course they hadn't; his mom had cleared it out as soon as he was in the coma. She'd known she could've been exposed now that her son was no longer willing to help keep up the ruse. And yet she hadn't been able to kill him.

Of course she hadn't—even now she was clinging on, unable to let go. Five months unconscious under the glow of the hospital lights because she couldn't let go. Dozens of emails appearing out of nowhere because she couldn't let go.

She would've done anything to reel him back in. It was Alex who had to cut the strings.

Mr. Evans stepped back and said, "No further questions."

CHAPTER 43: TRIAL DAY

Back in the conference room, they waited while the jury deliberated. Mr. Evans busied himself by reviewing documents at one end of the table, and Alex's dad sat at the other end. Alex sat down somewhere in the middle and buried his head in his arms.

Nothing was going to be normal after this. Every medical episode would be met with suspicion. His dad would always wonder if it was fake. And who could blame him?

"Alex," his dad said.

There was no way he could face his dad now.

"Hey." His dad rapped his knuckles on the table.

Alex glanced up.

"I can't imagine how terrifying it was to say all that." His dad shook his head. "To let it out."

Alex looked back at the table, the swirls of wood grain burning into his vision.

"You did great."

"I don't understand." Alex could barely force the words out. "I... I admitted... I worked *with* her." He put his head in his hands, dug his fingers into his scalp. "I let this go on for *years*. I knew, I *knew*, and I didn't—"

"Alex. Alex!" His dad stood up and came toward him, grabbed him by the shoulders. "Hey. Take it easy."

Alex sucked in a shaking breath.

"Listen to me." His dad's gaze was warm. "The things she said… about how you would always be sick, about how you were too mentally ill to know the truth… I can't imagine what that did to you. What she did…"

He looked away for a moment.

"It's hard for me to imagine. And I bet that's how it feels for you too. Like your world has been crumpled up and turned upside down. But you… you found a way to make it right-side up again." He put his hand over Alex's. "That's something else. That's brave. I'm still trying to figure out how to do that myself."

Alex's shaking hands went still. His dad didn't hate him. He'd called him *brave*, a word Alex knew he didn't deserve. And yet there it was, floating in the air between them.

Alex gripped his dad's hand and looked up at him. "You mean that?"

"A million times, kiddo." That *kiddo* felt like an affirmation—that his dad still saw him as his son, not some monster that'd been living in their house for years. "I'm proud of you."

Mr. Evans's phone buzzed at the other end of the table. He leaped to his feet and said, "They're calling us back."

They were brought back to the courtroom, where the incessant chatter seemed to grow louder and louder until it was all white noise. Mr. Evans was speaking with the judge, and Alex recognized the sharp tone of the defense attorney, and through it all came the sound of her voice. Speaking at the defendant's table, as warm as a summer day.

"*Are you sure?*" she was saying, so soft, so calm—

Alex fell into his chair behind the prosecutor's table.

Something in the tone of her voice made it sound like she didn't believe any of this was happening. Then again, she was mentally ill. Munchausen syndrome by proxy, factitious disorder imposed on another. She was sick.

So was he.

Ella had looked at him and seen nothing but a monster—but that was too simple, too easy. The true crime afficionados wanted a neat narrative, and putting scare quotes around mental illness was the simplest way to do that. The evil mother who was so sick she lied to the world, the serial killer off his meds, the murderer who did what the voices told him to: People devoured those stories. They were fun, dramatic, simple. And totally wrong.

His mom was sick, yes. But he was too. And neither of those things made them who they were. They made their own choices, and she'd made hers long ago.

"Has the jury reached a unanimous verdict?" the judge asked.

Someone answered in the affirmative. Alex gripped the sides of his chair.

Footsteps, whispered words. The sound of paper being unfolded.

"The jury finds the defendant guilty on all counts," said a voice, and the room exploded into noise.

One second. She was there, rising on unsteady legs, the bailiff trying to lead her out of the room—

Two seconds. Alex got to his feet—

Three seconds—

Her words filtered into his head, as if dropping out of the air like snowflakes.

Whatever you do, know this: One day, I want to see you grow taller than me.

It was clear now, standing just a few feet away, that he had.

CHAPTER 44: AFTER

Notes 2: Things I Will Never Know

- ➔ Am I a monster for letting this go on for so long?
    - Maybe.
- ➔ Am I ever going to not be like this?
    - Unlikely.
- ➔ Am I ever going to feel like a decent human being?
    - God, I hope so.

Notes 3: Things I Know Too Well

➔ When it's early spring, and we don't think there are going to be any flowers in bloom, but then we go to the park and there's a single freaking marigold sitting there behind a bush like it's pulling a prank. And Mom, your face lights up, and I see that battle in your eyes, how you're questioning whether you should pull the flower out so you can bring it home and treasure it. But of course if you do that, the flower will die. I saw that battle inside you. I saw it all the time.

➔ You. You. You.

Notes 4: Things I Want to Know

- → How much German Dad picked up while he was living there.
- → What Logan's video game will be like when it's done.
- → If Bryce is going to start some new hobby now, like carpentry.
- → If Naomi is going to study abroad in China in college.
- → Me.

CHAPTER 45: AFTER

After the trial, things were different at school. It wasn't so much that people stopped bothering Alex—if anything, it got worse, ever since the public had learned he really *had* been involved—but the tight feeling that lingered in his chest, the sick dread in the pit of his stomach, just... vanished.

Sure, people made strange comments and gave him even stranger looks. Sure, Ella looked like she wanted to stab him in a dark alleyway, and yeah, that would be great fodder for another podcast. But he got through the day. Every day.

His dad still called him *kiddo*, and Logan, after he'd learned about the entire thing, didn't care in the slightest. *Yeah, okay,* Logan had said, *so can you play my newest level now?* Alex had blocked his mom's email address, and now every time his phone buzzed, it didn't feel like he was going to explode.

Sure, the comments on the now-abandoned *Lethal Lullaby* accounts were unhinged. Sure, *Liar's Dose* had been halfway vindicated, given that it told a strange shade of the truth.

But after school Alex met Naomi and Bryce at the Shitwreck. And he could breathe.

"Are you sure this plan is gonna work?" he asked Bryce, the air bitter and cold as the three of them trudged through the bare woods. "I know you want to win the next cosplay competition, but I think if you bring *real* snakes, they're gonna throw you out."

"Nah, it'll be great. I just need to keep them alive until I get to the con in DC tomorrow." Bryce beamed. He and Naomi had taken Alex's side of the story surprisingly well when they'd recorded it. They didn't turn away after he told them the truth. They didn't see a monster. They just saw him.

Alex rolled his eyes at Naomi. "I was in court for *one day* and now he's kidnapping snakes."

Naomi fiddled with her phone. "Oh, but it'll be great content."

Naomi was starting a vlog in Mandarin, and she was trying to convince Alex to start one in German. Maybe he would. He'd need to learn whatever long German word there was for *MyFriendIsAboutToDo-SomethingEmbarrassingButIt'llBeSoFunToWatch.*

In some ways, with everyone talking about him, Ella on the verge of murder, and the growing frenzy of tabloid articles about his family, things were worse than ever.

Except now he had allies.

On a foggy morning a few days later, after school had let out for winter break, Alex went downstairs to find his dad and Logan in a heated discussion about laser tag tactics, and whether one could shoot two guns at once, and how hot *could* a real laser gun get, exactly?

"Laser tag?" Alex sat down on the couch.

"Heh, yeah." His dad tied his shoes. "Logan asked me a few weeks ago. With the trial over and school out, we finally have time. I was going to see if you wanted to join, but I don't know if it's your kind of thing."

"No, that's cool. I'm meeting up with Bryce, anyway," Alex said. His dad and Logan needed to spend more time together. Logan had never gotten a real parent out of their mom, and Alex wasn't going to let that happen again.

Logan held back a smile. Yep, Alex was going to tell him *told you so* for the rest of his life.

The two headed out through the garage, Logan already rambling about tactics. Alex got to his feet and pushed the front door open. On their doormat, there was a newspaper: **"MONSTER MOMMY" CASE GOES TO TRIAL: NEW REVELATIONS UNCOVERED IN COURT.**

For a second, he found himself back in the lawyer's office that September: **HARROWING NEW DETAILS IN "MONSTER MOMMY" CASE.**

The article beckoned, as if urging him to pull the paper open, to wreck himself on every word and sentence.

Instead he took a breath, stepped over the newspaper, and went outside.

ACKNOWLEDGMENTS

I have a lot of people to thank who helped make this book possible.

My editor, Sally Morgridge, for her incredible insight and feedback as we navigated edits on this book. She tore this novel down and then built it back up, and it is so, so much stronger for her efforts.

My agent, Ismita Hussain, who believed in this project from the beginning and whose editorial eye rescued it from being a rambling, messy story with no coherent plot.

Thank you also to Chelsea Hunter, who designed a beautiful cover that really captured the heart of the book. Beatriz Ramo, thank you for bringing that cover to life—your art made my jaw drop when I saw it! Major thanks to my copy editor, Chandra Wohleber, and a huge thank-you to the Holiday House marketing and publicity team for bringing this book to readers.

Thank you so much to an extraordinary group of beta readers who have helped me grow so much as a writer, and who I have learned so much from: D.L. Stille, Tim Turner, and Blair Hanson. Thanks also to my marvelous CP group: Fiona, Quiarah, Tamara, and Alexis, who always keep me motivated and who provided amazing feedback on this project.

Another huge shout-out goes to my sensitivity reader, Lara Ameen. Your care for the subject shows, and your expertise is deeply valued. Any errors that remain are my own.

To my parents, thank you for raising me to be a reader—I've always found kindred spirits between the pages of books. To my brother, thanks for being weird. Your own stories continue to inspire me.

To my wife, thank you for everything. You make every moment an adventure.